WITHDRAWN

BREAKING
THE
DANCE

CLARE O'DONOHUE

D0029586

MIDNIGHT INK
WOODBURY, MINNESOTA

Breaking the Dance: A World of Spies Mystery © 2019 by Clare O'Donohue. All rights reserved. No part of this book may be used or reproduced in any manner whatsoever, including internet usage, without written permission from Midnight Ink, except in the case of brief quotations embodied in critical articles and reviews.

FIRST EDITION
First Printing, 2019

Book format by Samantha Penn
Cover design by Shira Atakpu
Editing by Nicole Nugent

Midnight Ink, an imprint of Llewellyn Worldwide Ltd.

This is a work of fiction. Names, characters, places, and incidents are either the product of the author's imagination or are used fictitiously, and any resemblance to actual persons, living or dead, business establishments, events, or locales is entirely coincidental.

Library of Congress Cataloging-in-Publication Data
Names: O'Donohue, Clare, author.
Title: Breaking the dance : a world of spies mystery / by Clare O'Donohue.
Description: First Edition. | Woodbury, Minnesota : Midnight Ink, [2019] |
    Series: A world of spies mystery ; #2.
Identifiers: LCCN 2018052801 (print) | LCCN 2018055348 (ebook) | ISBN
    9780738756974 (ebook) | ISBN 9780738756547 (alk. paper)
Subjects: | GSAFD: Spy stories. | Mystery fiction.
Classification: LCC PS3615.D665 (ebook) | LCC PS3615.D665 B74 2019 (print) |
    DDC 813/.6—dc23
LC record available at https://lccn.loc.gov/2018052801

Midnight Ink
Llewellyn Worldwide Ltd.
2143 Wooddale Drive
Woodbury, MN 55125-2989
www.midnightinkbooks.com

Printed in the United States of America

Acknowledgments

I made my first (but hopefully not last) trip to Argentina to research this book. It is an amazingly beautiful country and there was inspiration everywhere. I first have to thank two people I met in Buenos Aires—Saul, who taught me how to make empanadas, and Marco, who showed me the basics of tango. I also discovered writers and painters I'd never been aware of before, and fell in love with Ushuaia, a city that may be at the end of the world but is most certainly worth a visit. I did as much research as possible, and loved every minute, but any mistakes in the book are evidence I did not do enough and come with my apologies.

A book is made up of many people working together to make it real. For me that includes my agent, Sharon Bowers; Midnight Ink's acquiring editor, Terri Bischoff, and my editor, Nicole Nugent; and everyone at Midnight Ink. Thanks to my mom, Dennis, Jack, Cindy, Steven, and Mike for dealing with a writer in the family. And thanks to my friends who offered support, served as early readers, and forgave me for the many times I cancelled plans so I could research and write this book.

Finally, I want to thank Kevin, for his many Finn-like ways.

The revolution is not an apple that falls when it is ripe.
You have to make it fall.

—*Che Guevara*

Zurich, Switzerland

Declan Murphy stood outside the Fraumunster Church and watched. It was September, so there were only a few tourists wandering the area near him. Enough, he thought, to keep him from looking out of place, but not so many that he would have to be worried about being overheard. It was just the amount of foreign voices and selfies he would have chosen, if that sort of thing were possible to control.

Not that Zurich was ever really a city for tourists. The winding pathways filled with shops selling fondue pots were a misdirection. Most tourists came to the city for a day before heading off to Lucerne or the Matterhorn.

The people who stayed usually did so for one reason. Zurich was a city of money. Not always made honestly. Often hidden. It was a city where everyone spoke four languages and kept secrets in each of them.

It was not his favorite place, if only because it reminded him too much of himself.

When it was time, Declan walked inside, up the center aisle, past the massive pillars, to the choir. He was not a religious man. He and God had given up on each other a long time before, but he did like churches. So much sin and forgiveness comingling among the cool air and whispered voices. So much pointless hope.

He took a seat to the left and looked up at the windows. The church was built on the remains of a ninth-century monastery, but that's not what brought people in. It was the windows. Extraordinary stained-glass windows designed by Marc Chagall when he was in his eighties. Declan breathed out, feeling slightly more free in their presence. Certainly more at peace than he'd felt since he'd left Ireland. Each window was dominated by a color—red, blue, green, yellow— that, in the early morning light, bathed the church with drama and excitement. It was how art was meant to be. Public and private all at once, for everyone who cared to see it. He knew he was a man of few principles, but at least he was consistent in this one belief.

As he sat, watching the softness of the light play off the gray stone of the church's floor, a man slid next to him.

"*Guten Morgen.*"

Declan nodded at his new seat-mate, a small man with a Turkish accent. "Morning," he said.

Like Declan, the man's eyes were on the windows. He took a deep breath, as if meditating. "You've had losses."

Declan bit the inside of his lip. "Months ago. I've put it behind me."

"You are in need of friends, I think."

"I'm in need of money, mate."

The man looked puzzled, but Declan felt no need to explain. "There are those who would pay well for the book," the man said.

The book. An address book that had been almost within his reach before it was gone. "It was taken by two Americans. Amateurs."

"They have it?"

Declan shook his head. "I don't know. Either they have it or they handed it over to Blue."

Again, the man looked puzzled. This time Declan helped him out.

"They thought it was Interpol. They don't understand the finer points of the game."

"Do they know what the book means?"

"I don't think so. I don't think Blue knows, either."

The man let out a breath. Declan hadn't realized until that moment that the man had been nervous. He allowed himself a half smile at the thought, at knowing he wasn't the only one with muscles constantly tense, eyes always on the alert.

"You drew attention to yourself recently," the man said. "Blue is after you."

"I'm a small fish."

"But you could point toward the bigger fish if you wanted to."

"I just want to get off this bloody continent. And I need a bit of cash."

The man nodded. "Our *porteño* friend needs some aid."

"I'd heard there was trouble."

"The job was bigger than he could handle. It's brought unwelcome attention, and most are deciding to stay away."

"Leaving our friend desperate for help." Declan felt a little thrill at the idea.

The man nodded. "He has a reputation, you know this, for being reckless. Think through carefully before you say yes."

"But there's money to be earned."

"Yes, there is money."

"And it's spring in Argentina."

"A time of renewal. A fresh start."

As the man spoke a woman moved toward the windows, looking up with the kind of awe that made Declan envy her. Seeing something beautiful for the first time is unlike any other experience.

"Send me the details," Declan said.

As he got up, the man grabbed his arm. "If things go wrong, I cannot help you. And, from what I understand, there's no one left in Ireland who can offer you any assistance. You'll be completely on your own."

"Not entirely," Declan said. "There are two people who owe me a favor."

"Capable people?"

Declan raised an eyebrow, amused at a memory he wasn't intent on sharing. "Surprisingly so."

One

The days were just starting to get shorter. By six o'clock the sky had taken on a streaky pinkness, but even that was yielding to the coming darkness. Outside there was the laughter of students enjoying both the September warmth and the freedom of a Thursday afternoon. But Hollis Larsson was still in her office at Bradford University, still typing, a half-dozen books on the United Nations crowding her desk.

It wasn't her already delayed book on the history of the UN that she was writing, though. Instead she was adding the final touches to her lecture on Interpol. She'd become fascinated with the subject, the first time in years she'd been excited to teach her students about the complexities of international relations.

But it was what she couldn't teach them that interested her the most. A short mission to Ireland for Interpol just a few months earlier had turned into an adventure, both dangerous and exciting. She could still recall the thrill of uncovering a killer, though the fear she'd felt at the time had faded a bit. From the safety of her small Michigan town, it seemed like a dream. If it was, it was one she and Finn had shared and kept as a secret between them.

She leaned back in her chair, stretching her spine to relieve the tension that lived there these days. Too much sitting. There was some report somewhere that it was worse than smoking, which seemed impossible and plausible all at once. At least with smoking there was the high of nicotine and the noir beauty of wisps of smoke. Sitting was just an ache, a rounded spine, and an increasing waistline. But it couldn't be helped. She had research to do—and not the kind she could pawn off on a grad student.

This research was about Blue, the group that lived somehow within Interpol, or beside it. In Ireland it had been brought up more than once, and in a way that made it clear it was a secret entity. It was intriguing. Interpol was founded in the 1920s to allow for police organizations to better coordinate international investigations and catch criminals. Blue seemed to operate in the gray area between what is specifically illegal and what isn't—more CIA than police. But why would it be needed?

She couldn't answer the question despite months of trying. There was nothing she could find. No whispers in academia anyway. Even people who had devoted their lives to understanding Interpol had never heard of any *intelligence* organization operating across international borders. Cooperation between countries' intelligence agencies, yes, but working as one group? One retired professor she contacted actually laughed at the idea.

"We can't even get the FBI and the CIA to coordinate, and we're all Americans," he'd said. "Do you honestly think that the Brits, the Aussies, the Germans, and who knows who else would team up in some secret group?"

"Maybe if the threat were significant enough," she'd countered.

He laughed again. "Intelligence agencies guard their territory like mothers guard their young. Wouldn't happen. Couldn't happen. Where do you come up with these ideas?"

She didn't say. She didn't know if she could trust him with the truth that she'd been in the center of a Blue operation and knew of a threat that could potentially crash the world's financial markets. She and Finn had decided early on that going public would only put them in more danger. She let the retired professor think she was over-reaching.

"Don't go chasing shadows," he'd advised her. "I know these days academics want to make a name for themselves, get on all the cable news shows with bestselling books. But don't ever forget, Hollis, we're teachers. And what we teach are facts, not theories."

And now, sitting alone at her desk, she had to admit, aside from limited personal experience of Blue, all she had were theories.

"Maybe it is a joke," she said out loud, with nothing but the dust bunnies gathering under her desk to hear her. Maybe the agents who spoke of Blue were just playing some game. She shut off her computer for the day and stood up for the first time in hours. Her hip creaked a little. At forty you just couldn't miss three weeks of yoga and expect to stay flexible.

"Dr. Larsson?" A woman about her age peaked her head into the office. "Can I bother you for a moment?"

Hollis waved her in. The woman in turn waved to someone behind her and in seconds she was joined by a man. Both dressed in jeans and Bradford University t-shirts, with overeager grins and the nervous expectations of the parents of freshmen. Hollis didn't know either of them, but she knew immediately the conversation she was about to have.

"I'm Anne," the woman began. "Our son Jim is a student of yours and we're just wondering how he's doing."

"The semester just started. I don't even know everyone's name. Jim...?"

"He had a quiz," the man said. "He got a C. He wasn't a C student in high school and it worried us. So we thought we'd both take the day off work and drive here from Grand Rapids."

"Not just for this," the woman corrected him. "Jim needs some new clothes and we also thought maybe we could stock his fridge. I don't want him living on pizza."

"What can I help you with?" Hollis asked with a practiced tone of patience.

The man nodded. "Sorry, Professor, my wife worries. He's our oldest, you see. We thought maybe Jim might need some extra tutoring. Or maybe he's partying too hard and he needs a stern warning. I remember my college days."

"Arthur!" the woman said. "He doesn't party," she assured Hollis.

Helicopter parents. They got worse every year.

"He's just adjusting to the workload," Hollis told them, as she'd told many parents before them. "It takes time for all freshmen to find their sea legs. I'll keep an eye on him and if there's any concerns about his grades, I'll be in touch." She had no intention of following through on that. If her guess was right, she wouldn't need to; Anne and Arthur would be checking in regularly.

Hollis turned off her desk lamp and moved toward her office door. The parents moved with her, luckily, until they were all in the hallway. Hollis locked the door and smiled. "Nice to meet you both. I'm sure Jim will adjust. They all do."

"He said your husband is a teacher here," Arthur said.

"Yes, world literature, but Jim wouldn't have a class with him. Not yet, anyway. He mainly teaches graduate students."

"It sounds fascinating," Anne gushed. "You with world politics and your husband with world literature. You must have wonderful conversations over dinner. Maybe Jim will want to major in that."

"Who can make a living with a literature degree?" Arthur said, less as a question than an obvious statement.

"Take care." Hollis smiled and turned in the other direction. As she reached the stairs she heard Anne telling her husband he had been rude, and wondering, loudly, how that would affect their precious child's grades.

She had several students named Jim, but she only taught one freshman class, Intro to World History. It wouldn't be too hard to figure out which one of them belonged to Arthur and Anne. But that was next week's problem. She had a long weekend stretching out in front of her and she wasn't going to waste a moment of it thinking about school.

Two

Hollis walked from Mason Hall across the campus to the faculty parking, crunching leaves under her feet as she stepped. As she did, she knew that someone was following her. She was always listening for steps that patterned hers, slowing when she slowed, quickening when she stepped up her pace. Usually the pattern broke after a few yards as the person behind her moved away. Not following her, she would realize, just walking behind her.

But this time there was no break. The steps stayed the same as hers from almost when she left the building, through the quad, and even through the shortcut she took across the library's front lawn. Every time she turned, the steps behind her turned.

She listened carefully. It wasn't two pairs of steps, so it was unlikely that the parents were the ones following her. Besides, they would hardly just follow;

they would likely be shouting her name, flagging her down to show her photos of Jim as a baby or high school valedictorian or something else that would send their son into therapy for years.

This was one set of footsteps. And whoever they belonged to, they were beginning to move faster. They were catching up.

In just a moment she would reach the parking lot. Her car was in the second row, fourth from the right, as always. She could move quickly and be inside before the steps caught up with her. Or she could turn around and face what she knew would be trouble.

She decided to turn.

"Dr. Larsson." It was Angela, the grad student who was working as her teaching assistant for the semester.

"Were you following me this whole time?"

"I was …" She hesitated. "I was trying to catch up." Angela stretched out her hand, in which she held a tan envelope. "I've got a letter for you. It seemed too important to wait until next week. It might have something to do with the donation."

The donation—a multimillion-dollar endowment to the university that had been made a month earlier. The fact that it was anonymous hadn't meant much; a lot of wealthy people donated anonymously to avoid future requests for money. It was that it was so specific in its endowments—the International Studies department would be expanded; a library would be built next to Meyers Hall, which housed the English Department; and the Art School would receive desperately needed funds to remodel a crumbling building and update their technology. She and Finn would both benefit from the money, or at least their departments would, so it shouldn't have nagged at her, but it did. Whoever the donor was had to be someone who cared enough to focus on three normally overlooked departments. Though even with that tantalizing clue, the identity of their benefactor seemed a mystery to everyone. It had become the talk of the school.

Hollis reached out for the envelope. It was a plain four-by-six envelope that felt padded on the inside, the kind that could be picked up by the pack in any store. It was thick, but the contents were bendable. Papers, perhaps. There was no return address, nothing distinguishing. Hollis's name and address were hand-printed in block letters, the sort of thing that could have been done by anyone. But it likely meant it wasn't junk mail, which usually came with a pre-printed label. Intriguing maybe, but not much to go on.

"Why did you think this was too important?"

Angela looked down at the sidewalk for a moment. She was smart and worked hard. She'd traveled extensively, something to do with her father's line of work, and she had a passion for international relations. Her ambition was to work in diplomacy, but she had one small problem: she was painfully shy. After only a few weeks of working together, Hollis had already learned to be patient. If she asked a question and waited, she'd get an answer. If she tried to force an answer, Angela would retreat. She felt a special responsibility to help this talented young woman reach her potential, but if she were being honest, Hollis also struggled with an urge to shake information from her. Especially when she was tired and anxious to get home.

Nevertheless, she stood waiting, hoping that Angela would explain.

"It was hand-delivered to the front desk by a guy I know," Angela said. "I brought it to your office, but you had left."

"What guy?"

"His name is Tommy. He's getting his master's in history. I've almost got him convinced to switch to international studies. I think he would really like taking a class from you."

That was the most she'd spoken since Hollis had interviewed her for the position.

"He delivered it, but it isn't from him?"

"No. He said he was paid twenty bucks to bring it to you."

Hollis looked down at the envelope again. No stamp. That was a pretty significant detail to miss, she scolded herself. "Did he say who paid him twenty bucks?"

Angela shook her head. "Should I have asked?"

"No. Not important. But text me his contact info, just in case." Hollis stuffed the envelope in her purse.

"Aren't you going to open it?"

"Eventually. Thanks for bringing this to me."

"If I can help..."

"You already have. Enjoy the weekend, Angela." Hollis turned and walked the rest of the way to her car. As she slid into the driver's seat, she saw that Angela was still standing where she'd left her, watching.

Three

As tempted as Hollis was to open the envelope in her car, she drove out of the lot. Whoever paid Angela's friend to bring the letter to her could be there, somewhere, waiting for a reaction. She wasn't going to give them the satisfaction.

Instead she drove her usual route, watching her rearview mirror for any signs she was being followed. She wasn't an expert at such things, but she had been paying attention ever since Ireland.

She checked the rearview mirror so often she almost hit a student who had run into the street to catch a Frisbee. She slammed on the brakes. The guy opened his mouth to yell something at her, then they both realized he was one of her students, and he closed his mouth without uttering a word. She mouthed an "I'm sorry." He waved and ran back on the grass. He sat third from the left in her class Intelligence During the Cold War. She made a mental note to grade his next paper generously.

The news came on the radio, with a headline about a gaffe some congressman had made, followed by several minutes about upcoming elections. She was about to turn it off when they switched to international news. She used to listen because it was part of her job to know what was happening in the world. Now she listened in case some art forgery or jewel theft would give her a clue as to what Blue might be fighting these days. Instead, the news was about financial instability in Argentina, where there were rumors the government would not be able to pay back loans to the World Bank. A near repeat of an issue the country had in late 2002. Hollis turned the dial to music.

The rest of the ride was uneventful but beautiful. The trees were still full of green leaves, the air still warm, and there was a slight wind that swept away any of the day's humidity. At first she wondered if the envelope had something to do with Blue, but by the time she got to the parking lot of Finn's boxing gym, she'd convinced herself the letter was some student's idea of a joke, or an odd plea from her publisher about the UN book.

That was okay, she told herself, she was happy with life as it was. And even though she wasn't chasing bad guys, or running from them, other things had changed for the better. She and Finn had become much closer, and all it had taken was being chased by a killer. Probably not the course of action a marriage counselor would have recommended, but there was no ignoring the results.

As if on cue, Finn walked out of the gym right on time, punching the air and sort of skipping toward the car. He jumped in the passenger seat and kissed her, perhaps a little too passionately for a mini-mall parking lot.

She took a moment to look at him, tall and fit, with all of his blond hair still on his head, if a little messy. He still had a bright smile and he was still a good kisser. And most importantly, he seemed as pleased to see her as she was to see him.

"I take it you had a good class," Hollis said.

"My cross–uppercut combo is the best my trainer has seen from any of his students in years."

"Impressive. Do you have enough strength left to open an envelope?" She pulled it from her purse and handed it to him.

Finn held it in both hands, turned it over, then turned it back again. "No stamp."

"Angela said it was hand-delivered. It feels like papers to me. I could bend it a bit."

"And you didn't open it?"

Hollis couldn't explain why, exactly. "At first, I thought maybe it might be from Interpol and if it was, I wanted to wait for you."

Finn's eyes flickered. A sign that he was as excited by the idea as she was. But then he shrugged. "Why would they get in touch with us? It was a one-and-done kind of mission in Ireland," he said. "And if they did want our help again, why not just call?"

Both good points. But Hollis tapped the envelope. "Then open it and we'll forget all about it. Maybe get Chinese for dinner?"

Finn slid his finger under the flap and sliced through the envelope. He pulled out a brown bundle.

Hollis couldn't get a proper look. Finn was covering it with his hands. "What is it?"

He lifted his hand to show her. "More wrapping. Seems a bit overdone. Who wraps paper to put it in an envelope?"

"Let's find out what they sent first, and judge their packaging etiquette later." She reached for it, but Finn wouldn't let go, so she moved closer to get a better look.

Finn undid the tape and slowly pulled off the brown paper. "Huh."

It was as good a reaction as any to what was inside the envelope. Two American passports. Finn opened the top one to the inside front cover and pointed to the photo of Hollis. "Did we lose our passports, and someone sent them back?"

Hollis grabbed the other one and opened it. Finn's face stared back at her. "These aren't our passports. This is Tim McCabe's passport."

Finn looked again at the one on his lap. "This is for Janet McCabe."

"But they're our pictures."

They both sat for a moment and stared at the little blue booklets. "I don't get it," Finn said. "Why would—"

A loud bang. They both ducked low in their seats. Hollis reached for her purse. "I'll call 911."

"What was it? It didn't sound like a shot."

"It sounded like one to me."

Finn raised up a little, and Hollis watched from a crouched position as her husband started looking out at the parking lot. Another loud bang. Hollis flinched but Finn didn't.

"It's a shopping cart," he said. "Every time the door opens to that grocery store, it bangs into the cart."

Hollis sat up. "No need for emergency services, then."

"Not for that. But these passports … I mean, Holly, this is super creepy stuff. Maybe we *should* call the police."

"And say what?"

He shook his head. "I don't know. That our lives are more complicated than they appear."

Hollis looked closely at the passport Finn held. "I know this picture. It's my work ID photo." She picked up the other passport and opened it to Finn's photo. "Yup. This is your work ID picture."

"Someone hacked into the university's security department and used our photos for fake passports."

"Looks like it."

Finn let out a long breath. "I'm no expert on identity theft, but when someone makes a fake passport they use the names but different pictures, not the other way around. And they don't usually send it to the victims, do they?"

"Maybe there's an explanation in the envelope."

"Like an instruction manual?"

His tone was mocking but Hollis ignored it.

Finn reached back into the envelope and pulled out a folded piece of plain white paper. He opened it slowly.

Hollis leaned over to see. "What does it say?"

"That depends on how well you remember your high school Spanish."

She looked at the paper. He was right. A short handwritten note in Spanish. She recognized a word here and there, but nothing of significance. The only thing that stood out was *BsAs*.

"That's short for Buenos Aires." She scanned the note again and found another word of interest—*muerte*. "That means death."

"Someone sent us two fake passports because there's been a death in Argentina?"

"It doesn't just mean death," Hollis remembered. "I think it can also mean murder."

Four

With the help of an internet search, it took less than twenty minutes to translate the note. Finn ordered their usual beef with broccoli, chicken cashew, and steamed pot stickers, while Hollis sat at their kitchen table, typing in the words she could make out. Some of the note was scribbled, as if the author were in such a hurry that he couldn't be bothered to make it legible.

"Here's what I think it says: *Oscar Solari is in trouble. A murder in our Buenos Aires group. You owe him. Listen only to me. Twenty-four hours. Tomas Silva,*" Hollis read. "*Beware Jorge Videla.*"

"Oscar Solari," Finn repeated. "That's Xul Solar's real name."

Hollis looked at him, completely blank.

"Xul Solar was an Argentinian painter. Very surreal work. He was into astrology and tarot, invented languages. Very revolutionary and uncompromising."

"He means Declan Murphy," Hollis said. "Revolutionary, uncompromising, artist. It's him. Plus, the line about how we owe him. It has to be Declan."

Declan was an art thief and forger, but he had also saved Hollis's life, so it was true that they did owe him. But to Hollis's mind, they had nearly paid him back already by not turning him in to Interpol, and by giving a description that would make him almost impossible to identify.

Finn, though, focused on a different line in the note. "He said 'our group.' Does he think we're part of The Common Treasury?"

"He might be referring to himself and Declan."

"I hope so." Finn said. "This Tomas, he wants us to use fake passports to go to Argentina and help Declan? No. Absolutely not."

"Maybe it isn't TCT," Hollis said.

"Of course it is. They're a group of forgers, aren't they? Forgers and hackers and art thieves and anything they can think of to upend the world financial system. Who else would send us fake passports?"

She didn't have an answer. "I wonder why he thinks we could help."

"We're not doing it."

"I'm not arguing with you," she pointed out. "There's nothing we can do to help unless Declan needs to identify an obscure sixteenth-century poet or understand the intricacies of diplomacy during times of undeclared war."

"I think we're more useful than that."

She laughed. "Now who wants to help?"

Finn grabbed the note and the passports off the table, put them back in the envelope, and threw them in the trash.

"I'm not sure that solves the problem."

Finn grunted. "You want to go along with what this fellow is asking?"

"That's not what I'm saying. I'm saying that someone went to a lot of trouble to create fake passports for us, to give us assumed identities. I don't think just tossing them in with used teabags is going to get us out of this."

He grunted again, then lifted the envelope out of the trash and threw it on the kitchen counter. "So how do we get out of this? Because—and I want to be as clear as I can—we're not getting mixed up with a bunch of killers again."

Hollis tried not to smile because she knew it would only annoy him further, but the edges of her mouth turned up of their own accord. "You know I'm not on the opposing team, right? I don't want to do it, either. Besides, there's something more concerning in the note. *Beware Jorge Videla*."

Now it was Finn's turn to look blank.

Hollis and Finn had so many separate interests that she had once wondered what kept them together, but teaching was what they had in common. They loved being smart for each other, each bringing their own area of expertise to the table, each respecting the other's knowledge. It was something that certainly came in handy at moments like this one.

Finn took a deep breath. "I'm guessing Videla is a bad guy."

"Very. He was a senior commander during the period of state terrorism in Argentina, when anyone who disagreed with the government just went missing with no explanation to the families. Students, journalists, really anybody who spoke out against the government. They're referred to as The Disappeared."

Finn nodded, making the connection to a frightening time in that country's history. "Thousands of people, right? For about ten years from the mid-seventies."

"Yes. But Videla is dead. He was convicted of human rights violations. He died in a prison cell."

"Well, just like Xul was a clue to Declan's identity, obviously Videla is meant to be a clue to someone else."

It was a terrifying thought that someone would be compared to such evil, someone that they were being warned against. "Okay, so someone very bad, someone monstrous, is after Declan and he thinks that we can help. Or at least this Tomas Silva thinks we can."

"But we're not going to." Finn's voice was firm. "I won't allow it."

This only annoyed Hollis. "Okay, man of the house, aside from you putting your foot down, do you have any ideas?"

Finn walked out of the room, coming back a few minutes later with two more passports, their real ones. He tossed them on the table, sat down, and opened his, then opened the fake one and examined them both.

"What are you looking for?" Hollis asked.

"I want to see how good they are."

"Are you an expert in passports?"

"As a matter of fact, I have read quite a lot about it when I was doing research on a Thai forger named The Doctor," Finn said. "He was the best there was until his arrest a few years ago."

"Why were you doing research on him?"

She noticed a slight blush coming up from his neck. "I thought I might be able to turn our recent experiences into a book, or even just a paper," he said. "Haven't you thought about it?'

"I've been researching Blue," she admitted.

"You can't do anything on those guys."

"No, I know. I was just researching. You can't write about them, either."

"Not touching on anything we've actually been through," he said, "but on the subject of forgeries."

22

"I wonder if The Doctor was TCT?"

"I wonder if *everyone* is TCT. I like Declan, I really do, but if he murdered someone ..."

"We don't know that, just that there's been a murder."

"Okay, whatever he's done, that's his own problem. We're certainly not going to be able to help him," Finn said. "And what's with the hand-delivered package and the cryptic note? Why not just ring the doorbell?"

"I think it's self-explanatory."

Finn's eye twitched. "Okay, Professor, explain it to me."

"He can't just show up. Maybe someone's watching him. Or us."

Finn locked his jaw.

"Okay, *him*," Hollis placated. "Tomas needs to reach out another way and he wants us to be ready, with the passports. Obviously, we're supposed to get the word then head for the airport."

"Obviously." His fingers tapped the table, getting louder and angrier as he went. Hollis reached out and put her hand over his.

"We'll figure it out." Her voice was quiet and calm, but inside she was just as alarmed. It seemed impossible that they could help Declan out of a murder charge, or that he would even think to ask them.

"This all has to do with that break-in we had last week."

Hollis resisted the urge to roll her eyes. "There wasn't a break-in."

"I had David Wootton's *The Invention of Science* on the coffee table, opened to page 485. When I came back from class, the book was closed. You said you didn't close it. You told me you weren't even home."

"I said I wasn't home because I wasn't. I didn't close the book. You must have closed it and forgotten."

"When have I ever closed a book I was reading without a bookmark?"

23

It was a fair point. And a little odd, if she was being honest, that he was such a stickler about bookmarks. But long-term relationships required putting up with odd on both sides. Still, she found herself saying, "You sound a little paranoid."

"Do I?" His voice elevated before he could catch himself. "Fine. But the recycling was mixed up. The Tuesday paper was clearly under the Monday paper. And"—it was his summing-up-to-the-jury moment—"in our take-out menu drawer, the menu for the Mexican place was on top. That placed closed months ago, so obviously we haven't ordered from it recently. Why was it on top?"

"Are you done?"

He hesitated a moment, then waved a hand of surrender.

"I could have moved the recycling and the menu drawer, and it's possible, just possible that you absentmindedly closed your book."

"I didn't. And if you moved the menus around, you'd remember."

She probably wouldn't have, she knew, but there was no point in saying that. Neither of them was going to win this argument, so Hollis changed to the subject at hand. "Let's just assume that whoever sent us this package has a bit more in mind than rearranging our menu drawer. What do we do?"

"What if it's a trap?" Finn asked. "What we know about TCT is that it operates worldwide. The art forgery and all of that isn't just some guy trying to make a few bucks faking a Helmut Ditsch. This is about upending the value of art, of gold, of anything that puts wealth into a few hands. It's about rebalancing, or maybe just ruining, the world economy. To have that kind of power, you have to know people in high places, in government and law enforcement. And you have to be willing to do whatever it takes to reach your goals."

"Except Declan gave the impression The Common Treasury was more of a loosely organized collaboration between criminal groups than one central power."

"The mob in the 1930s could have been described the same way and look at the damage they did."

He was right, not that it helped. "Let's assume it is some kind of a trap," she said. "Why would we matter enough for them to go after us?"

"Because we know they exist."

They did know some of what TCT was about and had, perhaps wrongly, protected one of their members. That could make them allies, or it could make them liabilities. But there was a flaw in his theory, and it had to be said. "Sending us passports, a coded note that our friend is in trouble … it's a lot of effort," she said. "Why lure us to some foreign country if all they want to do is see us dead? They can kill us right here, right now, in our kitchen."

Finn sat perfectly stiff, almost frozen. "I don't know."

Outside, someone leaned hard against their doorbell, and both of them jumped.

"Stay here," Finn said. "Dial 9-1, and be ready to press the second 1, just in case." He stopped after a few steps. "Not that I want to be putting my man-of-the-house foot down."

She smiled even as she rolled her eyes. "All I'm saying is you don't need to treat me like a little woman who needs you to decide everything," she said. "But the usual exceptions apply. Spiders, heavy packages, and killers who are part of an international crime ring that come to our door ready to shoot us. Then you can go full testosterone."

He smiled. "That's a lot of pressure."

She watched him head toward the door. For most of their marriage, the worst either had faced was eye strain from too much reading. But the positive side of all this spy business was that she had gotten to see another side of her husband. When the situation called for it, Finn was brave, protective. It was extremely sexy. Most marriages don't get tested in dangerous situations. As Hollis watched him reach the front door, her hand ready to call for help, she felt a little sorry for those marriages.

The doorbell buzzed again, this time even longer. Hollis held her breath. She wondered why they didn't have a stronger lock on the door, or a big, vicious dog ready to jump at the throat of anyone who might show up unannounced. They hadn't thought they would need them, she knew. Ireland, and all that had happened there, was supposed to be behind them. Once they'd finished the mission, they never imagined the danger would follow them home.

But clearly that was naïve.

Finn looked out the peephole. Hollis waited. A moment passed before he turned back and smiled. He opened the door to the delivery guy from Sun Chinese.

Five

I t was surprising, but they both had an appetite. They sat in a trio. Finn on one side of the table, Hollis on the other, and the passports right in the middle. The food had been pushed to one side to make room. Finn took a long stretch to get the last pot sticker, made a halfhearted offer to split it, then popped it in his mouth.

"I'm not spending my life jumping every time there's a shopping cart or a doorbell," Finn said.

"As I said, I'm not on the opposing team."

"Did I say you were?"

"The tone of your voice..."

Finn's eye twitched. It was easy to spot when his annoyance level was reaching its maximum, but Hollis refused to take the blame for it—as much as she knew Finn wanted her to. She didn't ask for the package to show up, she didn't want to run off somewhere to save a man they barely knew from whatever bad choices he had undoubtedly made, and she was tired of the implied accusation that she was.

"We have to call Peter," he said. "You agree with me, right?"

The answer, she knew, was yes. Of course. Peter Moodley was an experienced member of the intelligence community, a former British spy, now working with the murky side organization Blue. At least as far as either Hollis and Finn could figure. Peter was a little hazy on details about his work, but that was what spies did. If anyone would understand what this was about, it would be Peter.

She pierced a piece of broccoli with her fork and stared at it. "We're off school tomorrow for Founder's Day. And my Monday and Wednesday classes are cancelled due to the model UN prep. We're in the semifinals."

"Congratulations. You haven't answered my question."

"I'm just pointing out that I have a light teaching schedule next week. You don't even teach on Mondays. We're at the start of a four-day weekend. I wonder if the Tomas fellow knows that."

"Because, like all criminal masterminds, he's a big supporter of education. Naturally he wouldn't want us to miss a day of teaching while we help a killer."

"Declan's not a killer." When Finn rolled his eyes, Hollis conceded the point. "Fine, he's killed at least once, but it doesn't mean he's an entirely bad person."

"You want to help him."

"I don't want to help him," Hollis protested.

"You still haven't answered my question." Finn said. "Do you agree that we need to call Peter?"

"The person in the note is going to contact us in twenty-four hours."

"Twenty-four hours from when he sent the note or when we read the note?"

Hollis wanted to ask why it mattered, but she bit her lip. Finn's attention to detail came in very handy more times than it was annoying. "I'm going to assume from when it was delivered. So, about three hours ago. Not that he'll be sitting with a stopwatch."

"And Peter?"

"I don't think he has a stopwatch, either."

She saw Finn open his mouth to say something, close it again, and bite his lip. Maybe they both did things that were annoying.

"Okay. To answer the question you keep asking, I think maybe we wait and see what he says first. Which is no more than …"—she looked at the clock on the microwave—"twenty hours and forty-three minutes from now."

"Because?"

"Because …" She struggled a bit. She wasn't happy to be dragged into this mess, but they had been dragged. Walking away from someone in trouble, someone who hadn't walked away when they were in need … no part of that felt right. "Because this Tomas guy is a friend of Declan. And maybe Declan really does need our help. And maybe we can really help him."

"Are we going to owe Declan for the rest of our lives?"

She looked at Finn, her eyes staring straight into his. "I will."

Finn leaned back in his chair, dropping his fork on his plate and letting the tinny clank echo for a moment. He shook his head, then sighed. "Fine. I suppose the upside is that if we get involved in whatever Declan has done, I don't think *the rest of our lives* is going to be a very long time."

Six

When Hollis was finished with two minutes on the electric toothbrush, then flossing, then mouthwash, she washed her face, added moisturizer, smoothed night cream under her eyes, and rubbed hand cream on her arms and elbows. At twenty, her nighttime routine had been kicking off her shoes and falling into bed. Now it could take up the evening.

She turned off the bathroom light and walked into the bedroom, where Finn was already propped up in bed reading.

"What's the book about?" she asked as she climbed into bed beside him.

"The history of weapons, from ancient times to modern warfare."

She was tempted to point out that he'd already read three books about weaponry, but Finn was a serial obsessionist. Last year there were months when all she heard about was ancient Rome. Each night as she would be drifting off to sleep, he'd tell her gruesome stories of executions and ambitious, insane emperors. It had gotten to the point where just looking at pasta made her slightly queasy. She had enough on her mind tonight, between the note and the fake passports; she wasn't in a mood for a dissertation on the new ways humanity had learned to kill.

She put her head on the pillow and her hand on his chest, feeling the steady in-and-out of his breathing. Her heart was pounding but his face was a blank. Finn looked like he'd spent the evening debating nothing more important than the ending of a favorite book. His ability to calm himself was slightly unnerving.

They'd decided that Tomas would probably send word somehow—another hand-delivered package, a coded text message—and they would be expected to follow instructions. Once they got the word, the first call would be to Peter. It seemed like a sensible plan. Well, a plan anyway. Nothing about any of it seemed particularly sensible. There had been talk, briefly, of getting in the car and driving for parts unknown. But they would have to come back at some point. Whatever needed to be faced might as well be faced now. Even Finn agreed to that. And if they could help Declan, all the better. Finn had just shrugged at that idea.

"Did you lock the door?" Hollis asked.

"Locked it, checked it, checked it again," he said. "Get some sleep. You don't want to yawn through your execution."

Hollis rolled her eyes. She wasn't sleepy. She was too nervous. But there was something else mingling in with the fear—excitement. Declan had reached out to them for help. Clearly a man with some serious survival skills saw beyond the dull Midwestern college professor persona. He saw people who could handle themselves in a dangerous situation. Of course, he was probably wrong. With that thought, the fear rushed back in.

She needed to calm down. She focused on the hand that rested on Finn's chest. She wasn't particularly in the mood for sex, but she needed something to clear the anxiety. She tapped her fingers on his stomach lightly, but Finn didn't react. She began moving her hand downward, slowly, until it rested at the lowest edge of his stomach. She looked up at Finn, but she didn't catch his eye. After a pause her fingers moved southward again, her fingers lightly stroking him over his pajamas.

Finn turned his head toward her and smiled. "I'd love to. But can I finish this chapter first?"

She nodded. Sixteen years of marriage.

———

After the chapter, after the sex, after Finn's *mission accomplished* grin had given way to sleep, Hollis lay in bed and stared up at the ceiling. She was trying to figure out the meaning of the note, but she couldn't concentrate. Eventually she'd drifted off to sleep, but something woke her up—and kept her up. The back of her neck was warm, while the rest of her was cold. She could feel each muscle tensing one by one, from her head through her shoulders, arms, and legs. She felt her breathing get shallow. Suddenly she couldn't catch her breath. She moved her hand over toward Finn. Maybe it—whatever *it* was—was bothering him too. But he was lying on his back, breathing heavily, happily. A man completely at peace.

She poked him.

He grunted a little, turned onto his side, and the heavy breathing began again.

She poked again.

"What?" It was half question, half whine.

"Something's wrong."

"I'm sorry."

"For what?"

"I know the drill." He rolled over to face her. "It's the middle of the night, so naturally you want to talk about the state of our marriage. I'm all ears, just tell me what I did wrong."

She bit her lip so hard that she could taste blood but at least she restrained herself from pointing out that this, right now, was what he did wrong. "I don't do that."

"So that's not what you woke me up for?"

"No. But I don't do that."

"You don't look for inconvenient times to talk to me about our relationship? Like how you didn't want to talk about our marriage at my grandmother's house at Thanksgiving, right before she served the turkey?"

"That was thirteen years ago. And your grandmother seated me at the kid's table. I still can't understand why you don't think that was wrong."

"She ran out of seats at the other table."

Hollis thought about it. She could argue her point, still right, that his grandmother was being passive-aggressive because she thought Hollis wasn't good enough for her perfect Finn, but she didn't. There were more immediate matters. "I think someone's in the house."

Finn sat up in bed and looked toward the door. "You think it's Tomas?"

"I don't know."

"But you heard something."

"Not exactly. I felt something."

"Oh." He put his head back on his pillow. "Remember my family reunion when you *felt* that one of my distant cousins was hostile because of the way he ate his burger? He turned out to be the nicest guy in my whole family."

"That was fifteen years ago, at least. Remember how you thought we should save money by spending our wedding night at your folks' house?"

"We were grad students. We got married three blocks from their house, and we couldn't afford another hotel night. Besides, we went to New Orleans on our honeymoon, so it's not like we moved in with them. What does our wedding night have to do with anything?"

"I'm just pointing out that it's not fighting fair if you keep our entire history in your back pocket to fling at me whenever it suits you."

"I thought you didn't want to talk about our relationship."

"I don't. There's someone in the house."

Finn pulled his head off the pillow, resting his body on his elbows, his eyes toward the door. They were both quiet. They waited in the dark and silence for almost a minute. But there was nothing, no strange noises, no creaks on the wood floors. "I don't hear anything, Holly. I could point out that this is why we should have called Peter immediately, so we wouldn't be worried about killers in the house. But I won't."

"No, you'll wait until our fiftieth anniversary to bring it up."

"There's no one in the house, okay?" He kissed her cheek. "We've still got about twelve hours before Tomas is going to contact us. We're going to get a good night's sleep and tomorrow we'll call Peter and he'll get us out of this mess." He patted her hip, then rolled over, his back toward her.

She stayed sitting up. Listening. The house was quiet but there was something wrong. She knew it. She poked Finn a third time, hard.

"Cut it out!"

"Finn, I'm not kidding. There's someone in the house. I can't explain why, but I can feel someone here."

"Then go tell them you *feel* it's time for them to leave."

Hollis stayed in bed another minute. She waited, listening for anything that sounded sinister, not that she was sure what sinister sounded like. Finn sighed a few times, angry sighs, but then he started to settle. Hollis had a choice to make. Try to sleep and hope that she was wrong, or go downstairs and find out that either she was right and their lives were in danger, or Finn was right and know that fifteen years from now he'd still be bringing it up.

She got out of bed hoping she was wrong. Living with Finn's smugness was still preferable to dying a horrible death. Though barely.

As she moved toward the bedroom door, as quietly as possible, Finn pushed the covers off and got up. He grabbed his cell phone. "I can't let you die alone."

"I appreciate that."

She turned the handle on their bedroom door and pulled it open. A slight squeak. The sort of thing that she'd never notice but now seemed like an entire orchestra was announcing that she and Finn were on the move.

Once in the hallway, Finn got in front of her, going down the stairs first. Hollis put her hand on his back, one step behind, but still close enough that if a bullet passed through him it would likely also kill her. Why did she think such things? It didn't help the situation. She shook her head, trying to wipe that image from her brain.

At the end of the stairs, they paused. Hollis could hear her own breathing, she could hear the clock in the kitchen tick slowly. But was there something else?

A sound. A shoe taking one step on their floor. Finn handed Hollis his phone. "9-1-1," he whispered.

But before she could press a button, a deep voice boomed in the darkness. "That won't be necessary."

Seven

It was an odd feeling, being relieved and terrified at the same time, but that was the effect he had.

Finn switched on the hall light. Peter Moodley was standing in their kitchen.

"I've put the kettle on," he said in a clipped South African accent. "Hollis, why don't you get the cups? And Finn, perhaps we could all use a biscuit if you have any."

Peter was someone used to being obeyed, and even though she objected to being ordered around in her own house, Hollis got out three tea cups, the good ones, and set them on the table. Finn had found some iced lemon cookies and was about to put them on the table in their package when Hollis stopped him, so he arranged them on a plate, shaking his head the whole time. He might have broken in, but Peter was still company and that required a little effort.

Peter stood by the kettle. Hollis was about to make a joke about watched kettles never boiling, but as soon as she opened her mouth the kettle whistled. Even water is afraid of defying him, she thought. Peter took out three tea bags from the box of Barry's tea that was kept in the cupboard next to the stove. Hollis wanted to ask how he knew they were there, but she didn't. She also didn't ask how he'd gotten into their home and if this was the first time. She didn't want to know. She did notice the gun holstered under his jacket, but she didn't ask about that, either.

Instead, Hollis and Finn sat at the table while Peter made a pot of tea, brought it to them, and poured each a cup. "You look well," he said.

"So do you," Hollis told him. Finn glared at her, but she shrugged. What was the point in being impolite? Plus, he did look good, actually. His dark-brown skin looked great against the pale pink shirt he was wearing. His head was still bald, but she could see a slight five o'clock shadow on his scalp, making clear he hadn't shaved his head because of a bald spot. Just some Peter-y control move, she guessed. His tall, muscular physique was still in peak shape. A gold watch, a Rolex maybe, on his wrist. A bit pricey for a government employee, but it suited him. And he looked rested. That part was odd. Spies don't keep regular hours. At least she assumed they didn't.

Still she was surprised that the nervousness she'd felt upstairs, the hot/cold certainty that something was wrong, had turned out to be Peter. It felt somehow worse than that. But, she reminded herself, she really had no idea what Peter was capable of. It could turn out to be very bad.

Finn got right to the point. "What do you want?"

Peter smiled, which sent a shiver down Hollis's spine. Peter was at his most dangerous when he smiled.

"When were you going to tell me about the letter?"

"In the morning," Hollis said.

"We were thinking about telling you in the morning," Finn corrected her.

It was Hollis's turn to glare. Finn had lobbied for turning the whole business over to Peter, and now he was talking tough. She tried to catch his eye, to see if this was part of a larger plan, but Finn was looking straight at Peter.

"We're not interested in getting mixed up with this again," Finn continued. "I was thinking it might be better to just toss the letter and the rest of it into the trash."

"That's not going to solve your problem."

"That's what I said," Hollis blurted out.

"What does it say?"

Finn squinted at Peter. "You know about the letter but not what it says?"

"I have many talents, but x-ray vision isn't one of them. We figured you were being watched, so we watched you …"

"Why are we being watched?"

Peter didn't answer. He just smiled and looked at Hollis. "Finn just said it might be better to toss 'the letter and the rest of it.' What's the rest of it?"

Hollis said nothing. She glanced toward Finn, who stared at her, then shrugged. Peter watched, his smile growing bigger.

"I miss this," he said. "The three of us playing cat and mouse." He moved his eyes from Hollis to Finn. "And other mouse. It reminds me of a tabby that roamed the neighborhood back home in Soweto. A big cat, always hungry. He would find himself a mouse and he would bat it between his paws." Peter swatted an imaginary mouse between his hands to demonstrate. "I would watch him as a little boy. He would play with the mouse like a toy. Sometimes the little creature would almost get away, but just as it was nearly free, the cat would scoop it back up and bat it around some more." He laughed. "I enjoyed watching that. I liked the way he took his time. But at some point, always, the terrified little mouse would finally realize that there was no escape and go limp. Then the cat would raise its paw high, and..." Peter raised his hand a couple of feet into the air. He paused, then he slammed his palm into the table. The teacups shook. So did Finn and Hollis. "He would break the mouse's neck and make himself a meal of it."

There was silence for a moment. In that silence, Peter took a bite from his lemon cookie.

"Can you just tell us what you want instead of scaring us half to death?" Hollis finally asked.

Peter laughed. "Where would the fun be in that?"

Finn got up from the table and went upstairs. Peter looked amused but said nothing. Hollis was not amused, but she also stayed silent. She was sure he wasn't going back to bed, pretty sure anyway, but she couldn't imagine what he was doing leaving her alone with Peter. She watched Peter brush crumbs off his shirt. As he moved she could see the handle of his gun. Peter's previous job in British intelligence, they had discovered in Ireland, was as a fixer—a man who got rid of anything that might cause problems for the government—inconvenient information, or inconvenient people. As pleasant as Peter could be, Hollis knew that if it was deemed necessary, she and Finn would become an unsolvable missing persons case for the local police. She wondered if Finn was thinking that too and was looking for a way they could escape.

It took several long minutes to find out.

Finn came back, the envelope in his hand. He dropped it in front of Peter. "Here. Now take it and do whatever spy stuff you do. Just leave us out of it."

Peter emptied the contents, going methodically through the letter and each passport before speaking. "I don't think that's possible, mate."

Finn sat at the table and poured more tea into his cup. "Why not? And don't give me some nonsense about how I'll be in danger without your help, because I'm in danger with it."

"I wasn't."

"And please don't say my country needs me."

"Better men than you have tried to take down TCT and failed."

"So we're off the hook."

"I'm afraid not." Peter put the letter in his pocket. "We might be able to find fingerprints," he said. Then he stacked the passports, put them back into the envelope, and slid them toward Finn. "You'll need these."

"Why? You just said we don't have the skills."

Peter got up, his chair squeaking as he pushed it back. He walked out of the kitchen and toward the living room.

Hollis watched him disappear from view. She looked at Finn, who was doing the same. "Do we follow him?"

"I'm guessing that's what he wants."

Hollis got up, but Finn kept sitting. "You know he's not just going to leave," she said.

Finn grunted. "I hate that guy." He took a giant swig of his tea and slammed the cup on its saucer making a pinging noise. As he watched the cup shake a little in the saucer, he blushed. "That move would have looked cooler with whiskey."

"You don't have to look cool for me."

"It would be nice if I didn't look like a complete idiot."

"You look impressive as hell," she said. "And much calmer than me."

He took Hollis's hand, kissed it, and they walked toward their living room.

"Okay, Peter," he said as they caught sight of him. "Let's get the 'show and tell' portion over with so I can go back to bed."

Peter pointed toward a corner of the room where the hall light didn't quite reach. "Not sure you'll want to sleep."

Finn took a few steps forward and gasped. Hollis couldn't see anything above the shoulders of the two men, so she pushed between them. Then she gasped too.

Propped up in an overstuffed floral chair was a body, with a dark stain on the chair near his head. A stain that even in the dim light could only be one thing—blood.

Eight

Hollis moved closer to the body. It was a young man, early twenties, she guessed, with long brown hair. His eyes were open and glassy. There was no point in checking for a pulse. He was dead. Very dead.

This was what had made her skin tingle earlier. This, not Peter. At least not just Peter. She could feel a shiver in her throat. The Chinese food that had been quietly digesting was now moving back up. She locked her jaw, closed her eyes, and tried to focus. She could hear Finn behind her, sounding relaxed and even a bit sleepy.

"Who is he?" he asked Peter.

"Not sure."

Hollis opened her eyes. There was no way she was going to be seen as fragile or afraid while the men discussed the murder with vague disinterest. But she wasn't just going to join in either, pretending this was somehow ordinary. Dead bodies at the Larsson household—just another Thursday night. She took a long breath, then reached into the dead man's jacket pocket and pulled out a cell phone and a slim canvas wallet. The first ID in the wallet was for Bradford University. Tomas Silva. History Department.

"He's a grad student," she told the men.

"I think he gets a failing grade in staying out of trouble," Peter said.

That was too much. Hollis spun around. "Is this funny? You killed this kid?"

Even at five foot eight, the top of her head only reached to Peter's throat. She wasn't intimidating, she knew that. But she was angry.

"He was here when I got here," Peter protested. "And I would lower your voice, Hollis. Your neighbors aren't aware of this young man, but shouting will draw attention."

Finn moved between Hollis and Peter. "You've been inside with us. How do you know no one has seen anything?"

Peter opened the front door and signaled toward a black van parked across the street. Two men got out. Hollis half expected them to be in black suits and trench coats, like in the movies, but they weren't. Both were wearing jeans and t-shirts. Nothing that would draw attention to them, except for guns tucked into their belts.

Fixers. That much she could guess. But what were they here to get rid of? The young man in the chair, or Finn and her?

Peter pushed Hollis and Finn back in the house. Hollis looked around. Her cell was upstairs, but she'd had Finn's at one point. Where? The kitchen, she remembered. She moved away from Peter toward the other room, and the table with tea, lemon cookies, and a cell phone.

Peter followed. As she grabbed the phone, he put his hand around her wrist. She twisted her arm to slip from his hold. Nothing happened.

She had a black belt in karate. She'd spent weeks getting out of wrist grabs just like this. She twisted again. Peter's grip held. Finn grabbed Peter's other arm, but he held Finn off just as easily. "Will you both be good children?"

"You're not going to hurt us," she said.

"Of course, I'm not," Peter said. "Stop twisting around."

Hollis wanted to keep fighting but what was the point? She nodded. Finn sighed. Peter let them both go.

"Don't call the police," he said. "You'll look like a fool."

"You can leave," Hollis said. "We'll tell the police we heard a noise and came down and found him."

"And they'll find that plausible?"

Probably not, she had to admit, but what were they supposed to do?

"I could tell them that an offshoot of Interpol wants us to get involved with an international criminal organization and somehow this kid was mixed up, so his body was placed in our living room as a threat. But that seems even more ridiculous."

"You think he was dead when he was brought here?"

"The alternative is that he broke in and sat in our chair. Then someone else broke in and shot him," Hollis said.

Peter considered it. "Why a threat?"

"Did you kill him?"

"I told you. No."

"It's a message of some kind. And not a happy one. If it's not you, then it's TCT."

Finn moved back toward the living room. "The body is gone," he said.

Hollis didn't believe him. It had been less than a minute since Peter had signaled the men. But when she followed Finn, she saw he was right. Where there had once been a dead man, there was now an empty chair, and where his head had been resting, there was a blood stain the size of an orange.

Hollis let a small noise, half gasp, half cry, escape from her throat. The nausea that had subsided while she was angry was returning. Was this her life now? Murdered college students in her living room, dangerous spies cleaning up the mess that even more dangerous criminals left behind?

Peter put his hand on Hollis's shoulder and she very nearly jumped. "We'll get that cleaned," he said.

"It's not my chair I'm concerned about."

But if she was willing to admit it (which she wasn't), she did like that chair. It was the first piece of furniture that she and Finn had bought after their wedding. It was a bit worn but still beautiful.

"Whoever did it must have walked up behind him and shot him in the head," she said.

"You think he was shot?" Peter asked.

"The stain is where his head was. Would you stab someone in the head? Seems like a place you would shoot someone."

"Logical. And I agree, not much blood. Another indication he was killed elsewhere and moved here," Peter conceded. "But it doesn't appear that they walked up on him and shot. The young man was held somewhere. Did you notice the bruises on his wrists?"

She hadn't and felt embarrassed about it at first. Then annoyed that she'd been expected to notice. All the questions weren't because Peter hadn't figured out what happened—he just wanted to know if she had.

"You think he was held, maybe tortured, before being shot?" she asked. "Tell me again that bringing him here wasn't some kind of a threat."

Peter, for once, seemed at a loss for words.

Finn didn't seem to be paying attention to the conversation. He had pulled back the curtain slightly and was staring out the window. Hollis couldn't tell if he was worried that someone might see a body being moved or just amazed by the efficiency of the two men.

"They're getting back in the van." He turned to Peter. "What are they going to do with him?"

"An alley, I imagine. Something that will make the police think it was a mugging. And since Hollis lifted his wallet and phone, in a way, they'll be right."

Hollis looked at the wallet on the coffee table. "It's Tommy. It has to be. Angela said her friend Tommy had dropped off the package, but she said someone had paid him to do it."

"He lied," Finn said.

"I suppose. But how can he be a master criminal? He's a grad student. Is he planning to take down the world's economy between classes?"

"Or he was paid to watch you," Peter suggested.

"And whoever paid him, killed him?" That didn't make sense to Hollis, but something else did. "Or you guys killed him, you or someone else in Blue. Which, if you did, you should stop lying about it. You hardly need to concern yourself with your reputation around us."

Peter's eyes widened. To Hollis, he seemed genuinely surprised by the insult. But he said nothing in his or his agency's defense. Instead he motioned for Hollis and Finn to sit down. Hollis did, but Finn put up a momentary show of protest.

"If 'Tomas Silva' is dead then this whole thing is off," Finn said.

"I don't think it's that simple," Peter said. "I'm going to leave now. If that was Silva, someone else will likely contact you. I want you to do what they tell you. Exactly what they tell you."

"What if they tell us to do something illegal?" Finn asked.

"We'll know, and we'll intervene. But the more you seem to be on the side of TCT, the more they will trust you and the less danger ..." He stopped.

"The less danger we'll be in," Finn finished for him. "Or we could say no. Tell whoever contacts us to call you, and take a nice long vacation somewhere no one can find us."

"There is nowhere you can go that they can't find you. And, for that matter, where we can't find you." Peter spoke evenly and softly, like he was talking to hysterical children. But Finn was calm, and Hollis realized her heart was now beating normally and her stomach was no longer roiling. She decided they were both in their safe place—taking an intellectual approach to the situation rather than allowing themselves to indulge in the fear that was just below the surface.

Finn looked over at Hollis. He said nothing, just looked into her eyes. She nodded slightly. He nodded back. It was all the communication they needed.

"It doesn't seem like we have much choice," he said. "For now. But the first chance we get to walk away, we will. And I want you to promise me that we'll never be bothered again. We go back to our lives and you stop breaking into our house."

Peter seemed ready to laugh but didn't. "I didn't drag you into this, Finn. Your Irish friend did. When you find him, do us all a favor and say the same thing to him." He wrote a phone number on a piece of paper, left it on the coffee table. "Dire emergency only." Then he got up, took the dead man's wallet and cell phone, and walked toward the door.

"I'll send the men back in for the chair," he said as he was leaving. "There's room in the van. We'll have it good as new in a few days."

"Don't bother," Finn said. "I always hated that chair."

Hollis didn't say anything until after Peter had left but once he was gone, she had to ask. "Since when have you hated that chair?"

"I just said that because I didn't want them to take it."

"So you like it."

"If I'm being honest, then no, I never really liked it."

"Yes, you did. You picked it out."

"You picked it out," he corrected her. "We'd been married for three months. I just wanted to make you happy, so I went along with whatever you wanted."

She tried to remember if that was true. It couldn't be. He was always disagreeing with her, wasn't he? "How do you feel about our china pattern?"

"White, with a narrow silver band and little white dots along the edge. Always loved it," he said, though it didn't sound genuine. "Do we have cotton swabs?"

"In the bathroom." She was about to ask why when Finn disappeared. When he returned, a dozen swabs in his hand, she realized what he was doing.

"We'll take this to Dr. Richardson," he said. "She's a DNA expert, probably the best at the university. Doesn't she owe you a favor?"

Hollis had helped Elaine Richardson with a grant proposal, just two colleagues offering support. It was hardly the sort of favor that would allow Hollis to show up with a bag full of cotton swabs asking for ... what?

"She's going to want to know why I need her to type these. And even if I come up with a reason, she's going to need to check the databases for a match. That's a lot to ask her."

She wasn't really explaining it to Finn, she was explaining it to herself, on her way to coming up with some half-acceptable reasons to show up with blood on cotton swabs asking Elaine to help her match the blood with a person.

It didn't matter anyway, Finn wasn't really listening. He was collecting sample after sample and dropping them into a plastic sandwich bag. When he'd collected about a dozen swabs in the baggie, he handed it to her.

"If we know who that kid was, maybe we'll be able to figure out what he was doing here, and that will help us with…" He paused. "With whatever comes next."

Hollis nodded. Finn needed to do something, have answers. She did too. They were *read first, ask questions later* type of people. Research, knowledge, it was always the way. Or, Hollis thought as she looked at the blood stain on the chair, it had been until now.

Nine

Elaine Richardson didn't even blink when Hollis showed up at her office with a baggie full of swabs.

"Thanks for coming in on a long weekend," Hollis said. "I owe you."

"I didn't do it for you. I'm always here when there are no classes. The only time I can get my research work done in peace." She looked at the baggie. "It'll take a week or so. I can have a grad student type it for me, but it'll still take up to a week."

"That's okay. I mean, it's silly. Finn is convinced that someone tried to break in last night and cut himself on a nail by the window. He even thinks he knows who it is, some student Finn says hates him, but I think it's just an animal. We have a lot of raccoons in our neighborhood. They're not friendly, are they?" Hollis wanted to stop talking but she couldn't.

She had rehearsed a reason for the request, and she couldn't stop herself from giving it, even though Elaine seemed perfectly fine doing the favor.

"Last week, an administrator who shall remain nameless asked me to match two saliva swabs. I think some girl showed up saying she's his daughter. He doesn't want to go through the normal channels because…" She smiled. "Well, because."

"The faculty are keeping you pretty busy with our little side projects."

"Never a dull moment. You just want to know if it's human or animal DNA?"

Hollis hesitated. She already knew the answer to that question, but she'd backed herself into a corner with the story. "Well, if it is human, which it probably isn't…"

"You want me to check it against the federal database?" Elaine raised an eyebrow, but there was a smile to go along with it. "That shouldn't be an issue. I'm working on a federal research project. I can slip it in with my samples."

"And that would include inmates, federal workers, like for example, I don't know, CIA agents and postal workers…"

"Interesting mix, but not entirely accurate. CIA, yes, but not all federal workers. The real gold is in those genealogy sites. Anyone who gives their DNA to one of those sites is offering up clues to their whole family tree. They're catching serial killers by finding people who share some DNA and then tracing it through the family tree to the actual killer. Amazing," she said. "I can sneak in a profile if I don't get a hit on the database."

Hollis wanted to say it wouldn't be necessary, but she couldn't. She had a feeling they would need the widest net possible to find the identity of the dead man. "It all sounds so fascinating. It might be fun just to see where it leads."

"I don't think people understand how much of our lives is now accessible to anyone with a computer. Not just financial records and the like, but if someone hacks into a DNA database, they could have the most personal information on nearly everyone in the country. Maybe even half the world. They could use it to create some supervirus targeted toward people with certain genes or something." She laughed. "I sound so paranoid. As if there's some villain out there trying to bring about chaos and destruction."

Hollis smiled though the whole idea seemed terrifyingly possible. "Thank heavens there isn't."

"I know! But in the real world, just a warning: If you think it might be a student here, it won't be in the federal database. Unless it's someone in the science labs, or someone who has signed up for one of our research projects. We take DNA swabs from those guys. If we're lucky and it's someone from here, I might be able to get results in a few days."

Hollis didn't know what to say, but she managed a smile. Finn could have done this much better, she thought. He had a way of being casual even in the worst moments. Hollis hadn't put in enough practice on her poker face. Elaine put her hand on Hollis's arm, and Hollis practically jumped.

"You're going to be right, you know," Elaine said. "You and Finn aren't the types to have enemies. Unless it's a *Procyon lotor*."

It took a moment for Hollis to realize Elaine was giving her the Latin name for raccoon. Academics can't help but show off.

Hollis handed Elaine a card. "Personal phone and email, when you get the results."

"Absolutely. Everything on the down-low. Makes me feel vaguely criminal." She laughed. "It's nice to have a bit of excitement once in a while."

"Yeah," Hollis agreed. "Once in a while."

It was almost two o'clock when Hollis left the science building. There had been no word from anyone unusual all morning. If that was Silva on their chair, then perhaps the whole thing was over before it could begin. In any case, she and Finn had been up since seven, waiting. They'd stared at the chair, debated what to do, made a breakfast they let go cold because neither felt like eating, and drank several more cups of coffee than either of them should have. But mostly they waited. And the longer they'd waited, the worse their anxiety got, so they'd made a plan. They were going to ignore everything Peter told them and run. They weren't spies, they weren't prepared to go off to save a criminal from himself. Before Ireland, it had sounded romantic, but the truth was that being scared, thinking that at any minute you might die, wasn't as fun as it looked in the movies. The more they talked about it, the more clear it became they were in over their heads. They had to run. Let Peter and Declan sort it out for themselves.

Finn was determined to get the DNA to the lab before they went anywhere. They knew that if they left together, it would set off alarms if anyone was watching, so they'd agreed Hollis would go on her own. She was the one who had helped Elaine, so they figured it would be easier for her to ask the favor. Even if she was followed, going to the university was not a suspicious activity. Hopefully.

Now she was supposed to go to the grocery store, just to get anything that would look like a normal day. Finn had suggested bread and milk, but that struck her as foolish. If they were going on the run, why let food spoil? She was planning on some frozen veggies and a few cans of soup. It would have the added benefit of being something she could throw at a would-be attacker if she needed to. Going to the store also meant she could use the cash machine inside. She was going to take out as much as the bank would let her, as well

53

as a cash advance on two credit cards. Whatever they could get would have to hold them until they were safe.

Then she was supposed to go home, to the second part of the plan. They'd make their escape through the basement window to the alley behind their house, run down the street to their favorite Italian restaurant, and get a taxi there to the train station and whatever train was leaving town first. There was the problem of when to call Peter. Neither of them had a lot of faith he'd back their play, but they'd have plenty of time to worry about that later.

Finn was home, still waiting until the last possible second for word from whoever Declan might send. They had decided if he did reach out, Finn would try to stall, buy them time to disappear. No matter what, they weren't going to Argentina. They were going to follow the plan.

But there was one place she had to stop, just to be sure.

Ten

Hollis was careful as she drove, watching out the rearview mirror, sure that no one followed her to Breyer Square, the small residential neighborhood just north of campus where a lot of the grad students lived.

But just in case, she parked around the corner.

"It's going to be okay," she muttered to herself as she walked down the street. It had to be okay.

When she got to the small frame bungalow on the corner, she rang the bell and waited. Angela opened her door, still in her pajamas, and she went pale at the sight of her professor.

"Are you okay, Dr. Larsson?"

"Are *you* okay?" Hollis asked.

"Why wouldn't I be? I wasn't supposed to go in the office today, was I? Oh my gosh. I'm sorry ..."

"No. It's fine. It's just you never sent me your friend's contact information. Do you have it?"

Angela opened the door to let Hollis in. The living room was small, furnished by Goodwill and Ikea. The only original pieces were a pair of paintings, both Van Gogh–esqe still lifes of flowers. The whole room was neat and very feminine. The amount of throw pillows alone would have sent Finn into eye-twitching mode.

They'd been married for nearly two years before she'd come home to garbage bags full of floral throw pillows that had once been on their bed. He told her he couldn't do it anymore, live with all the pillows. At the time she was confused. She remembered thinking he loved those pillows. But now, she smiled at the memory. He was right. When they were first married he had gone along with all her choices. Annoying as it was at times, she liked him better this way, sometimes cranky and opinionated, but honest. And in retrospect, it was far too many pillows.

"I got a call from him," Angela said.

"Tommy." Hollis's voice stuck in her throat. "What did he say?"

"He told me that someone dropped off a bag with cash in it, loads of cash. He said maybe ten thousand dollars. There was a note telling him to leave town. He thinks it has something to do with that envelope he brought for you."

"When did you speak to him?"

"Last night."

"When last night?"

"I don't know. Maybe ten."

That would have given the killer plenty of time to shoot Tommy and bring him to the house. It was after one when they went downstairs and found Peter.

"Are you sure it was ten?" Hollis asked. "Not later?"

"Yes, I'm sure. I was studying."

That would mean Angela was home on the night before a long weekend night reading about trade agreements and their effects on diplomacy. Hollis hoped, for Angela's sake, she was just trying to impress her professor with a lie.

"And that was the last time you heard from him?"

"Yeah. My roommates went to a party, so I had the place to myself for once." She nodded toward the hallway where there were several closed doors leading, Hollis guessed, to bedrooms. On each of the bedroom doors was a corkboard with notes. The only one she could read said, *Your turn to do dishes* with five exclamation points.

"They're home now if someone came ... I mean, you're not alone now?"

"Hungover and sleeping it off, but yeah." Angela was looking a little nervous. "What's going on?"

Hollis didn't explain. She was trying her best to stay calm and think about what to say next. "What does Tommy look like?"

Angela shrugged. "Ordinary. Sort of cute."

Not helpful.

Hollis tried again. "Yes, but black or white, short or tall, fat or thin, long brown hair or bald. Specifically, what?"

Angela walked to the coffee table, picked up a cell phone, and flipped through it for a few seconds. She turned the phone to face Hollis. "Like this."

Hollis stared at the photo. A good-looking black student with short hair. Not a white kid with shoulder-length brown hair, like the young man in her house. "This is Tommy?" she asked. "Are you sure?"

"Of course I'm sure. Why?"

Hollis handed her back the phone. "I thought I saw someone outside the house last night. A young man, white with brown hair. I wondered if it was your friend."

"That describes a lot of guys."

57

It did. "What's Tommy's last name?"

"Silva," Angela told her.

Yoga cleansing breath, Hollis. She tried it. It didn't work. If Tommy Silva was alive, then who was the dead kid in her chair? He had an ID with Tommy's name on it, but then again, she had passports with Janet and Tim McCabe's names on them. Whoever they were.

She felt herself go pale. If Tommy Silva was a real person, were Tim and Janet real too? Up until that moment she'd assumed they were just made up. If there were real people named Tim and Janet McCabe, they might be dangerous. Or, she realized, they might have wound up with bullets in their heads, just as the fake Tommy had in his.

"Please tell me what's going on, Dr. Larsson," Angela asked. "You seem really stressed."

"I didn't get a lot of sleep," Hollis mumbled. "This is the start of a long weekend. Maybe Tommy should do what the note suggested and go out of town. Maybe you should go together."

"We're not a couple."

"But you want to be."

Angela turned bright red. "Is Tommy in trouble?"

Hollis opened the door. "Call him and tell him to leave town today. You too."

Hollis walked out of the house, leaving Angela standing alone and confused. She could hear Angela call after her, ever eager to do something to help, but Hollis turned back and said again, "Leave town. Now. Promise me."

Angela nodded, but she didn't move from the door.

"I must sound crazy," Hollis muttered, but explaining herself to Angela was a problem for another day. Today was already chock-full.

She'd only delayed by twenty minutes or so. Not too bad. Now she would go to the grocery store and then home. And then, fingers crossed, she and Finn would be out of danger within the hour.

It had sounded like a great idea while they were sitting in their kitchen. Now she was sure there was a flaw that neither had anticipated. She just couldn't figure out what it was.

Eleven

"Dr. Larsson," a man said as she walked into the living room less than an hour later. "Let me take those." He pointed to the grocery bags in her hands. Before she had a chance to throw a can of chicken noodle at him, he'd taken them.

"Where's Finn?"

"The kitchen. Your husband was telling us you were at the office all day working on a book about the United Nations. How wonderful he turned out to have the wrong schedule."

He was a short man, stocky, and a little rough. He was in his seventies, she guessed, with dark brown hair that was clearly dyed, a tight smile, a strong Latin accent, and an air of absolute authority. But there was something off. His face was a bit puffy, a slight redness around the nose, and when he got close there was the unmistakable scent of stale whiskey.

He searched inside the bags and put them on the coffee table.

"Who are you?" She was waiting for him to say Silva, to tell her that Declan was safe but in trouble, to thank her for their help. But he didn't answer. And the longer he didn't answer, the more worried she got that he was the man they were warned about, the one the note referred to as Jorge Videla.

"What happened to the chair?" He nodded toward the blood stain that had now dried to a faded reddish-brown.

"My husband cut himself shaving."

The money she'd taken from the ATM was in her purse. She nearly offered it to him if he'd just leave them alone, but that wasn't likely to work, she knew. She also considered using the heavy bag as a weapon. He didn't look strong. She felt no doubt she could take him down. But that could lead to more trouble. If he'd come alone, where was Finn?

"I want to see my husband."

He smiled. "How about we go into the kitchen?"

He directed her to go first, and when she did she saw Finn standing by the refrigerator, his arms slightly raised, anger and terror in equal measure on his face. Behind him were two unsmiling men with guns, one of which was pointed at Finn.

"You okay?" Finn mouthed.

She nodded. He smiled a tight, sad smile. So much for the plan.

The man moved past her toward the gunmen. "I wanted to do this differently, but you had visitors last night, so here we are."

"And where is that?" Hollis asked.

"What an excellent question, Dr. Larsson. You both have a reputation for being quite intelligent. Well earned, clearly." He nodded toward the shorter of the two men, who left the room. Hollis could hear him walking up the steps to their bedroom.

"You don't have anything to drink in the house, do you?"

"Alcohol?" Hollis asked. "We might have some wine in the basement. If you want to send your friend downstairs…"

The man smiled. "He'll stay here, thank you."

He began opening the cabinets, disappointed each time. He walked out of the room and came back empty-handed. Finally he nudged Finn out of the way and opened the refrigerator. He stuck his head in for what seemed like a ridiculous amount of time but was rewarded only with a small bottle of green juice.

"What's this?"

"A combination of kale, spinach, carrots, and beets," Finn said. "I get it at the health food store near my gym."

The man frowned and put the juice back in the fridge. They waited. Hollis watched the other man, the one with his gun pointed at Finn's head. He was over six feet, and he looked strong. His hair was short, more stylish than a military cut, but still too short to grab in a fight. He was wearing a long white t-shirt and black pants. Nothing there she could use against him. And, obviously, even if she could, she'd have to get the gun away from Finn's head. And that seemed unlikely.

The gunman kept looking over at a photo of Hollis and Finn that a neighbor had given them, framed in one of those magnetic frames meant to stick on the fridge. It was a cute photo but nothing special. They were hosting a Fourth of July party and were posed behind the barbeque, drinking beer from red cups and flipping burgers. A pretty typical summer celebration, but the gunman couldn't take his eyes off it.

"What are we waiting for?" she asked.

"My colleague wants one more look. Just to be sure."

As he said that, Hollis noticed the other gunman looked confused. This wasn't what they were here to do. They weren't supposed to be looking for something. So why were they there?

"You haven't said your name," she said to the older man.

"Names have little meaning. You know that better than anyone."

He sat, as if he were too exhausted to keep standing. Hollis and Finn kept their eyes on each other. If she hadn't gone to check on Angela, she thought. If she'd just stuck to the original plan, they'd be at the restaurant at least, maybe even at the train station. They'd be safe.

It was ten minutes before the shorter gunman returned.

"*Nada*," he said.

The man nodded, but for a moment he seemed unsure, at least to Hollis. "Well, that's it then. I suppose we'll have to move forward anyway." He stood up.

"Move forward how?" Hollis asked.

The shorter gunman moved toward her. Hollis took a step back toward the front door, more out of instinct than strategy. As long as there was still a gun pointed at Finn, she wasn't going anywhere.

The gunman moved past Hollis, then turned. She could feel his breath on her throat. Hollis looked toward Finn, who managed a smile. She smiled back. Then her eyes moved to the man in charge.

"I am so sorry about this," the older man said.

And that was the last thing she remembered.

Twelve

The sound was low and steady. She recognized it but couldn't place it. She was cold. That felt familiar too. Her ears popped. She opened her eyes.

"Champagne? Or maybe you'd prefer water first."

The rough man was sitting opposite her, a smile on his face and a full glass of something bubbly in his hand. He extended it toward her, but she shook her head slowly. She was sitting in a large leather chair. At first, she thought she was tied to it, but as the grogginess lifted she saw that it was a seat belt. The steady noise, the cold, the ears. She was on a plane.

"Where's Finn?" she asked.

"We may have overdone it a bit on the chloroform," he said. "He's a tall man. We understand he's a boxer." The man shrugged. "He's sleeping it off on the bed in the other room." He nodded toward a closed door.

A bedroom? She looked around. The plane was small. Just ten seats toward the front, and only one of them occupied. The man who had chloroformed her. He nodded a greeting. She nodded back. They were polite, she thought. At least for now. Where she and the man sat, the middle of the plane she guessed, there was a couch and the two leather chairs. In the back, a bedroom. She'd always wondered what it would be like to fly on a private jet, on some adventure to an exotic locale. This was definitely not what she'd imagined.

She unbuckled her seat belt and got up. She was unsteady, but she managed the few steps to the bedroom door.

"You don't have any questions for me," the man said. "How odd."

"You can wait. I want to see my husband."

She pushed against the door with her shoulder, half expecting it to be locked. Terrified that if it wasn't, the room would be empty. But it was exactly as the man said. There was a queen-sized bed and Finn was on his back, snoring. Next to the bed, there was a chair. And in the chair was a tall man with a short haircut, a small scar on his neck, and a gun—the one who'd held the gun on Finn in their kitchen.

Hollis crawled onto the bed and lay beside Finn.

"He's out cold," the man said.

"That's okay." She wrapped her arms around Finn and put her head on his shoulder.

"You've been married a long time?"

"A very long time."

The man smiled a little, then got up. "I'll leave you alone." He closed the door quietly behind him.

She'd been kidnapped before. That was a heck of a sentence, she thought. She'd been kidnapped before. She and Finn had been taken in Ireland. Finn had been annoyed that the kidnappers had been more concerned about Hollis's black belt than Finn's size, so they hadn't even knocked him out. It bruised his ego. He'd be proud now.

She poked him.

He let out a grunt.

"Ssssh," she said. "I need you to wake up but quietly."

"Is it trash day?" he mumbled. "I'll bring the garbage out in a minute."

"What?"

The snoring started again, so she poked him again. He grabbed her hand and went back to sleep. She couldn't get out of it. Geez, he was strong. The Irish kidnappers had been wrong to think he wasn't a threat. She was about to poke him with the other hand when she had a better idea.

She put her mouth against his ear and whispered, "You are the sexiest man in the world, Finn Larsson."

The snoring stopped, but he didn't open his eyes.

"I get so turned on just looking at you," she continued. "All I want to do is take your clothes off."

He rolled over onto her. "I have an odd headache," he said, "but I'll play through the pain." He kissed her neck and moved his hands across her chest.

Hollis kept whispering. "The man from the house, do you remember?"

Finn stopped. He looked at her. She could see that it was slowly dawning on him—what happened at the house. He sat up. "Where are we?"

"A plane. A private plane."

"Going where?"

She shook her head.

Finn took a deep breath. "Buenos Aires. Before you got home, one of his goons went through the house. He said he was searching for guns, but all he took were the fake passports," Finn told her. "The guy in charge made a comment about how it was nice to finally meet me."

"What does that mean?"

Finn shook his head, then lay down again. "I feel dizzy."

"They chloroformed us."

Finn put his hand to his head and moaned. "You know chloroform can have long-lasting effects on the liver and the central nervous system."

"Let's focus on the short-term effects of being flown to Argentina by men with guns."

"Where are they?"

Hollis pointed toward the door.

"It's just the three guys from the house?"

"As far as I can tell. If they searched the house before I got there, why did they do it again?"

"I don't know. He actually seemed kind of surprised to find the passports. One of the gunmen said everything checked out, but the other guy didn't seem happy about it."

"He asked me about the blood on the chair. Did he ask you?"

"No. I thought at first he was Silva, but he wouldn't say his name."

"Not to me, either."

"But he called me Tim McCabe," Finn said. "He said calling myself Dr. Finn Larsson was a pretty smart cover. I told him I really was a World Literature professor and you really were an International Studies professor, and that Tim and Janet McCabe were fake people."

"And he didn't believe you."

"No, Holly, he did not."

"What if Tim and Janet aren't fake people?" Hollis asked. "I found out the friend of Angela who brought the package really is named Tommy Silva. And he's still alive. At least, it wasn't his body in our house. I was thinking maybe Tim and Janet..."

"Are international criminals? Spies?" Finn sat up. "And now that guy thinks we're them? Wonderful."

They had a choice to make. Stay in the room and wait until they landed or go out to the main body of the plane and ask their questions. Obviously, escape wasn't an option, though Finn spent several minutes looking for parachutes under the bed and trying to sort out the physics involved in jumping from a plane. Hollis just watched and waited.

"We're stuck," he said finally.

"We should ask who Tomas Silva is," Hollis said. "And explain that we really have no idea what's going on."

"Absolutely not. He's not going to believe we're amateurs ..."

"We are."

"But he's not going to believe that."

She didn't point out that no real spy would sleep through someone dumping a body in their home. Or walk into a trap the way they had, allowing gunmen to get the better of them in their own home.

But maybe they did. This whole spy business wasn't the glamourous, cocktail-swirling life she once imagined it was. The danger was real enough, though. That much she knew. And that was why it only made sense to tell the truth to the man in the leather chair and hope he could see that this was some ridiculous misunderstanding.

"We can try. He seems reasonable. Even a little sad. And he offered me champagne. He obviously wants us to be comfortable."

Finn rolled his eyes.

Hollis put her arms around him. "I was right about someone being in our house. Maybe I'm right now. I'm a good judge of character."

"Since when?"

"I married you, didn't I?"

"Sort of proves my point. Any other man would not go along with this ridiculous plan of yours."

68

"But you are?"

"It's either that or jump from at least a thousand feet in the air."

"You know how low private planes can fly?"

He blushed. His depth of knowledge really was impressive, she thought. She kissed his cheek.

"We'll explain what happened and he'll believe us," she said. "You'll see."

Thirteen

She laid out the facts, quickly but plainly. The man listened, amused. She could see Finn smile slightly, happy he'd been right about the man. His depth of knowledge was annoying.

"I knew you would say this," the man said, his soft accent getting stronger as he poured himself another glass of champagne. "Forgive me, but... professors in the American Midwest? It's such a wonderfully dull cover."

"It's not a cover," Hollis said. "We're really dull."

One of the gunmen snickered, which slightly annoyed Hollis. She wasn't used to having to defend the ordinariness of her life.

The man, too, seemed delighted by her. "And yet, you find yourself with the most interesting of friends."

Hollis looked at Finn. His shoulders raised slightly. He was wondering too. Which friend could also be a friend of this man? Declan, perhaps? Peter?

If the man was Jorge Videla, he was certainly not terrifying. Though perhaps that was the point. Even the most evil people can feign charm when they need to.

"You really do have us mixed up with two other people," Finn said. "As I told you, we're teachers. My wife is working on a book on the United Nations. She's way behind on it so she should be researching this weekend."

"Well, I'm pretty far along," she lied. Why she lied, she couldn't explain. But even on a plane with gunmen and a half-drunk man who thought they were killers, she felt slightly guilty about not getting her work done. Finn would never need an extension on a book.

"Point is, that's the stuff we think about," Finn said. "I'm in the middle of reading several really interesting books, and I have some papers to grade. I was going to surprise Hollis with a night at that Italian restaurant that just opened."

"I've heard it's expensive," she said to him.

Finn shrugged. "We haven't done anything exciting in a while, and I thought you would like it."

The gunmen were both laughing under their breaths now. The man turned to them and spoke rapidly in Spanish. One went toward the cockpit, the other to a phone at the front.

Hollis could hear the man on the phone, but she couldn't understand a word. She was really regretting her decision to drop Spanish after two semesters in high school and taking French instead. If she'd stuck out Spanish, she might be able to pick up at least enough to be sure who had kidnapped them.

"What's going on?" she asked, giving in to her frustration.

"Forgive me," the man said, looking back at the gunmen at the other end of the plane. "We want to make sure everything is ready for our arrival. This is a lovely play you're putting on for me, but it isn't necessary. Not anymore."

"What does that mean?"

"You know what it means, I think."

"Why did you come to our house?" Finn asked.

"I told you I would," he said, his voice soft and playful.

"You sent the note?"

The man nodded. He leaned toward them and waved a finger so they would move closer. When they did, he smiled. "We have friends in common."

"You're Tomas?"

The man smiled and stretched a hand out to Finn. "Tomas Silva. At your service."

Fourteen

"If you're Tomas Silva," Hollis said, "then you sent the passports too. You know we're not Tim and Janet McCabe."

"I was given the passports to pass on to you. I was told these were the names you went by out in the field. Señor and Señora McCabe. They had your photos on them."

"The passports are fake. We can show you birth certificates, work IDs, driver's licenses ..."

Tomas Silva shrugged. "All of that can be faked as well."

"But you were surprised—" Finn started.

"By the other passports you had, yes. The Larssons. Very good fakes. Best I've seen." He poured himself another glass of champagne, emptying the bottle.

"Those are the real ones," Hollis said. "Where are they?"

"I left them for you at the house. You won't need them on this trip and to be found with two sets of passports will only confuse our boss."

"Who is our boss?"

"He goes by many names. Sometimes he calls himself Jorge Videla."

Hollis's heart sank. If this man was Tomas Silva and he had sent the note, he warned them to stay away from the man called Videla. "Your note said there had been a murder."

"Where is my note, if I may ask?"

They couldn't say the truth. Instead Finn said, "We burned it. We thought it was safer to get rid of it."

Silva nodded. He might have looked relieved, or maybe it was just the alcohol.

"Who was murdered?" Hollis asked.

"It is a murder that has not yet happened, but that must happen. Because of the Irishman's error."

"Declan?" Hollis blurted out.

Silva didn't answer.

It had to be Declan. His error was going to get someone killed. The tone in Silva's voice was contemptuous. If he was Declan's friend, why not say so? And if he wasn't ... she didn't want to think about that.

The captain came on the speaker, saying something in Spanish. Hollis could make out only a few words, but she recognized *destino*. They were reaching their destination. If Finn was right, that meant they were in Argentina and more than five thousand miles from home.

"Perhaps you should sit," Silva suggested. But as they did, he got up and wandered toward the front of the plane, returning moments later with another bottle of champagne. "Can I tempt you?"

Both Hollis and Finn declined. Silva opened the bottle and poured himself another glass. "Have you been here before?"

"No," Finn said.

Silva settled back into his chair. "Buenos Aires is a place of many personalities. Our buildings are French, our food Italian, our language Spanish, and our ambitions American. We have had our dark moments, but we are a strong people. You will find us a resilient country of great history and culture." He seemed to be lost in his thoughts. Suddenly he leaned toward Hollis. "Do you tango?"

She swallowed. "No. I've seen it, I think. But we don't get to dance that often."

He sighed. "Promise me you will tango while you are in Buenos Aires. Once you know this dance, you know everything there is to know about my country."

The plane dipped. They were close to the ground, but Silva poured himself more champagne.

"You are aware we've been brought here against our will," Finn pointed out, though Hollis wished he hadn't. Silva seemed to be tiring of what he obviously saw as their pretending to be a couple of university professors.

"You are here—at great expense—to work," Silva said.

"Either way, I don't see much time for dancing."

"There will be time."

One of the armed men stood up, said something to Silva in Spanish. Hollis couldn't understand the words, but she did understand the gesture. The man took the champagne away but he had waited just a moment too long. The plane landed, the brakes caused them all to lurch forward and the gunman dropped the bottle on the floor. They watched as the liquid soaked into the carpet. Silva looked as if he were about to cry.

Once the plane stopped, the gunman gestured for Finn and Hollis to stand.

"These." The gunman pushed passports into Finn's hand. "Luggage at the bottom of the stairs."

"Better to be clever than strong, my friends," Silva said from his chair. Then, amazingly, he dropped off to sleep.

The gunman looked at him, disgusted, but said nothing about it. He turned back to Finn and Hollis. "Immigration. Customs. Okay?"

They walked to the door of the plane, waited for it to open. Hollis had a terrifying thought that a whole new set of gunmen was waiting for them, but the door opened to a set of stairs and a tarmac. It was a private airport, as far as she could tell. There were a few other small planes parked and one just taking off, a building, and aside from that, fields. Nowhere to run. Finn was looking around as well and when their eyes met, it was clear he'd made the same assessment. They had to just go along with the gunmen for now.

At the bottom of the stairs, as promised, were two carry-on-sized roller bags. One black, one light blue. Finn took the handle of the black one, so Hollis grabbed the other. At a small desk just inside the building a woman sat waiting behind a counter.

"Passports," she said.

Finn handed them over. The woman looked at the photos carefully, then paged through. It hadn't occurred to Hollis earlier to see if there were other stamps in the book, but as she watched the woman she saw that there weren't.

Finally, the woman looked up. "Business or pleasure?"

"Pleasure, I guess," Finn stumbled.

"You're not sure? You think you might have business here?"

Hollis could see the hesitation in Finn's eyes. He was just about to tell the woman they'd been kidnapped, she was sure of it. But what if she couldn't be trusted?

"No, he's sure," Hollis stepped in. "Just a little queasy from the plane. It's pleasure. We're excited to be here."

The woman glanced toward her, tapped her fingers for a moment. Behind them the gunmen, minus any visible weapons, were walking up to the Immigration counter. Silva was noticeably missing.

Hollis yawned. "Sorry, jet lag. We're anxious to get to our hotel."

"It's a long flight from the United States." The woman stamped each passport and returned them. "Welcome to Argentina, Mr. and Mrs. McCabe."

They walked from the counter just as the gunmen reached it. Hollis leaned into Finn. "We need to stay farther ahead. Once we're out of here..."

"There have to be taxis or something. Or someone..."

But first there was a severe-looking man at Customs. Hollis braced herself. She had no idea what was in the luggage. There could be drugs, she realized. Or priceless antiquities. Or bits of a body... She and Finn kept walking. She waited for the man to stop them, but he just nodded as they passed.

"That was easy." The exit from the airport was just in front of them. She could even see a line of yellow and black cars. They had to be taxis.

"We don't have any money," Finn said. "I didn't have my wallet on me. And your purse..."

"Maybe we can ask the driver to take us to the American Embassy and they'll pay for the car. We'll call Peter..."

Finn kissed her head. "Genius, Mrs. McCabe. If we can just get in a car, we might actually be close to finished with this thing."

They exited the airport building into a hazy morning dew. The flight from Michigan had to have taken twelve hours at least. There was an hour time difference, so that would make it about five a.m., she guessed. She wanted to take a moment and get her bearings, but there wasn't time. Finn grabbed her hand and they walked quickly toward the front of the taxi line. A driver got out of the cab and popped his trunk. Finn lifted one of the bags, and the driver grabbed the other.

Hollis opened the door to the backseat.

"This is the wrong car, Mrs. McCabe." It was a strong male voice with a heavy accent but one she hadn't heard before.

She didn't want to turn around, but she knew there was no point in ignoring the voice. When she did turn she saw a tall man about sixty, in a dark blue suit, with silver hair and a small, tidy mustache. If he was a hitman, he at least dressed well.

The taxi driver yelled at the man in Spanish, then in English, "Go away. My fare."

"No," the silver-haired man said. "Mine." He took both bags and gestured forward, to a black sedan waiting just ahead of the taxi line. "I know where you will go."

"Where is that?" Finn asked.

The man smiled. "Where I take you."

Hollis took one last look at the angry taxi driver, cheated out of his fare, and got into the backseat of the sedan.

Fifteen

The drive seemed to take forever. Lots of fields, with only a house dotted here and there. Buenos Aires was a major city, she knew that. She'd read somewhere that nearly forty percent of all Argentinians lived near their capital city. So, where were they? Hollis began to wonder if they were being driven somewhere quiet to dispose of their bodies. Finn seemed to read her mind.

"If they wanted to kill us they would have done it in our kitchen, remember?"

She leaned into his shoulder. "It's all going to be fine. Silva promised us there would be time for tango."

Finn laughed.

Hollis kept her head on Finn's shoulder, her eyes closed, for what seemed like an hour. Then the car started to slow. She looked out the window and felt relief. Buildings. Beautiful buildings, actually. Silva was right, it looked like Paris. Or what she imagined Paris would look like. The buildings seemed to be in Art Nouveau style, and all the apartments had balconies. On the ground level, there were cafés with small tables on the sidewalk, and boutiques with gorgeous clothes in the windows.

She had never thought about what Buenos Aires would be like, but even so, it surpassed all she could have imagined. It was gorgeous.

Finn looked over at her and smiled. "We should have come here sometime. It looks like a great place to explore."

"We are here."

"I meant as a vacation, not a kidnapping."

"It's an odd kidnapping, though." She nodded toward the driver, who was humming along to haunting guitar music on the radio. "Look at this car. Plush leather seats, bottles of water in case we get thirsty, plenty of room to stretch out. And we're not even handcuffed."

"I have a feeling at some point the hospitality will end. Who knows what's at the other side of this ride."

"What's the plan when it does end?"

"I was thinking when he stops the car, if you can, just get out on your side and run. I'll do the same on mine. Find anyone who can help you and get to the embassy. I'll do the same."

"I don't want to separate."

He thought for a moment. "Okay, if we can we'll both head toward the back of the car and run together. But Hollis, promise me, if there are guys waiting for us and there's any chance you can get away, I want you to run."

She bit her lip. It wasn't a promise she could make. "We go together, or we stay together," she said.

This was not the kind of argument most married couples had, she thought. The *what to do in case someone is trying to kill us* argument. They'd had it more than once.

"We don't stay together if there's trouble," Finn was insisting. "I'll do something to distract them and you run."

"You're putting your foot down again. I'm just as capable as you are ..."

"Of what? Getting killed?"

As he spoke, the driver pulled over and turned to the back seat. "Your hotel." He pointed toward a small black sign with gold lettering that read *Hollywood Hotel.*

The only people on the street were a mom with a stroller and an elderly couple. None of them seemed particularly deadly. Maybe the guys with guns would be inside the hotel?

The driver got out, took the luggage from the trunk, then opened the door to the backseat. It was all so oddly formal, Hollis thought.

On the sidewalk the man shook Finn's hand. "Enjoy your stay," he said. "And *gracias, señor.*" Then, he turned to Hollis. "The Prodigal Lady enjoys visitors."

Hollis nodded. The man smiled. Then he got back in his car and drove away, leaving them on the sidewalk.

"Am I the prodigal lady?"

"Maybe his English isn't very good."

"I'm so confused. We could just hail a taxi from here and we're home free."

Finn wasn't listening. He was looking at a small piece of paper in his hand. "Grab the luggage. We need to check in."

Hollis followed him into the hotel, trying to grab for the paper, but Finn had formed a fist around it.

The hotel lobby was modern and sleek. Black and white tiles, silver light fixtures, and abstract paintings. But aside from a young man behind the reception desk, it was empty. Off to the right was a bar, with lights low, and to the right, white leather chairs and low round tables, also empty. If they were being watched in this expensive hotel, someone was doing a very good job of staying hidden.

At the reception desk the young man smiled. *"Buenos Días,"* he said. *"¿Como puedo ayudarte?"*

Finn handed over the passports. *"Buenos Días. Estam ..."* Finn struggled. *"Regis ..."*

"My name is Matias," the young man said. "Are you checking in?"

"I'm sorry, my Spanish is very rusty."

"No mind, sir." The young man looked at their passports. "Señor and Señora McCabe. We have the very best room set aside for your visit with us."

"We'd like a different room," Finn told him.

"But this is the very best."

"That's okay. Anything else will do."

"But I cannot give you a refund of the difference in price."

"I don't care." Finn spoke in an even tone, but he was firm. It reminded Hollis of the many times she used to suggest they travel, and he would respond with the same quiet stubbornness. Well, the joke is on him, she thought. He's seeing the world whether he wants to or not.

Matias looked flustered. He seemed about to protest again, but instead went to the computer, tapped on the keys, and made two key cards. "This is a lovely room. Not as nice as the suite we had for you. It is reserved for a couple from Amsterdam who arrives tonight. Their honeymoon. Since you are now occupying their room, may I give them your suite instead?"

"Absolutely. Just tell me where our room is."

Hollis watched the whole exchange in silence. Something in that note had spooked Finn, but she knew there was no point in discussing it in front of Matias. She wondered if the hotel clerk was in on the kidnapping. The fact that he'd been polite and helpful wasn't really a clue either way. Silva and the men at the house had been polite, but they also had guns and chloroform. She tried to see if Matias had a gun, but the counter was too high.

"You are in room 512," Matias said. "I can have the bags—"

"We can get them."

Matias nodded. "If there's anything you need..."

"How long are we staying here?" Hollis asked. "We made our plans so long ago and I'm sleep deprived."

"Of course. Three days, Señora."

Finn was already several steps ahead of her, pressing and re-pressing the elevator button. His jaw was locked, his eye was twitching, and he was biting his lip so hard she worried it would bleed. Whatever the note contained, it was obviously the end of the luxurious portion of their abduction. And what came next, she could only guess, was not going to be good.

Sixteen

The room was as high-end as the lobby, furnished in shades of white and tan, with accents of red in an upholstered chair and in a single throw pillow on the bed. Hollis locked the door and glanced into the bathroom, about twice the side of their master bathroom at home, outfitted with a marble tub.

"Swank," she said, but Finn didn't look over.

He left his suitcase by the door and dropped onto the bed. He flung the throw pillow onto the floor. He still hadn't unclenched his fist, so Hollis let him have a minute to process what was in the note. She opened the door to the balcony and walked out to take in the view and the breeze. There was traffic noise and people chatting on the street below, and somewhere in the distance there was music. A lone guitar, as far as she could tell, playing a tune filled with longing. She closed her eyes and tried to block out the voice and traffic and listen only to the music. This, all of it, had her feeling light-headed. They were in Buenos Aires, in a luxury hotel—against their will. It didn't go together, it didn't make sense.

"Don't you want to know what's in the note?"

She turned. Finn was still on the bed, but his fist was open, the paper visible in his hand.

"I'm almost afraid to ask based on your reaction."

He held it out, but before she could take it, he said, "'Tim and Janet are dead.'"

"What?"

"It's got to be a threat. That's why I switched rooms. Maybe it will buy us some time."

"If it were a threat, wouldn't the note say, 'Tim and Janet are going to be dead'?"

"Only if it were written by a grammarian."

Hollis read the note. That's what it said, all it said. "It feels like a puzzle."

"In what way does a death threat feel like a puzzle?"

"Declan didn't come right out and say he was in trouble. He sent clues. Clues that were matched perfectly to one of your areas of expertise, art, and to mine, world politics. That can't have been by accident."

"You're assuming the note came from Declan?"

She *was* assuming that, she realized, but with absolutely nothing but a feeling. "The driver said the prodigal lady enjoys visitors. Maybe that was a clue too."

"It makes no sense. It's not politics, it's not art, so ..."

"Maybe he meant to say something else and it just got mixed up in the translation. It's possible we're not kidnapped. Maybe Declan used his friend Silva to get us down here before Peter could set up some kind of surveillance. He is a wanted criminal and Peter is after him. It explains why no one seems to be watching us." She was starting to feel hopeful.

"Or whoever is after Declan brought us here hoping we'll lead them to him. And once we do, they'll kill us all."

And the small bit of hope was gone. "Or that," she admitted. "Silva said it's a murder that will happen. Are we here to stop it?"

"He said it's a murder that *must* happen." Finn got off the bed. "If there's a clue, then it's probably in those," he said, pointing to the luggage.

Hollis grabbed his hand before he could take one of the cases. "What if opening it is how Tim and Janet get dead?"

"Options?"

They stared at each other. Neither spoke.

"I guess we have to take the chance," Hollis said.

Finn took the black one and hoisted it onto the bed. "Stand back in case it's a bomb that gets triggered by the zipper."

"Just a sec." She reached her hand around his neck and pulled him close to her. Her lips met his lightly. "Be careful."

She took a few steps back. They both took a deep breath. Finn slowly unzipped the case, took one last deep breath, and opened the lid.

"Clothes," he said.

Finn dumped the case on the bed, rifling through the clothes, checking pants pockets, inside the shoes, even inside the toiletry kit, but coming up empty-handed. "No clues. Nothing but clothes."

"You sound disappointed."

"I'm not. It's just, I don't know, you threaten to kill a person and then you pack him a suitcase full of jeans and t-shirts," he said. "I feel like I'm in the middle of some strange prank. I keep getting my adrenaline going and it turns out to be nothing."

"That's good, remember? Not getting killed. That's kind of our goal here."

Hollis began her own search, carefully folding each garment as she did. It wasn't just t-shirts and jeans, she saw immediately. It was some nice stuff. She held up a light blue shirt. "This is a Battistoni," she said. "Expensive. And your size, perfectly." She put it aside and looked through the rest of the clothes. "Trousers, jeans, shirts, all designer. Even the underwear is designer."

Finn grunted. "I don't wear stuff like this."

"Tim McCabe must." She grabbed the blue suitcase. "I wonder what Janet wears."

That suitcase, too, was filled with designer clothes. Several dresses, tops, pants, and a rose-colored cashmere and silk sweater by an Italian designer. It was all so beautiful, and so far beyond their budget that she had never even held clothes this expensive, let alone worn them.

"Who are Tim and Janet McCabe that they can afford this stuff?" she asked, holding up a French-lace bra with matching panties.

"About to be dead people, remember?" He pointed to the lingerie. "That would look good on you."

She dropped the clothes back in the case. "It's strange that I'm enjoying this."

"Yes. It's definitely strange."

There's something that makes all of this make sense, she decided. The multiple Tomas Silvas, the private plane, the prodigal lady, the nice clothes, the fancy hotel in Buenos Aires ...

"We either see this through or head to the embassy right now."

Finn hesitated. "If we go for help that may be the signal to end us."

"Okay, so we play through," she said. "It's just after six. Let's nap for a couple of hours and then get out of here. Walk around. See the sights."

"Play tourist?"

"Play Tim and Janet, playing tourist. We can sit here and wait for whoever is behind this to find us, or we can go out there and see if someone approaches. Maybe Declan or one of his friends. Or Peter."

"Moving targets?"

"If this is the work of Declan's enemies, we're targets whether we move or sit."

Finn stood there. She waited for him to protest, but he didn't. "It's not a terrible idea. At least we'll get to see a bit of Buenos Aires."

They kicked off their shoes and lay on the bed, still made, as if they'd have to jump out again. Hollis slept on and off, but as the city woke up, the sounds of cars and people wafted in from the balcony. Every noise reminded her she wasn't home. Finn didn't do much better. When the room clock said nine a.m., he got up.

"Now or never," he said.

Within twenty minutes they were ready. Finn wanted to stay in his own clothes, but Hollis talked him into a pair of jeans and the light blue shirt she'd admired. Hollis dressed in a pair of gray pants, a black silk blouse with a black cardigan, and a pair of ballet slippers. In the jewelry pouch she found a beautiful diamond bracelet, and a pair of matching earrings. There was a gorgeous tan leather Prada bag. She didn't have a wallet to put in it, but she grabbed a few tissues and a lipstick. Worth carrying, she thought, if only to show it off. She almost took the rose-colored sweater but had a momentary flash of the beautiful garment covered in blood. She put it back in the suitcase, trying not to focus on what that image would really mean.

Seventeen

The shoes, though very cute, had limited arch support. Clearly Janet didn't walk much. Hollis decided not to let that bother her and focused instead on any too-long glance from a stranger, or a car that pulled just a little too close.

But neither happened. All she saw as they walked the streets of their Palermo neighborhood were fashionable people hurrying toward what were clearly important appointments. Like in every major city, most were looking at their phones, or listening to music through earbuds. No one seemed to be paying them much attention at all.

Just as she had seen from the car, the city was lovely. Every other business seemed to be sidewalk cafés with people enjoying coffee, between them clothes shops or small groceries. They turned down a side street that had large trees on each sidewalk, with branches that reached out to the middle to create a canopy.

As people walked by them she heard Spanish mainly, but then other languages—English, French, Arabic, Chinese. An elderly woman walking a poodle smiled at her. She smiled back. A couple of teenage girls sat on a step, giggling to each other about whatever teenage girls giggle about these days, but they looked up and smiled when she and Finn walked by. What a friendly place, she thought. Hollis began to forget what she was doing in Buenos Aires, she was just happy being there.

"Maybe here," Finn said, pointing toward a main street. "If Declan or someone is trying to find us, maybe if we stick to the main roads it will be easier."

They turned onto the busier street and walked for twenty minutes, ready to be approached, before Finn stopped on the sidewalk, looking tired and annoyed.

"What now?"

She looked around. "Something to eat?"

"We don't have any money," he said. "No cash, no credit cards, no cell phones. No way to get money. We can't jump in a cab or stop for a cup of coffee."

Hollis looked around. "If we see a phone somewhere we could reach Peter. I'm sure he'd take a collect call."

"Shouldn't he be reaching out to us? Shouldn't he be watching us right now? Wasn't that the promise he made?"

"Maybe he lost track when we were put on the plane."

"That does not inspire confidence."

She leaned into his chest. Going back to the hotel didn't strike her as a great idea. But her initial enthusiasm about wandering the area was starting to wane. Was it possible they'd been dumped in the middle of Buenos Aires with the assumption they knew what they were doing?

"Five more minutes," she decided. "We'll walk a little farther and if no one approaches, we'll go back to the hotel and order room service. At least we can put that on the bill."

"And who pays for that?"

"We'll worry about that at check-out." She could see Finn about to say *if we check out* so she put her hand up to his lips. "We will get out of this."

"Did I say anything different?"

"You were about to."

"I should at least get to say it."

She looked up at him and waited.

Finn sighed. "You've ruined it now. But next time I want to be doom and gloom…"

"I promise not to get in the way."

They walked, passing pizza places and empanada stands. Finn's stomach growled, and the lightheaded feeling Hollis had earlier attributed to confusion now seemed more closely linked to hunger.

Toward the end of the block she saw a sign for the Eva Perón Museum. Under normal circumstances she would have run to see what exhibits were on display for Argentina's most famous first lady, but they were just pretending to be tourists and an hour in the museum was hardly going to get them closer to finding Declan.

Finn saw the direction that Hollis was looking and squinted. "Eva Perón," Finn said. "She was an actress, wasn't she?"

"Yes, in the forties. She did a handful of movies before she met Juan Perón," Hollis said. She felt herself turn red. "I'm so stupid."

"What did you do?"

"*The Prodigal Woman* was one of her movies. It was a clue. I knew it was a clue."

"I'll bet the museum gets lots of visitors," Finn said. His voice had a bit of excitement in it that quickly disappeared. "And I'll bet there's an entrance fee."

There was no way Hollis was going back to the hotel now, no matter how badly her stomach insisted. "Maybe we can just explain that we're big fans of hers."

"I'm pretty sure that anyone going to the museum would qualify as a fan, and honestly I don't know much about her other than what was in *Evita*."

"We can try."

She took Finn's hand and started pulling him toward the museum. He took a few steps then stopped. No matter how hard she pulled, he wasn't going anywhere. His superior strength didn't generally annoy her. It actually came in handy when heavy boxes needed lifting, or she wanted to be held close. But right now, as she tugged on his hand, his strength combined with his stubbornness was infuriating.

"Even if they don't let us in, maybe there'll be something at the entrance that will help us," she said. "Standing here isn't getting us anything."

"I disagree." Finn held tight to Hollis's hand, then lifted it.

"What are you doing?"

"I'm looking at the solution to our problem." He nodded toward the bracelet on her wrist. The diamonds sparkled in the morning sun, shining a light on the sidewalk that seemed to Hollis like a bat signal.

"Do they have pawn shops in Argentina?"

He didn't answer, but he didn't have to. Now it was Finn dragging Hollis, walking almost too fast for her to keep up. Then he stopped, and she slammed into his back.

"Seriously, you are half a foot taller than me," she snapped. "I feel like a terrier being walked by a Great Dane."

"Sorry. How about in there?" He pointed to a coffee shop.

"Even without knowing ten words in Spanish, I can tell that's not a pawn shop."

"They might know where there's a pawn shop," Finn said. "Or we can give them the bracelet and they can give me a pastry."

———

Once inside the coffee shop, they could have been anywhere back home. There were people sitting at tables with half-finished coffees and sandwiches pushed to the side, their focus entirely on laptops.

Finn and Hollis walked to the counter, where a dark-haired woman in her early thirties was putting round croissant-like pastries on a plate.

"*Hola,*" the woman said. "*Que te gustaria?*"

Finn hesitated. "*Hola. Hables* ... um ... *usted* English?"

She smiled. "Yes. I can speak English. Would you like a table?"

"No, thank you. We're looking for a pawn shop. Do you know of one?"

The woman studied Finn, then Hollis. Hollis couldn't tell if she was just curious or suspicious.

"We were mugged," Hollis jumped in. "We've lost our money and credit cards. I have this bracelet"—she held her hand up—"we thought if we could pawn it ..."

"*Eso es terrible!*" The woman pointed toward a table. "Where did this happen? I can call the *policía* for you."

"That's not necessary," Finn said. "We, um ..."

"We already called them." Now it was her turn to struggle. Lying was more complicated than it seemed, especially when the recipient was a kind-looking person hoping to help.

"Someone lent us a cell phone," Finn jumped in. "The officer said we would need to fill out paperwork. He didn't sound hopeful."

The woman shook her head. "Please, sit. Have a coffee. Are you hungry?"

Finn and Hollis glanced at each other, and that was enough for the woman to take Finn's arm and point them toward a table.

"Sit please. Buenos Aires is a lovely city. I'm so angry this has happened to you. I'm Gabriella. Please you let me feed you and I'll find a shop for you. Do you need a phone to call anyone else? A friend maybe?"

"Maybe coffee first," Finn said.

Gabriella rushed away, clucking to herself in rapid Spanish.

"It isn't a lie," Hollis said to make herself feel better. "Not exactly. It's not Buenos Aires's fault we're without money."

Finn just nodded. "I'm starving. I don't care who gets blamed, as long as I get fed."

Within minutes they were served toasted ham and cheese sandwiches and coffee. Gabriella walked away and came back with milk and sugar, glanced at the table, then brought chocolate-covered cookies she called *alfajors*.

They ate the sandwiches without speaking, practically without chewing. When there were only crumbs, Hollis turned to the cookies. She took a small bite and realized she'd discovered heaven. Two chocolate cookies, with dulce de leche between them, covered in chocolate.

"When we pawn this bracelet, I'm going to buy a barrel of these," she said.

Finn bit into one. He nodded. "Money well spent."

When the food was gone, and the coffee finished, they each sat back in their chairs. Gabriella returned. "I called my boss and he is going to be here in five minutes. He says if it is real diamonds, he will buy the bracelet. He says he will give it to his girlfriend." She rolled her eyes. "He will have to decide which girlfriend. I will bring you more coffee and cookies." She put a cell phone on the table. "And you call anywhere you need. It's okay."

"Thank you," Finn said. "You have no idea what we've been through."

"*De nada*," she said. "Your day will get better from here."

But out of the corner of her eye, Hollis saw a man walk into the restaurant. He was watching them. She had no idea who he was, but she was sure he was trouble.

Eighteen

Finn drank his second cup of coffee and tried to catch a glimpse of the man. "I don't recognize him. Maybe he's just a man."

"I have a feeling," Hollis said. "And don't mock it."

"Wasn't going to. We could call Peter."

"Do we know his number?"

"It was on a piece of paper in the living room." Finn laughed, but it was more annoyed than anything. "If that guy is watching us, our options are narrowing. Instead of chasing down this *Prodigal Woman* clue, we call the embassy and ask them to put us in touch with Interpol. Maybe they can do a better job of helping us get out of this than Peter could."

Hollis opened her mouth to speak and it was Finn this time who put up his hand.

"Don't say *what about Declan*. I don't care about that guy. I care about you and me. That's it."

"I wasn't going to say it."

"Yes, you were."

He was right about that and about their priorities, so she didn't bother to argue. And there was that guy, just sitting there, his eyes only looking away when they met hers. He'd pretend to look at his phone or at a newspaper but in a way that was so obvious she was sure he was there to watch them. But for whom?

She sipped her coffee and tried to make a plan for a quick exit. It had been several minutes since they were told the owner was on his way. All they had to do was wait and hope that nothing happened.

A few minutes more, the coffee was finished. The man was still looking, and Finn was getting a telephone recording at the embassy.

Hollis sat back in her chair and tried to focus on deep, cleansing breaths. In and out. It also gave her a chance to look at the other patrons in the restaurant: a couple in their twenties laughing, a pair of middle-aged women chatting quietly over coffee, a mom and two kids, a woman alone reading a book. And then that man. Still watching. Still pretending he wasn't.

"Señor?" A heavy-set man about fifty approached their table. "I'm Saul. Gabriella has told me about you." He shook each of their hands, but held onto Hollis's, looking closely at the bracelet. "Come in the back with me, okay. I don't like to do business in front of others."

Hollis looked around but the waitress, Gabriella, was nowhere to be found. Finn got up first, following the man. Hollis went last, glancing back just one more time. The man dropped a few coins on the table and walked out the door.

Saul walked to the back of the counter and stopped at a small doorway that led to a darkened back room. He motioned for Finn to go ahead of him, but Finn paused. "We'll follow you."

Saul smiled and went first.

"This is a good idea, right?" Hollis said.

"No, it's a terrible idea, but we're going to stick with it." Finn walked through the door into the back room. Hollis took a breath and followed him.

Immediately there was a wall, and then a turn to the left, and another turn. Hollis put her hand on Finn's back and kept following. She saw a light ahead and soon a small kitchen filled with banged-up stainless-steel appliances and a shadowy figure smiling at them.

Looking perfectly at home, Peter was leaning against the commercial oven. He handed a stack of peso notes to Saul, who stayed in the kitchen but retreated to the shadows.

"You're alive!" Peter said, though he didn't sound too worried.

"Was it you who kidnapped us?" Finn asked.

"Not me. Not Declan's people either, at least as far as I can tell." He pulled a large envelope from his coat and handed it to Finn. "About two thousand dollars' worth of Argentinian pesos, credit cards in the names of Tim and Janet, and a couple of burner phones."

Saul looked disappointed. "You are not selling me your bracelet?"

"You're not in on this?" Hollis asked.

Saul just looked confused.

"No," Peter explained. "My man—"

"I knew he was watching us!"

"You always do, Hollis. It's your superpower. That and getting into trouble," Peter said. "He's been following you since you left the hotel. Discreetly. He texted me, and I came to help."

Finn handed him back the envelope. "We don't need pesos. We need a lift home."

"Not possible, mate. This mission is a go, so we're going to have to see how it plays out."

"This mission to help Declan?" Hollis asked.

"This mission to capture Declan. He's pretended to be just an ordinary bloke, a small player in a big game, but I know he's more than that."

"Based on what?" Finn asked.

"A feeling."

Finn threw up his hands. "Another one with feelings. I don't want to help Hollis save Declan, but I'm even more opposed to helping you put the guy in jail."

Peter's body stiffened. "You're on his side?"

"I'm on my side. I'm on Hollis's side. I'm on the side of not getting killed and on the side of going home before my Monday class."

"You don't have a class on Monday," Hollis said, the words slipping out before she could stop them.

Finn turned toward her. "This is so not the time to be the person in charge of the schedule."

She nodded. "He's right, Peter. We're in way over our heads. Neither one of us can figure out what the plan is. We got chloroformed, then woke up on a private plane with men carrying guns. Then we were dropped off at a fancy hotel. Not one part of that makes sense."

"But you look good. That blouse suits you."

She didn't want to, but she blushed.

"We survive the mission, we get to keep the clothes," Finn said. "Is that supposed to be an incentive?"

Peter tilted his head slightly, either annoyed or amused, Hollis couldn't tell. "Obviously you were brought here to do a job. And if I had to guess, it's the people looking for Declan. Word is someone wants him dead and you're here to do it."

"The murder that must happen," Hollis said.

"But if they're looking for Declan, they have to know we're friends, or you know, at least friendly with Declan," Finn said. "Why would they want us to kill him?"

"I don't think they want you. They want Tim and Janet McCabe."

"Who are Tim and Janet McCabe?" Finn asked, straining to keep his voice at a normal level.

Peter shrugged. "They're not on our radar. But whoever they are, they travel well"—he pointed toward Finn and Hollis—"and clearly they dress well."

Finn sighed. "When we can't kill Declan, or whatever it is the McCabes are supposed to do, I have a feeling these nice clothes are going to be covered in blood."

"I know this is a risk, and we'll stay as close as we can. Remember, Declan Murphy wanted you here," Peter said. "He thinks you can handle this, so I do too. Besides, if I pull you now, I'll probably never get close to him again." This time he handed the envelope to Hollis. "Remember the dead body in your living room? Until this is over, going home is no safer than staying here."

Hollis looked over at Finn. "What about a gun?"

"No," Peter answered for him. "I know it seems like a good idea, but it's more dangerous for an inexperienced shooter to have a gun than to be without one."

"I'm not inexperienced," Hollis said.

Peter wasn't buying it. "You haven't shot a gun since you were training at Langley. That was, what, fifteen years ago?"

"Seventeen," Finn corrected him.

"When's the last time you shot at anything, Finn?"

"Never, but I've been reading a lot about weapons lately," he said. "So we aren't marksmen, so what? Hollis is right. You're using us as bait. I want a little insurance we're not going to get gobbled up before you have a chance to hook your fish."

Peter shook his head. "A bad guy is going to take the gun off you. Then you'll be in real trouble."

"A bad guy will come with his own gun."

Peter thought for a moment. He muttered something, then reached behind him and pulled out a Sig Sauer 9mm. He sighed, moved to hand it to Finn, then changed his mind and handed it to Hollis. "Try to remember your training if you need this."

She felt the weight of the weapon in her hand. It had been a long time since she held a gun, and she'd only shot it at paper targets. She had no idea if she'd have the courage to shoot it at someone.

"The phones have speed dial," Peter said. "The number one spot on each phone is the other phone. I know how you guys like to keep tabs on each other. The number two spot is me. The number three spot is my colleague from out front. Just in case I'm not reachable."

"Why won't you be reachable?" Finn asked. "You've got plans to take polo lessons or something?"

Hollis lightly bumped against Finn to get his attention. He looked at her, annoyed. Her eyes widened. Finn blushed.

"Okay," Finn said. "Sorry, Peter. If something happens to you, we have a contact. Thanks for that."

"But be careful," Hollis added.

Peter rolled his eyes. "Use the phones before you use the gun. Promise me."

Finn and Hollis both nodded. It sounded like a reasonable idea in theory.

Gabriella appeared, saying something in Spanish to her boss. Saul nodded toward her and glanced to Peter. "You will all go now?"

Hollis put the gun into her nearly empty purse, then took the cash—a stack in hundred-peso denominations—split it roughly in half, and handed one stack to Finn along with one of the phones and the credit card with Tim McCabe's name on it. She stuffed her half next to the gun. The bag was heavy on her shoulder.

"We think we're supposed to go to the Eva Perón Museum," she told Peter before turning to Finn. "Is that still the plan?"

He glanced at Peter, frowned, then back at her. "The museum."

Peter moved toward the front of the restaurant, but Gabriella stopped Hollis and Finn. "There are two men out front. I don't like how they ask questions. There's a back door if you want to go that way."

Hollis slipped off her bracelet and put it in Gabriella's hand. "Thank you for your kindness."

Gabriella nodded. "I think you're in more trouble than a mugging."

Nineteen

It was only a few blocks, but they ducked down one street, walked a bit, turned left, and walked a bit farther before doubling back. If Gabriella was right about the men at the restaurant, it was likely they were being followed. But because they hadn't seen who those men were, it was impossible to know if they were the gunmen from the plane or someone else who was after them. At one point they saw a man watching them, or who appeared to be watching them, so they turned and ran several blocks before doubling back a second time.

By the time they got to the museum, they were both breathing hard. Finn leaned against the wall, wheezing a little before his breath returned to normal.

"When we get home, you need to go to the doctor for a check-up," Hollis said. "We're at that age when heart disease starts to become a thing."

"I'm fine."

"Wasn't there a guy about forty in the physics department who had a heart attack last year?"

"He was a smoker. I'm fine."

"Just get a stress test."

"This, right now, is a stress test."

She put her hand on his chest. "When we get home, I'm making an appointment."

"If we get home," he said. He grabbed her hand and they headed into the museum.

Hollis's own heart began beating a little fast but for a different reason. She was sure the answers about what had brought them to Argentina were in this building.

But by the time they'd gone through the exhibits, past the beautiful dresses, the recordings of Evita's speeches, the large paintings and photographs of her from nearly every period of her life, Hollis's optimism had begun to fade.

Everyone else in the building seemed like a tourist. No one approached them, or even seemed to take much notice of them. She scanned the faces of everyone they passed, but no one looked back.

"Was she Evita or Eva?" Finn asked.

"Eva. Evita was a nickname."

"That's not a clue then."

"I don't think so."

"We're doing something wrong." Finn pulled Hollis toward a corner, letting people moved by them. "We can't just wander around hoping to bump into someone. We have to think about a specific meeting place. What do you know about Eva Perón?"

"Not much," Hollis admitted. "She was a poor child from a town a couple of hundred miles from here. She ran off with a musician, but he abandoned her once they arrived in the city. I think he was married ... or maybe that's just a story. She might have come to the city alone," she said, trying to remember. "I'm sure if we walked through the museum again and looked at the exhibits ..."

Finn shook his head. "You remember her story. You have a great memory. Just think."

She wasn't sure she deserved his confidence. At home, she would know this stuff cold, but here with the gun in her purse and people chasing them, she wasn't sure. She had a sudden empathy for *Jeopardy!* contestants. She always knew the answers from the safety of her couch.

"Okay," she said. "However she got here, once in Buenos Aires, I know she got jobs on the radio and eventually in movies. She had a lot of boyfriends, men who could help her." Her brain was moving slowly. She felt she was dragging the information from a fog. "I can't remember much. I'm sorry," she admitted. "All I know is that eventually she met Perón. He was older than she was, a lot older."

"You're a lot older than me, and it works for us," Finn said.

"I'm two months older than you," she said. "And you can't run a few blocks without getting winded, so really, I'm younger."

Finn smiled.

It took a moment, but Hollis caught on. "You think if you tease me about something, I'll relax enough to focus?"

"Did it work?"

It had. She could catch her breath a little. "She was someone who was incredibly good to the poor, opening hospitals and giving away sewing machines so women could start their own businesses. She helped Argentinian women get the right to vote. But she was corrupt. She spent millions on clothes and jewels while the economy was suffering. She and Perón allegedly sold ten thousand blank Argentinian passports to Nazis looking to escape postwar Europe," Hollis said. "She was complicated."

"Sounds like Declan," Finn said.

"Yeah, there is a certain 'end justifies the means' approach to both of them. Maybe that's why he sent us here."

"But he couldn't have sent us to the whole museum. He sent us to one particular place."

"*The Prodigal Woman*. That was the clue," Hollis said. "Maybe there's a movie poster or something."

Finn looked around. The room they were in had some of Evita's clothes along with enlarged photographs of her wearing them at various state occasions. Nothing in the room spoke to her film career.

That section, though small, was toward the beginning of the exhibits, Hollis remembered. They made their way back. She noticed they weren't the only ones moving in that direction. Two men were also quietly making their way back toward the entrance, instead of following the set path of the exhibits the way the other tourists were doing.

Once in the area that highlighted Evita's acting career, Hollis and Finn looked around. There was a photograph of Eva from *The Prodigal Woman* among several others of that time period.

"Maybe there's something behind it?" Hollis suggested.

"If we touch it, we'll draw too much attention." Finn nodded toward a security guard parked at the door to the room.

"So do we just stand here?"

"If I can distract the guard—" Finn started to say. But before he could move, a tall dark-haired woman of about thirty, in a long black dress, far too overdressed for wandering the museum, walked toward the photo and looked closely.

"Wonderful movie," she said. "Have you seen it?"

106

"No," Finn told her. He glanced at Hollis, before adding, "We had it recommended by a friend, though."

The woman smiled. "You seem to have a lot of friends. Too many." She glanced behind her. "It's a shame what happened to her after her death."

Finn looked confused, but Hollis knew what the woman was talking about. Eva Perón's body had been moved after her husband lost power, even finding its way to Milan. It was only after Juan Perón's return to the presidency that the body came back to Argentina and was finally buried in Buenos Aires.

"It's safe now," Hollis said.

"Well," the woman responded, "it's safer. Poor Evita. Life is very short, and death is long, and you have as your companion only a small dog." She smiled and walked away.

Finn leaned toward Hollis. "We were speaking in code to a spy," he said, "which I hate to admit was pretty cool."

"A spy ... or a member of TCT," Hollis said. "Or one of Declan's girlfriends, or some combination."

"Okay, but whoever she is, I'm not sure exactly what information we got from her."

"She just told us where to go next. Recoleta Cemetery."

"You sure?"

"That's where Evita is buried. There's obviously something at her grave."

Finn took Hollis's hand. "The trick will be getting there without taking anyone along with us."

Hollis and Finn looked around the room, pretending to be interested in the other exhibits. There was a young British couple at the far end of the room, the security guard, and a man in his seventies. None of them had been in the restaurant, nor had she noticed any of them in the other part of the museum.

How could they escape being followed if they had no idea who was following them? Hollis squeezed Finn's hand. "What do we do?"

"I have a plan, but I don't think you're going to like it."

"Better or worse than your idea to save some money by spending our wedding night at your parent's house?"

"Worse," he said. "Much worse."

Twenty

"Then let's not do it," Hollis suggested.

"You stay here. I'm going to go to the men's room. Watch to see if someone follows me. If no one follows me, then just wait for me in the gift shop."

"And if someone does?"

"Take a taxi to the cemetery. I'll lose the guy and meet you there."

"I hate this idea."

Finn ignored her. "Hopefully, I'll meet you in the gift shop. If you're not there, I'll see you at the cemetery."

"If there is someone, text me when you lose the guy."

Finn walked slowly away from her, toward the entrance to the museum. She scanned the visitors to see if anyone made a move. It wasn't crowded, but there were enough people wandering to make tracking everyone a challenge. She saw a familiar face walk into the room—the man from the restaurant, the one she now knew was Peter's man. But he stayed put. His eyes were on her.

Hollis saw Finn pause and look up at a sign that pointed toward the men's room, then he walked inside. At first it didn't seem as if anyone was following, but then she saw a young couple separate. The man walked straight toward the men's room.

YOUNG MAN, BLUE SHIRT, she texted. Then another man walked in that direction. OLDER, BLACK JACKET.

Hollis waited to see if anyone else followed but no one did. How long should she wait? She looked over at the man from the restaurant. He was texting.

A minute passed with no one else going in or out of the men's room. Finn's plan was solid, she knew that. Easier for one of them to get to Eva Perón's grave unnoticed than two.

Two minutes had passed. She glanced toward the gift shop. He'd be annoyed if she ignored his plan and just waited for him anyway. They had the phones. He'd be okay, she told herself. His boxing teacher had praised his technique.

She walked outside. She half hoped she wouldn't be able to find a taxi, but there were several. She picked the middle one just in case the first one was a TCT driver. It was getting hard to live with so much suspicion.

"Recoleta Cemetery, por favor," she said.

The man nodded and drove off. She took one last look through the back window but saw no sign of Finn. He'd be okay, she told herself again.

The drive was longer than she expected. Buenos Aires was a large city, spread out. And each neighborhood had its own personality.

While Palermo had seemed trendy, Recoleta had an "old money" air to it. The avenues were wider, the buildings even more Parisian, the shops much more expensive.

She kept her burner phone on her lap, waiting for a reassuring text from Finn. But there was nothing. After ten minutes she sent him one. OKAY? But there was no response.

"He's okay," she muttered to herself, but she no longer believed it.

"Here," the driver said, pulling up in front of a stone wall.

Hollis pulled out a fifty-peso bill.

"Too much," the taxi driver said. "I get you change."

"It's okay."

She wasn't paying attention. There was a man getting out of the taxi behind her, and he looked a lot like the shorter of the two gunmen on the plane to Argentina. She'd been so focused on Finn that she'd missed someone keeping track of her.

"Could you drive a block, turn the corner or something?" she asked the driver.

"But this is the entrance." He pointed toward an elaborate art nouveau gate, through which tourists were moving in and out.

"I'm trying to avoid someone."

The taxi driver smiled. "Okay with me then. I'll bring you somewhere."

As the car pulled away, she looked into the rearview mirror and saw that the man getting out of the taxi was gesturing angrily. He tried to get back in the taxi, but a well-dressed woman with a purse dog jumped in ahead of them. Hollis's driver was around the corner and back in busy Buenos Aires traffic before he'd found a replacement.

She was about to ask the driver where he was taking her when the car screeched to a halt. "This is a shop all the tourists like," he said. "You spend twenty minutes in there, your friend will forget you."

"The cemetery is where?"

111

The driver gestured to the rear window. "We are at the back." He pointed to a stone wall. "Follow the wall around and you'll find the gate."

"Is there another entrance?"

"No, you go in where we were. You have to pay there."

Hollis went for her wallet, but the driver shook his head. "You have paid me already. Enjoy Argentina."

The driver peeled away, leaving her on the sidewalk outside a small shop with leather jackets in the window. Still no word from Finn. She almost texted him her location, but what if someone else had his phone?

It was a bad idea, splitting up. Much worse than spending their wedding night at his parent's house.

She walked inside the shop and was immediately greeted by a smiling saleswoman.

"*Hola!*"

Hollis nodded.

"I'm Nina," the woman said. "I can help you find what you're looking for."

Hollis glanced back at the street, then into the shop where there were rows of suede and leather jackets, belts, wallets, and handbags. "I'm just looking."

"We have some wonderful purses," she said. "It's from capybara hides. Do you know the capybara?"

Hollis looked at her phone. Nothing yet. "No."

"It's the world's largest rodent. They are very popular in Argentina." Nina brought her a light tan crossbody bag with a mottled texture. It was beautiful. From inside she pulled a postcard with a photo of a sweet-faced animal, one that looked more like a giant, sleepy Guinea pig than a rat.

"He's too cute to wear as a purse," Hollis said, handing it back. The price tag was a factor too. Even doing a general exchange from pesos to dollars, the cost was several hundred dollars.

"I know what you want," Nina said.

"I want Finn," Hollis muttered. But Nina was digging into the racks of leather coats. Hollis thought about texting Peter. When she'd walked out of the museum, Peter's man hadn't followed. That was good, right? He was with Finn.

"Try this on." Nina slipped a soft brown jacket onto Hollis before she had a chance to protest.

"I'm not in the market for a jacket."

"But it looks so wonderful on you."

Nina turned Hollis to face a full-length mirror. It did look wonderful. The jacket was light, but it felt warm. The suede was soft to the touch, and the color was somewhere between a light caramel and toffee.

"The nice thing about goat suede is that it can get wet. You just hang it up to dry, give it a brush if you want, and it's good to go," Nina kept talking while Hollis used the full-length mirror to look out the window.

She glimpsed someone. Not Finn. The gunman who had followed her. He'd walked the perimeter of the cemetery, she realized, probably wondering, as she had, if there was another entrance. The good news was he hadn't seen Hollis. Yet.

"It's lovely," Hollis said. "But I need to leave."

"The sleeves are a little long on you. Perhaps we can go upstairs, and I'll adjust them."

The man moved toward the shop. It was hard to tell looking through the mirror's reflection, but it didn't seem that he knew Hollis was there. He was just, she hoped, doing a general search.

"Upstairs?" Hollis asked.

Nina pointed toward a staircase at the back of the shop. "We do our alterations."

"Okay."

The man reached the window of the shop, looking in. Hollis stayed in front of Nina, walking quickly until she reached the stairs. Just as she was out of sight, she heard the door to the shop open and another salesperson greet that customer with a cheery, "*Hola!*"

What she couldn't hear was the person reply.

On the second floor, Hollis kept listening for voices while Nina introduced her to a tailor, who began marking the jacket with chalk.

"He'll take it in for you a little. You have such a slim figure," Nina said. "It will be ready tomorrow. We can deliver to your hotel room. Where are you staying?"

"Hollywood Hotel in Palermo." Everything was a blur. Half her brain was focused on her purse and the gun inside, just in case the man came upstairs, and the other half silently begging to hear the reassuring ping of a text from Finn.

"How would you like to pay?"

Hollis put her hand in her purse, making sure not to expose the gun. She felt around until the hard corners of the credit card were in her grasp. If nothing else, buying the coat on credit would alert Peter to where she was.

Nina took her card and went downstairs. By that time the tailor had finished his work and took the jacket off her.

"Tomorrow," he said.

She nodded. Hopefully I'll be alive to receive it, she thought.

The tailor waved his hand toward the stairs and nodded. Obviously, it was time to go. There was no other exit from the small room. She'd have to go back down to the main shop. She put her hand in the open purse, gripping the gun, and took each step slowly.

At the bottom of the stairs, she peeked around the corner. A woman and a teenage girl were picking out handbags, but they were the only customers there. The gunman wasn't in the store, at least as far as she could see. Hollis checked her phone one more time. Still nothing from Finn.

Nina handed Hollis back the credit card. "Are you okay?"

"I seem to have lost track of my husband. He was supposed to meet me."

"Husbands! He probably didn't want to come shopping and now he will regret that he doesn't have a wonderful souvenir." Nina smiled. "Wait!"

She was gone and back in a few seconds. In her hand she held a wallet made of the capybara hide. "This will let him know you were thinking of him."

All it took was a slight nod from Hollis and Nina had taken back the credit card, rung up the wallet, and placed it in a small bag. In less than ten minutes, she'd spent over six hundred dollars. At least it wasn't her money.

There was nothing left to do but go to the cemetery, find Eva Perón's grave, and hope that Finn was there.

Twenty-One

Hollis walked along the stone wall of the cemetery, turning one corner and then another until she was back at the entrance. She kept looking but didn't see the man again. At the entrance she slipped into a large group of American tourists who were taking a tour, the fastest way to find the grave, she assumed.

"Stay together," the guide, a man in his twenties was saying, "the cemetery is called 'the labyrinthine city of the dead' and with good reason. It's very easy to get lost if you wander down one of the walkways that branch off from the main path. This is a lovely place to visit, but let's not have anyone make this their permanent address. Not yet anyway."

The group laughed. Hollis didn't. The purse strap was digging into her shoulder, the zipper was open, and her hand was tucked inside, her fingers on the gun. In her other hand, she had her phone out, waiting for anything from Finn.

The cemetery itself was beautiful, filled with art deco mausoleums. Some of the buildings had elaborate marble carvings on them—vines, leaves, statues of angels and beautiful gowned women. Hollis made a mental note to come back someday when every hair on the back on her neck wasn't standing on edge.

"This is a fourteen-acre cemetery, founded in 1822, and there are over forty-five hundred vaults," the guide continued. "Families not only have to pay for the construction of their mausoleum, but they are also required to pay for upkeep, which can get quite expensive. For some families this becomes impossible. If the line dies out or if the descendants no longer can afford to pay for the upkeep, the bodies are removed and reburied elsewhere, and the mausoleum is put up for sale. Being buried in Recoleta still has some prestige, but not quite what it did a hundred years ago."

"What if no one buys the grave?"

The guide smiled. "Perfect timing." He pointed toward a simple white crypt that looked neglected and empty. "They begin to decompose, much like the people meant to be inside."

The crowd laughed again and moved forward. Ahead there was a crowd of people all gathered around a wall of brown marble. The guide edged the group closer until Hollis could read the sign above the door—Familia Duarte—Eva Perón's maiden name. To the side there were plaques for various members of the family buried within. Eva's was among them.

Hollis looked around. No Finn. She'd been holding it together pretty well because she assumed, she wanted to assume, he'd be at Perón's grave. But he wasn't. She looked for a possible clue, but there was nothing. It wasn't the grand mausoleum she'd been expecting. There was no hiding place for a clue or a person.

Now what? Could he have gone to the hotel? Still no text. He had to be at the hotel.

"I want to show you another grave that attracts quite a lot of visitors," the tour guide said. "It's a dog and its master, the only dog buried in Recoleta Cemetery. It's quite a sad story as to how it got here."

Hollis was about to break away from the group, but the dog… the woman at the museum said something about death being long and having only a dog as your companion. Could that have been the grave she and Finn were supposed to find?

Hollis followed the group, her heart pounding, scanning every face she passed. Down one row and then another until they found the mausoleum. It was a modern building, with a life-sized bronze statue of a young woman, her hand resting on the head of a dog.

As the guide described the tragic circumstances—"She was on her honeymoon in Austria when an avalanche struck the hotel."—Hollis looked around. No Finn, no package or note or anything that might tell her where he was or what to do next.

She was trying not to cry, but it was all she wanted to do. Sit down on a marble step and cry. But it wouldn't help. This is why she'd decided not to be a spy all those years ago after she'd finished her training at Langley. Spies don't cry, even when they really want to. Instead, she wandered into the path around the corner. There were more tourists looking at more graves, but no Finn. At the edge of a group of tourists, with his back to her, though, she saw a full head of brown hair—not her blond-haired husband, but still a relief. She knew that hair, and the twenty-something man that was attached to it. And she was ready to kill him.

She walked over, slapping him across the arm. "Declan!" she whispered. "Where's Finn? You better know the answer because I have a gun in my purse."

The Irishman laughed. "Nice to see you too, Hollis."

He put his hand on her back and guided her to a marble crypt, emptied and decaying, similar to the one the guide had pointed out. The white plaster had grayed, and in parts it had come off, exposing brick. At the center there was a door at least seven feet tall, a solid iron piece with stylized iron flowers and leaves decorating it. Above the door was a small stained-glass window of a lily. The crypt was impressive to look at, but creepy, especially since the door was slightly open.

"Inside," he said.

She trusted that Declan wasn't likely to kill her, but a dusty, spider-filled grave?

From inside she heard a voice: "Hollis, just get in here."

She nearly fainted. She ran inside and in a dark corner she saw Finn. She wrapped her arms around his tall, thin frame. He was holding her as tight as she was holding him. She didn't want to let go but she needed to look at him. To see his face.

And when she did he looked fine. Perfectly fine.

"What happened to you?" he asked.

"What happened to me? You never texted me after you got away from the man who was following you."

"Why would I text you?"

"I told you, right before you went to the men's room. That was the plan."

Finn took a deep breath and glanced toward Declan, who stood in the corner, one hand on the half-shut iron door that shielded them from view. Declan just shrugged. Hollis felt a little dizzy. The stress and the dusty air were getting to her. She leaned against the marble tomb in the center of the crypt.

"This is empty?" she asked.

"Does it matter?" Declan said. "If there's someone in there, he won't mean you any harm."

"I've just been so freaked out that Finn didn't answer my texts."

Finn grunted. His eye twitched. "The plan was for you to watch if someone followed me," he said to Hollis, "and meet me in the gift shop if the coast was clear or take a taxi here if it wasn't."

"And I said text me. I added to the plan."

"I didn't hear you."

"Of course you didn't." Her relief was now turning to irritation.

"You were supposed to come directly here," Finn pointed out. "I've been here for almost an hour, freaking out because I couldn't find you. I went to Perón's grave and then I remembered the thing about the dog and asked someone about it. That's when I found Declan."

Declan nodded. "Yeah, Hollis, we've been sick with worry."

She rolled her eyes.

"No. Honestly. I know I've dragged you down here, but it was important. I need the address book."

"What address book?"

"The one you took from the antique shop in Ireland," Finn explained. "I told him we handed it over to Peter."

"Get it back," Declan said.

"I don't think we can. It's just the names of TCT members, right, in some sort of code?"

"It's a bit more than that," Declan said.

Hollis looked to Finn for the explanation that Declan was obviously not going to give.

"He won't say any more," Finn said. "Believe me, while you've been wandering Buenos Aires I've been trying to talk him into explaining himself."

Declan's jaw hardened. "Silva was supposed to explain that I needed the book."

"Who is Silva, by the way?" Hollis asked. "Is he a college age kid or a middle-aged man? Is he black or white? We have more than a few candidates ..."

"Sshh ..." Declan closed the door until it was almost shut. "I think I just saw Peter walk by." He waited. After a minute he relaxed. "He's moving away now."

Finn moved forward. "Don't let him leave. We can end this whole thing now. Peter can get you out of harm's way ..."

"And into a prison cell. No thank you."

Hollis took the gun from her purse and pointed it at Declan. "Let us out of here."

Declan smiled. "Lovely. You brought toys."

"You have to answer our questions," Hollis said, not entirely sure if Declan would answer them, gun or not.

"Fire away," Declan said, then put his hands up in mock fear. "Questions, I mean. Not bullets."

"Who are Tim and Janet McCabe?" Finn asked.

"You are."

Hollis took the safety off the gun. She remembered that much anyway. Whether she could shoot was another story.

"Okay," Declan said. "They're fixers. They were hired to kill me."

"Silva said there was a murder that must happen. That's you?"

"I don't think so." Declan waved his head around as if he were debating with himself. "I mean, yes, I'm meant to be dead. But I think there's a second murder and I'm trying to stop that one from happening. It's not my fault, any of it. Actually, it's your fault, in a way."

"In what way?" Finn had lost his patience with Declan's riddles.

"You two are in love, really. I hadn't seen that much in my life, hadn't believed in it. But now I do. And I'm trying to keep someone in love from getting killed. That's why I need your help."

"So we're here to kill you *and* someone else? And you want us to save the other person," Finn said. "So does that mean it's okay to kill you?"

"Obviously not, Finn," Declan said. "And after what I did to save your wife..."

Hollis stepped in. "Why does someone want you dead?"

Declan sighed. "That book was meant to get to someone. It was very important. But you took it before I could. I tried to explain, but TCT isn't an organization that accepts an explanation. He still wants me dead."

"Who?"

Declan glanced again outside the crypt. "The man who doesn't exist."

Finn grunted. "I know you like this guy, Holly, but can I just punch him?"

"Fine by me."

Declan put his hands out in front of him. "I was in the military, Finn, special services. I could probably kill you before you get in one hit."

"He's been taking boxing lessons," Hollis said. "He's the best in his class."

Finn turned red.

"Have you now?" Declan smiled. "That's grand. That will help with your credibility as a hitman. Though Hollis will have to learn to hold a gun better than that."

"I'm holding it just fine."

Declan shook his head. "Your fingers are all wrong. Let me show you."

He reached out a hand and had the gun before Hollis could protest. He turned it on them.

"What just happened?" she asked.

It was just what Peter had warned and Hollis was furious that they would have to explain the blunder to him.

"If you had been holding it properly, I never would have been able to take it from you," Declan said. "But there's a lot to learn in the world of professional hits, and you're only getting started."

"Give me back the gun and I'll learn everything I need to know."

"I need that book," Declan said. "Give it back to me and then you can punch me. It's a win-win."

"Or I can punch you now," Finn said.

"Americans are such optimists. Try if you want, Finn."

The two men stood looking at each other for a moment but neither moved.

"I am sorry about this," Declan said, glancing outside. "The one bright spot is that I don't think this place is soundproof."

"What difference does it make if it's soundproof?" Finn asked.

Declan didn't answer. He slipped outside the crypt and shut the door behind him, leaving Finn and Hollis inside.

Twenty-Two

"There's no latch anywhere?" Hollis asked from behind Finn.

Finn spun around. "For the tenth time, the usual residents of this place don't need a way out," he said. "So, no, there's no latch."

"We'll scream again."

"We've tried that." He grunted. "Declan was wrong. It does seem soundproof."

Hollis looked at the bars on her cell phone. No service. The usual residents of the place didn't need unlimited texting and calling plans, either.

She leaned against the tomb again, but this time her legs wouldn't hold her, so she slid onto the floor. It was dusty. There were bugs. She didn't care.

"I'd cry if I had the energy," she said. "This has been a really crappy day."

Finn stopped grunting and sat next to her on the ground. He put one arm around her and with the other he opened the flashlight app on his phone. It helped a little. Once the door had closed, the only light was from the small stained glass window over the door.

"I'm sorry," he said. "I really didn't hear you say to text you."

"Didn't you see my texts?"

"I'm seeing them now. You sound really worried."

Hollis rested her head on his shoulder. "You must have been worried too."

"Yeah. What happened?"

"One of the gunmen from the plane followed me, so the taxi driver took me around the corner and I ducked into this shop." She realized she was still holding the small bag, so she rested it on Finn's lap. "I bought you a wallet."

Finn reached into the bag. "It's nice."

"It's capybara. It's native to South America."

He smiled. "I love how you took time out to souvenir shop."

"Do not mock me," she said. Though she was relieved that he was here, with her, able to tease her. For a long time that afternoon she'd wondered if she'd ever have the chance to be annoyed at him again. "I bought some stuff because that way I could use the credit card, which I knew would alert Peter to my location. That's probably how he found us here."

He kissed the top of her head. "Genius," he said. "What else did you buy?"

"What?"

"You said 'some stuff.'"

"A goat suede jacket. They needed to do alterations, so it will be delivered to the hotel tomorrow. Not that we'll be out of here by then."

He smiled. "Try to think positively."

125

"You think we'll get rescued?"

"No, but at least if someone goes to our room to kill us, we won't be there."

Hollis leaned in as close to Finn as she could. There was a large spider on the wall. If she didn't look at it, she told herself, it would just go away. But then she thought of something worse. "The couple from the Netherlands will be in our room. If someone is coming to kill us, they'll kill an innocent couple on their honeymoon instead."

"I guess we have to do something." Finn pulled his arm away and stood up. He took off a shoe and slammed it against the wall, killing the spider. He scraped the dead bug onto the floor put his shoe back on.

"Wow," Hollis said. "Have I told you lately how wonderful you are?"

He blushed. "Wait until I get us out of here. You'll think I'm Superman."

Hollis stood up and started examining each wall for anything that could be used to pry open the metal door. There was nothing. But she did feel a small amount of warm air in the corner. There was a tiny hole in the marble, not even big enough to stick a finger through, but it did mean there was some oxygen getting in. Maybe they could use a stone to dig at the hole until it was large enough that their screams would be heard. She searched around until she found a small stone with a sharp edge and started scratching at the wall. It would take hours, she realized, maybe all night. The cemetery would close at dusk and the only people left in the place would be permanent residents.

Finn had other plans. He put his cell phone over his head and threw it at the stained-glass window. It hit the marble instead and shattered.

"Give me your phone," he said.

"But if it breaks how do we call Peter?"

"I don't have anything else to throw."

She nodded. She scrolled through the numbers on the phone. Still no service but there was a listing of the contacts. Number two on the speed dial was Peter's cell. "20245," she said. "Memorize that."

"20245."

"I'll memorize the other five. We'll be able to call him once we're free."

She handed Finn the phone. He took a deep breath. For a moment, she flashed on him in college, playing basketball. She would sit in the stands and watch him center himself before he took a free throw.

Finn took a deep breath, raised his arm and threw, his entire body lurching forward with the effort. This time the phone hit the glass. But then it slid to the floor and shattered. The window remained intact.

They both stared at the stained-glass window in silence. There had to be another way out, Hollis thought, she just didn't know what it was.

"I'm sorry," Finn said, so quietly Hollis almost didn't understand the words.

"We'll get out."

"How?"

It was a good question. Hollis leaned against the tomb for the third time and bit the inside of her lip. "What's our worst-case scenario?"

Finn narrowed his eyes.

"Okay, aside from death," Hollis said. "We spend the night here. We keep working at the small hole in the wall and by morning someone finds us. That's kind of a funny story we'll tell someday."

"What story will the honeymoon couple get to tell?"

The couple. She didn't even want to think what trouble they'd be in. "Declan will come back once Peter is out of the cemetery, don't you think?"

"No."

"He wanted us down here. He wants the address book..."

"Which I told him we can't give him," Finn said.

"How desperate is he?"

"Apparently his life depends on turning that book over to some guy who doesn't exist."

"That doesn't make sense," Hollis said.

"Yesterday we were having Chinese food in our kitchen. Today we're locked in a mausoleum in Buenos Aires. Nothing about this makes sense. And that story about how he's trying to save someone in love?" Finn rolled his eyes.

"It is possible he's telling the truth."

"Then why send gunmen to our house and chloroform us? If we're here to help, and Silva's in on it, why do any of that?"

She couldn't come up with an answer. And the way Declan spun tales, she wasn't sure whatever answer he would give them would even be true.

There was a banging noise from outside the door. Hollis grabbed Finn's arm, and they moved to the corner near the door. If it was someone intent on hurting them, maybe they could push him and run.

"But this time we run together," Finn said.

The door creaked open. A small man of about sixty looked at them both. "*¿Qué estás haciendo aquí?*"

Finn let out a long breath. "*Gracias*. We got locked in here."

The man looked both confused and frustrated. "A child, he says a bird hit the window, trapped inside."

"It was my phone," Finn said. "I threw it at the window to get attention."

Hollis gathered her purse and the wallet, along with as many pieces of the phones as she could. "I'm sorry," she said to the man.

"Okay," the man said. "Go now."

As they walked back onto the path, the man shut the door behind them with a clang that made Hollis jump.

The man looked at them one last time.

"I am sorry," Hollis said again. "Thank you for coming to our rescue."

He shook his head. *"Turistas!"*

"At least we're okay," Finn said.

Hollis nodded. "We have to go back to the hotel and make sure that couple who has our old room is okay."

"That way to the exit?" Finn pointed to his left.

Hollis frowned. "I think it's the other way." As she looked to the right, she saw the gunman from the plane walking toward them.

"Run," she said to Finn.

He didn't ask why. He just grabbed her hand and they took off.

Twenty-Three

They ran on what they thought was the main path, but soon they hit a dead end and had to turn back. Hollis got turned around. All around them were rows of marble crypts in light grays and ivory. Up close, each was a masterpiece of design, but it was a dizzying, and slightly unnerving, reminder that death was everywhere.

"What if we go to the left?"

"We've been left."

"Then we'll go right."

"I think we've done that too." Finn leaned against an iron railing and put his head down. "I know. Doctor's appointment when we get home," he said.

Hollis wanted to let him rest, but she couldn't. "Let's go left."

Finn stood up. "When we find Declan, I'm going to kill that guy for doing this to us."

"Which part? Bringing us down here as a pair of assassins or locking us in a crypt and leaving us to die?"

"I'm good with both reasons."

Finn took a few steps and peeked around the corner. "It seems like the cemetery is getting quiet. Just a few tourists around. Maybe the gunman figured we left and stopped chasing us."

"The weird thing is I don't know if he was chasing us. He saw us, but we ran so quickly I don't know if he ran after us or not."

"Then let's get out of here and worry about that later," Finn said. Hollis heard voices. "Sshhh."

"He worked as a grave digger for over thirty years, carefully saving his money to have this mausoleum built with a statue of his likeness," a voice from another row was saying. "When it was finished, the story goes, he went home and killed himself, so he could be buried in it."

Hollis pointed to the right. "I remember that story from the tour."

"You took a tour? You went souvenir shopping and you took a tour. Tell me again how worried you were about me."

She ignored him. "The entrance is back that way."

They moved quickly, passed two tour groups, joining them when they felt unsafe, then discarding them to move closer to the front. Eventually the white pillars of the cemetery's entrance came into view. There was no sign of the gunman, of Declan, or of Peter. For a moment Hollis felt relief, but this was just one step. There was no way of knowing what was waiting for them at the hotel. What was waiting for that poor unsuspecting couple from the Netherlands.

They hailed the first taxi they saw and sank into the backseat. As they rode back toward Palermo and the hotel, Hollis ran through possible scenarios with Finn, even though his eyes were closed, and his head was against the back of the seat.

"If they've arrived, we can knock on their door and explain that the room has bugs or something, which is why we moved. That way they'll go downstairs and get a different room," she said.

"Fine."

"But if they haven't arrived, maybe we tell the clerk that we've decided we want our old room back."

"So someone can come shoot us?"

"Do you want them to shoot innocent honeymooners?"

"Yes, Hollis. That's what I want."

Full sarcasm. He was feeling better. "I'm open to ideas."

He put his arm around her and pulled her close to him. "My idea is that for the next twenty minutes, while we're safe in this cab, I want to hold my wife."

She snuggled next to him. "I want that couple to have as happy a marriage as we have."

"Setting the bar kind of low." She poked him. He laughed. "Bugs if they're already in their room, switch back if they haven't arrived. Everything will be fine," he said.

She knew he was saying that just to get her to stop worrying, or just to stop talking about being worried. He needed rest, and as she closed her eyes she realized she did too. And food. The sandwiches had been hours ago. Finally being out of danger, however temporarily, allowed for her body to return to normal functioning, and it was shouting that she was hungry.

"Room service," she said, more to herself than Finn.

"Steak," he answered. "The steak is famous in Argentina."

"And dulce de leche," she said. "And a very large glass of red wine."

"Save a honeymoon couple, eat dinner, find Declan and kill him. Nice to have a plan."

Hollis didn't bother to mention that so far none of their plans had worked out.

Twenty-Four

The hotel bar was filling up when Hollis and Finn arrived. Some of the patrons were quite dressed up and others were in jeans and t-shirts, but they all looked incredibly stylish. It made Hollis aware of the spider webs on Finn's pants and the crypt dust that clung to them both.

"Our lives are weird," she said.

"Huh?"

She shook her head. "Save the couple, room service, shower," she said instead.

"Kill Declan. Don't forget the most important part."

"Which, oddly, is what Tim and Janet are supposed to be doing."

Finn stopped just short of the elevator bank. "But they're dead. I was thinking of the note. Tim and Janet McCabe are dead because Declan killed them and substituted us. What better way to make sure he isn't the victim of a hit than to have his friends play the hitman?"

Hollis smiled.

"Not friends," Finn corrected himself, "but you know what I mean."

Behind her she heard footsteps. Matias was running toward them with a large silver envelope in his hand.

"Señor McCabe," he said. "This has arrived for you both." He handed the envelope to Finn and glanced at their dusty clothes. "You are enjoying your visit?"

"Very much," Hollis lied. "Has the honeymoon couple checked in yet? We thought we'd drop off a bottle of wine for them."

"How kind of you! Yes, they arrived a few minutes ago." He frowned. "It's still okay that I gave them the room you had paid for?"

"Yes, fine. Perfect." She tried to smile but she had images of gunmen waiting for the happy couple. She only hoped that they were still at gunpoint, and not already dead.

In the elevator, Finn handed Hollis the envelope. It had *Señor and Señora McCabe* in beautiful script written across the front. Inside was an invitation to a party.

"Tonight at the Café Tortoni," Hollis relayed. "A car will be sent for us. It says black tie. I saw a dress in the suitcase, but nothing fancy enough. I wonder if there's time to buy something."

"Our lives are weird."

"That's what I said."

"When?"

"As we were walking into the hotel."

She could see that Finn was psyching himself up for whatever awaited them, so she didn't press the point. His memory was a thing of wonder, she decided. He managed to remember every line he read in a book, and every mistake she made fifteen years ago, but not something she said just seconds after she said it.

The doors to the elevator opened. Finn took her hand. "Ready?"

"As I can be."

They walked the short hall to a double door suite. Hollis could hear noises inside. Grunts and some muffled shuffling.

"Should we break in?" she asked.

Finn tried not to laugh. "Listen."

It took a moment. The grunts, the shuffling... and just in case she wasn't sure, she heard a moan. "Matias said they only arrived a few minutes ago," Hollis said.

"They are on their honeymoon."

"We weren't like that."

"You were terrified my mother would hear us."

Hollis laughed. "You put a pillow over my face to keep me from making too much noise. You almost smothered me on our wedding night."

He kissed her cheek. "I hope they have as many wonderful memories as we do."

They listened a moment more. Still the same noises. "They seem pretty happy."

Finn pulled her from the door. "Doesn't mean they're not in danger though."

"So, what do we do?"

Finn looked around. "We could pull a fire alarm. Or call from our room and say there's an emergency or something."

Hollis looked around. No fire alarms close by. "Isn't that cruel? Shouldn't we let them, you know, finish?"

Finn leaned against the wall. "How long do you think that will be? I really want my steak."

The elevator door opened. The taller gunmen from the plane stepped into the hallway. Finn stood straight, and Hollis stood next to him trying to look tougher than she felt. Could they tackle him, she wondered?

As he got closer, she realized he looked as nervous seeing them as they did seeing him. He was wearing a navy-blue European cut suit, slim against his muscular body. It was hard to see where he'd have hidden a gun, but that didn't mean there wasn't one somewhere. Even though he was the taller of the two gunmen, he was still an inch or two shorter than Finn. He looked young, no older than his late twenties. And, though it seemed impossible, he almost looked shy.

"Your room, please," he said, pointing toward the door.

"This isn't our room," Finn said.

"Yes, it's your room."

"We moved," Hollis explained. "A honeymoon couple was checking in and we decided to let them have the luxury. They have nothing to do with any of this, do you understand?"

The man looked at her, puzzled. "Yeah, okay. Where is your room?"

So much for being safe in a different room, Hollis thought.

"Let's go to the bar downstairs," Finn said.

"No, please. Your room."

It was crazy, but Hollis said it anyway: "I'm going to need your gun."

He looked at her.

"Your gun. Otherwise we take the elevator to the bar, and you follow us on the next one."

"But ... Señora ... Why would I hurt you? I want to *be* you."

Finn took Hollis's hand and walked to the elevator.

The man put his hands in the air. "Frisk me," he said. "No gun."

It was especially crazy, but Hollis did it. She ran her hands across his torso, his arms, and down each leg, checking his socks for hidden knives. He was really muscular. She wondered for a moment what he looked like under the suit, but she put that thought out of her mind.

She turned back to Finn. "He's clean."

The elevator door opened, and Finn motioned to the man. "We're on the fifth floor. Take the elevator first, and we'll meet you there."

The man stepped in the elevator, looking thoroughly confused. He looked at Hollis as the doors closed.

"What was that?" Finn asked. "All the touching?" He ran his hand down her torso. She swatted it away. "You were very thorough."

"I was appropriate. We're hired killers. Hired killers frisk people to make sure they're not carrying, don't they?"

"I'm sure it's in the handbook."

"My point is he obviously knows who we are," Hollis said. "Who the McCabes are. He may have hired us."

"His boss, maybe. That guy is strictly muscle."

"He really is," she said.

Finn just rolled his eyes. "At least we got him away from the couple, and he knows that's not our room, so I think they're safe." He pressed the down button.

"The way he was acting, I don't think that he was going to harm them."

"Yeah but the trauma he would have inflicted banging on their door while they were in the middle …" Finn smiled. "End of the marriage right there."

Hollis took a few steps back and listened at the door. "They've stopped," she whispered. Then she heard a moan. "No, started up again."

"Envy them?"

"We do okay," she said. "They should pace themselves. A lifetime is a lot longer than it seems on the wedding day."

The elevator doors opened. She noticed that Finn had pressed the fifth-floor button. "Were going to meet him? We're not going to run?"

"Where? Like you said, we're hired killers and our job is to get rid of Declan. As long as we go along with that, we're safe," he said. "I think."

Twenty-Five

On the fifth floor the gunman was waiting for them.

"My colleague," he said, gesturing toward the elevators.

It was an oddly polite word choice for, as Finn had called them, "muscle." But Hollis took her cue from her husband and said nothing, just waited.

A moment later, the elevator door opened and the other gunman from the plane walked out, carrying a garment bag and a small suitcase. His suit was just as tight-fitting but a medium gray. He had a white shirt, unbuttoned at the top with no tie. Both men looked far less menacing than they had on the plane. But that didn't mean anything, Hollis reminded herself. Declan never looked menacing either.

"We should frisk him too," Hollis said, pointing to the second gunman.

"Frisk, not feel him up." Finn took the bags from the man. "Holly, you look through these. I'll pat him down."

She blushed a little at his saying that in front of the men. They'd been together since freshman year of college, with only a short break after graduation. They each had their meaningless moments of fantasy. He went through an Olivia Munn phase the year before and Hollis hadn't said a word.

She zipped open the garment bag. A tuxedo, and behind it a gorgeous black cocktail dress that appeared to have sequins sewn in by hand. She couldn't wait to get a better look at it. She put it aside and opened the suitcase. It held two pairs of shoes, one black pair for Finn and a pair of medium-heel black pumps with a strap across the ankle. Next to the shoes was a rectangular black velvet box. Inside was a diamond and ruby necklace, with diamond and ruby drop earrings, and a pair of silver cufflinks with an image of the sun engraved on them. The flag of Argentina, Hollis realized, had the same design. Someone was making sure they would be properly dressed at the party later.

She handed the men back the cases. "What are your names?"

The taller man smiled. "I'm Eduardo. This is Bryan."

"You enjoy your work?"

The men looked at each other. "It's steady. And no two days are ever the same."

"We're Tim and Janet."

Eduardo held out his hand. "Lovely to meet you, Señora McCabe. No one ever asks us about ourselves."

"We like to know who we're working with."

Bryan nodded. "Your room?"

Finn pointed down the hall. "Five twelve."

The men walked first and Finn glanced toward Hollis. "You have to make friends with everyone?" he whispered.

She shrugged. It couldn't hurt.

———

Once in the room, Eduardo reopened the suitcase, carefully put the shoes on the floor and the jewelry case on the dresser. Then he pulled at a corner of the suitcase and revealed a secret panel. Finn and Hollis exchanged glances. It was too late to do anything but watch. Eduardo pulled out a small black plastic box. He opened it. Two guns. Two very real guns.

Hollis held her breath. They should have met in the bar downstairs.

Eduardo handed the box to Finn. "Boss said you might not have brought your own. We explained that things were a little, um, confusing in Michigan."

"We need to apologize for that," Bryan chimed in. "Clearly you knew things we didn't. If we were kept informed, we could have done the job ourselves."

"It was not the way to bring us here," Finn said. His voice had authority, a touch of annoyance. "Why did it happen that way?"

Eduardo frowned. "It was a decision made by another. I hope you won't hold it against us."

Bryan wandered the room, glancing in the bathroom and out onto the balcony. "This is your room?" Bryan said. "I was told you had been given the very best. People of your stature should not have small rooms."

"It's actually quite nice," Hollis started to protest.

"It's a room," Finn jumped in. "We like to keep options whenever we're on a job."

Bryan smiled a tight smile. "Smart."

Finn placed the gun box on the desk. "You were following us earlier today in Recoleta."

"Just trying to make sure you were okay," Bryan said. "Considering the betrayal..."

Eduardo nudged Bryan, and Bryan swallowed hard.

"We'll send a car at eight," Eduardo said. He reached into his pocket and pulled out a cell phone, which he handed to Hollis. "Untraceable, of course. In case you need anything from us..."

"We're fine," Finn said. He walked to the door. "Eight o'clock."

Hollis let her breath out as the men walked out the door and Finn locked the bolt. "It's almost five now," Hollis said. "We can rest for a bit before we get ready. I know I could use a few minutes off my feet." Janet McCabe's shoes were leaving her feet with a dull ache. "Maybe we could order some room service appetizers. I assume they'll have food at the party and we don't want to be rude and not eat."

Finn walked back to the desk, closed the box with the guns in it, and sat on the bed. He said nothing, just sat there staring at something, Hollis couldn't tell what.

"You okay?" she asked.

"I can't do it, Holly. Gunmen. International assassins. Spies. Getting locked in crypts. Wearing a tux..."

She did not even smile at the last one. She knew better.

"You're doing really well. You seemed so calm in front of Bryan and Eduardo."

"I was faking," he said. "I'm a teacher. Ask me anything about the literature of Argentina and I can go all day ... Jorge Luis Borges, he was amazing. If you haven't read *Ficciones*, you should."

"I did," she said, sitting next to him on the bed. "Years ago."

"Read it again." His voice was high, stressed.

She stroked his back. "Juan Jose Saer is good too."

"He's a genius. Cesar Aira, Victoria Ocampo, Julio Cortazar ... I could go on all day."

She knew that was true. "Lie down," she told him.

"I feel like I'm speaking in another language. I'm just not built for this. From the moment that Eduardo guy got off the elevator my hand was shaking."

"You hid it well."

Finn's eye was twitching. He pushed back in the bed and lay on his back, his head on the pillow. Hollis moved too, positioning herself on her side so she could get in close to him. He put his arm around her and she put her hand on his chest, her forehead against his neck. They stayed silent for several minutes, just breathing at a normal rate for the first time in more than twenty-four hours. She wanted to say it would be okay, but that was dumb. Would it be okay? She had no idea.

"I can't do this," Finn said.

He wasn't in the mood for a pep talk, so she said nothing.

"I know you like all of this stuff."

"I don't," she said.

"You like it more than me. I want to be home, reading about people who risk their lives on international missions of intrigue. I have no idea what I'm doing."

"From where I'm standing, you're doing a really good job."

"That's a pretty worthless recommendation. You don't know what you're doing, either."

She laughed. "And yet, we fooled Eduardo and Bryan. I think they're afraid of us."

"Who were Tim and Janet McCabe when they were alive? They must have had quite a reputation."

A thought occurred to Hollis and her body immediately tensed.

"What?" Finn asked.

"What if someone at this party knows Tim and Janet McCabe? If they do have reputations in TCT, someone has probably hired them before."

"I can't do this. I won't walk into a party with no idea of who has hired us and who will kill us."

Hollis rolled onto her back, mimicking Finn's position—tense and staring at the ceiling. "And what about the betrayal? Who was that?"

"Declan. It has to be Declan."

That made sense. It wasn't comforting, but it made sense.

"And even if no one at the party knows the McCabes," Finn continued, "at some point whoever hired them to kill Declan will want proof that he's dead. What do we do then?"

"We'll think of something."

"And the other person who's supposed to be killed. Who is the other person? Are we supposed to know or is someone going to tell us?"

"I don't know."

"I can't do this," he said again. "I can't walk into a party and try to be a hired killer in front of a bunch of criminals. I won't be able to keep up the pretense."

As the thought settled in, Hollis realized, neither could she. But in less than three hours, they were going to have to.

Twenty-Six

As Hollis walked into the shower, she could hear Finn muttering, "I can't do this." When it was his turn and she was putting on makeup, she could hear, "I can't do this." She put on the French lingerie and slid the cocktail dress over her head. Finn walked out of the shower, dropped his towel on the floor, and said, "I can't do this."

"I laid your tux out on the bed." Hollis picked the towel up and put it on a hook in the bathroom.

"Holly ..."

Hollis came back into the bedroom.

"Our host is the man who hired us to kill Declan."

"That's my guess." She put on the diamond-drop earrings and ruby and diamond necklace. They were heavy in the way that practically announced their extravagance. "Do you think we'll have to give this stuff back?"

"*That's* your concern?"

"We can both freak out, if you'd prefer."

"I'd prefer that, yes. I can't do this."

"I know. But you can. You have to," she pointed out. "What are our options?"

"Change our names and leave the country."

"Not to state the obvious, but haven't we already done that?"

"I thought Peter would be of more help," he said.

While Hollis was in the shower, Finn had gone to the bar for a drink. But he'd also borrowed a cell phone from a stranger and called Peter, looking for an escape plan. Not only had he not offered one, he seemed thrilled they were going to meet another member of TCT, someone high enough on the food chain to order Declan's murder. Whatever calm had come from the short nap was immediately negated by Peter's directive to go ahead with the evening's plans.

Finn pulled on his underwear, grunted, muttered, and then put on his pants. He held up the shirt. "This isn't going to fit."

"Put it on."

"It isn't going to fit."

"Put it on."

More muttering. He put the shirt on, and it fit beautifully. It was a narrow cut, like the suits that Eduardo and Bryan wore, and it accentuated his slim body.

Much to Hollis's surprise and delight, there was no further commentary. He put on his socks and shoes, then his cufflinks, and his jacket. He held out his arms. "So?"

"Gorgeous. Sexy as hell."

"Better than Eduardo?"

She smiled. "Every day of the week. Do you want me to Google how to tie a bowtie?"

"I know how to tie a bowtie. I'm not a barbarian." He stared for a moment at the black rectangle, then put it around his neck, one side slightly longer than the other, and quickly twisted it into a bow.

Hollis watched in amazement. "How have I never seen you do that?"

"Because the last time I wore a bow tie was on our wedding day."

"And you remember from that?"

"I remember everything."

She could have pointed out that it wasn't exactly true, but she didn't. Instead she offered him her back, and he zipped up her dress, kissing her neck.

"You are stunning," he said.

"We're a very attractive couple. Well, Tim and Janet are, anyway." She noticed the room's clock. "It's almost eight."

"What do we do about those?" Finn pointed toward the plastic box and the two guns.

She opened the lid of the box and looked again. The guns were Walther PPKs, and there was a small box of ammunition. It was serious, spy-level, ammunition. But it was also not the sort of thing that could go unnoticed in a small handbag or a slim-cut suit.

"I think this is meant for later," she said.

"Miss Manners would object to bringing weapons to a party?"

"Miss Manners and whoever is hosting the party."

Finn closed the box and put it in the suitcase, which he zipped up and put in the closet. "Just in case the maid turns down the bed."

Hollis's shoes took a moment to put on, as she struggled with the stiff strap, but they were comfortable at least. On the same hanger as the dress had been a shawl, black embroidery on black silk cloth, and a black satin handbag. She put some money, the cell phone, and the credit card in it. As she was grabbing her lipstick, she noticed Finn pacing.

"You okay?" she asked.

"No. I'm exhausted, terrified, angry, and completely in over my head. You?"

"We can call Peter again..." She lifted the phone from our purse.

"Not from that phone. Never from that phone. They could be listening in."

"We'll go back to the bar and call."

"And he'll tell us the future of the world depends on our going to this party."

"So we go?"

She knew what the answer was all along, but it was better to let Finn work it out for himself. She'd learned that after years of doing it the hard way. The first time she told him they had to have two Thanksgivings, just to keep the peace in both families, it turned into a fight that practically ended their marriage. So, she knew now to give him options and keep talking until he chose the right one. It was, frighteningly enough, a technique employed on world leaders by members of their senior staff.

Finn paced a moment more before stopping. He kissed Hollis's head. "It'll be fine." He put the keycard in his pocket and moved toward the door.

"Wait," Hollis said suddenly, pulling out her phone. "We should take our picture."

"To send to Peter?"

"No. We never look this nice. I'd like to have a photo of us looking like this."

Finn walked back to her and took the camera. "Smile," he said as he snapped. He didn't take his own directive. He scowled for the photo, then handed her back the phone. "Souvenirs, tours of the cemetery, and now holiday selfies. You manage to find a way to enjoy everything, even when common sense says you shouldn't."

"I'm taking that as a compliment."

"Exactly my point."

———

The same driver who dropped them off, who sent them to the Eva Perón Museum, was waiting for them outside the hotel. He smiled but said nothing. It seemed more than likely that Declan was behind the clue, but obviously the driver didn't work for Declan. Hollis thought about asking who the host of the party was, and if they were in danger. But whatever reason the driver had to help Declan might not extend to them. So instead, she sat back and watched the lights of Buenos Aires.

They passed beautiful buildings and watched couples strolling in the spring evening. Argentina would be moving into spring and summer soon, just as back home in Michigan they would be moving into fall and winter. The transition was Hollis's favorite time. The uncertainty of whether to bring a sweater was an annoyance to Finn, but she liked the not knowing. Even tonight, walking into who-knew-what. She was, along with the terror, a little excited to attend a grand party in a sequined cocktail dress and meet the mysterious man who had invited them there.

She watched out the window as the driver turned and slowed down, stopping in front of the Café Tortoni, a large café with a marble façade and an art nouveau sign out front.

The driver opened the car doors and extended a hand to help Hollis out of the car. "Señora McCabe," he said. "You look lovely, if I might say."

"*Gracias.*"

"*Espejo,*" he said. "It is the best move."

As he had done earlier, he said nothing to clear up his statement. He just got into the car and drove away.

"What does that mean?" Hollis asked.

Finn grabbed the phone from Hollis's purse, and searched. "It's a tango term. Means to mirror the movement of your partner."

"I should follow your lead?"

The door to the café opened, and a tall, elegant man close to seventy emerged. He had a full head of gray hair to match a neatly trimmed gray mustache. His tuxedo was classic, white shirt and black suit, but he had a white pocket square and a light blue carnation that suggested a bit of originality. He walked out onto the sidewalk, a broad smile on his face.

"Señor and Señora McCabe!" he said. "I'm so grateful you have come to my party."

"I don't think I'm the partner the driver meant," Finn muttered just loud enough for Hollis to hear.

Twenty-Seven

Stepping out of the street and into Café Tortoni was like moving from one world to another. There was a long bar on one side of the room, marble pillars running down the center, and café tables everywhere with three or four chairs tucked in intimate groupings around each table. Even from the doorway, Hollis could see that it stretched far back, in multiple rooms, with small stained-glass panels separating areas. Art nouveau decorations and dark wood on the walls made the café look, not just plucked from Paris, but Paris circa 1900.

"She is beautiful," the elegant man said. "Gorgeous." He seemed pleased.

"I'm Tim McCabe," Finn said, putting out his hand.

"Carlos Gardel." He bowed a little before shaking Finn's hand, then Hollis's. "You have honored me with your presence."

"Is this yours?" Hollis asked.

"Oh, no." He blushed. "This is simply my favorite place in the city. Once a year I throw a party for some friends and rent out the whole restaurant."

Hollis looked around. Bryan and Eduardo were at a table near one of the walls. There was a short, bald man in black, wearing a long white apron, holding a tray. But that was it.

"Are we early? We were told to be ready at eight."

Carlos shook his head. "You are my party," he said. "I did not wish to share you with too many others."

At least they wouldn't have to worry about being recognized, Hollis thought. She saw Finn let out a breath. Maybe they could do this.

Carlos signaled the waiter, who nodded and disappeared, only to return moments later with a bottle of champagne wedged into an ice bucket, and four champagne glasses.

"There's at least a fourth person coming," Hollis said as the waiter poured the champagne.

"My wife. She takes too much time to ready herself, I'm afraid." His eyes moved up and down Hollis's figure. "You look exquisite and manage to be on time."

"The job demands it," she said without thinking. She almost added that students won't wait for a late professor but caught herself.

"That's good to hear." Carlos poured them each a glass of champagne. "I am of course interested in the property more than the man. But that is not my decision, you understand."

"We appreciate the gift you sent," Finn said. "It was an odd extraction from the US and left us no opportunity to gather our ... belongings."

Carlos looked, for the first time, unhappy. "This is my fault, entirely. But I'm grateful you'll be able to end one headache for me, and I assure you I will end the other."

Hollis sipped her champagne, unwilling to push the point further. Peter would want as much information as they could give him, but there was all evening. After a second sip, she felt a little lightheaded. She put her hand on a chair's back to steady herself.

"I'm afraid we haven't eaten much today," she explained.

Carlos signaled the waiter again. "That I can fix." He walked Hollis a few steps from Finn and put his hand on her back. "Your work is so interesting to me. And you seem, if you'll forgive me, so unlike what I was expecting."

"Ordinary?"

He smiled. "Yes, in a way."

"Better to blend in."

"Of course. You came highly recommended. How long have you known our mutual friend?"

She paused. "Long enough to earn his trust." It had sounded like the perfect answer in her head, but as she spoke, she realized the friend could be a woman. There was no backtracking, so she hoped for the best.

"What I'm asking won't trouble you? To have asked his help in finding you then to use it against him, you understand this is not my normal way of doing things, but the item is too valuable, the reward too tempting."

"I understand. Business is business."

He nodded. He seemed relieved by the answer. She was just happy to stop talking about their "friend."

"It's quite a beautiful place." She glanced around the room. "Almost from another time."

"Timeless." Carlos breathed in the place. "It has been opened since 1858. Everyone has come here, and still comes here, to talk politics and life, to have a coffee … to be seen. Jorge Luis Borges had a regular table."

Hollis nodded toward Finn. "He's one of my husband's favorite writers."

Carlos's face lit up. He turned to Finn, still standing near the champagne. "'Any life is made up of a single moment…'"

"'The moment in which a man finds out, once and for all, who he is,'" Finn responded.

Carlos laughed. "One of my favorite sayings of Borges."

"Mine too."

"Let me find out who you are," Carlos said.

"I'm just a man who likes to read," Finn said.

"We have that in common." Carlos abandoned her for Finn. The men sat at one of the small tables and Hollis could hear them talk about books.

Hollis looked to Finn, waiting for a sign of distress, but he seemed relaxed. He was wrong. Not only could he be in a room with killers, pretending to be one of them, he was good at it.

While the men talked about books, Hollis explored the place on her own. There were paintings and sketches on the walls from different time periods and in different styles, like might be collected over generations, and likely were, she imagined. There were also photos on the walls from more than a century of visitors and events. Waiters from the turn of the twentieth century stared out at her from one large photograph, looking quite ready to take her order. In another Albert Einstein leaned against the bar. And in a picture hanging toward the back, Robert Duvall smiled from a table.

In the corner of one of the many rooms, there were three figures in wax, a man and a woman seated, and a man standing next to their table.

"Borges," a voice behind her said.

Hollis turned. It was Tomas Silva, looking sober and unhappy.

"Did you know that Borges was blind?" he said. "Not his entire life, but by his late thirties the light began to fade for him. It did not stop him from becoming a great writer."

"Very inspiring."

"Do you know the other figures at the table with Borges?"

"No."

"The poet Alfonsina Storni," Silva said. "And the tango legend Carlos Gardel."

Hollis stared at the figure of the man who was standing, younger than the two others, wearing a gray double-breasted suit with a white pocket square and a light blue carnation in his lapel. Carlos Gardel. She leaned in and saw a small plaque. Her eyes went immediately to Gardel's name, and the inscription 1890–1935. Of course the elegant man chatting with Finn hadn't given his real name. Why should anything be that simple?

"He was the best tango singer in the country's history," Silva continued, with the melancholy tone of a man who was in mourning. "He died in a plane crash. Too young."

"Very sad."

Hollis was unsure what to make of Silva. He seemed exhausted and unhappy. It was unlikely that he would be able to do anything to help them, but perhaps he didn't need the help. He was at this very exclusive party. He clearly had a connection to the man calling himself Carlos Gardel, so that had to be worth something.

"It's a shame that someone with so much to offer is taken suddenly."

"A sacrifice stays hidden only so long," Silva said. "Once it is on display, the world can judge its worth. Remember this."

Hollis was a life-long solver of crosswords, but even she was growing tired of the endless puzzles. If he was on their side, she longed for him to say it.

Instead he said, "I need a drink."

"There's champagne," Hollis said. Based on their experience on the plane, Silva was easier to handle when he was drunk. He seemed to agree. He moved away from her toward the front room and the bar, leaving her with wax versions of three Argentinian legends and a very real problem of what to do next.

Twenty-Eight

The waiter arrived holding out a tray of mini empanadas, stuffed mushrooms, and cheese puffs. Hollis was tempted to take the whole tray, but she took only what would fit on a small napkin.

"We barely had lunch," she explained.

The waiter smiled, then moved toward the front. Hollis decided to follow. Carlos was hugging Silva, keeping him from the large scotch he'd poured for himself.

"Silva and I began in the streets together," Carlos told Hollis and Finn. "I had the ambition, he had the talent for theft. Brains and brawn. We were a great team."

Better to be clever than strong. Silva had said that on the plane. Obviously, he felt Carlos had gotten the better end of their partnership.

Silva finished his drink, despite the hug. Once free, he poured himself another and drank it in one gulp. "Do you remember the time we stole an Emilio Pettoruti from the gallery moments after it sold?"

Carlos laughed. "There was a huge argument between the gallery owner and the man who had bought the painting as to who should take the loss. I stood there watching while my friend here loaded the painting in his car."

"Pettoruti was a cubist, wasn't he?" Finn asked.

"A man of considerable knowledge," Carlos said. "Far more than I expected from someone of your ... other talents, Señor McCabe. I'll tell you about that painting. It was so hot, I had it in my apartment for five years before I could move it."

"It hung in your dining room," Silva said. "I missed it when it was gone."

"Me too. But the money helped me get over it."

"You did make a killing," Silva said.

"Just the beginning."

Silva curled his mouth into a pained smile. "I missed some of those good times when I was away."

Carlos nodded. "You're here now. And times are good." He poured Silva a third scotch.

"Things have gotten easier since globalization," Finn offered. "No need to sit on specialized goods. There is always someone half a world away who will pay."

"But there is another price we must pay." Carlos turned to Finn and Hollis. "It becomes harder to fulfill expectations when they get so high. That is why I'm so grateful for your help in procuring the item."

Silva drank, but slower this time.

The door opened, and a woman slid in wearing an exquisite red silk chemise, cut to skim her tall slim body the way a dress from the jazz age might have done. Hollis recognized her immediately as the woman from the museum who'd directed them to the cemetery—to Declan. The woman looked over at Hollis and smiled. "I'm his wife," she said, nodding toward Carlos. "You must be Mrs. McCabe."

"Yes. Nice to meet you."

"Teresa, finally, you're here," Carlos said.

He kissed her cheek, more ownership than affection. For her part, she made no pretense to enjoy it. There were May–December marriages, and Hollis tried not to judge, but Carlos was old enough to be Teresa's grandfather.

Teresa grabbed two glasses of champagne, drinking one in a gulp. "I see you've invited your old friend," she said, glaring at Silva.

"He is always welcome," Carlos told her.

Teresa turned to Hollis. "Did you enjoy the clothes I picked out?"

"You picked them?"

"I was given instructions to help you fit in."

"They're gorgeous."

"The dress fits you well," she said.

"It does," Carlos agreed. "I told my wife to spare no expense, and clearly—probably for the first time since I proposed—she heeded my instructions."

Teresa ignored him. "Have you seen any of the city?"

"The Recoleta Cemetery," Hollis said to let her know that they had figured out her clue at the museum. There was no point in lying about it anyway. Bryan had followed them there. She wondered if she should mention the museum, but she left it up to Teresa.

"I hope you see more," Teresa said. "Carlos and I met at a *milonga*, a club to dance the tango, but there are so many other things to see and do in the city."

"The pink house," Silva suggested.

"Yes, our president's home," she agreed. "It's where Evita did her famous goodbye speech."

Silva began to sing the lyrics to "Don't Cry for Me, Argentina" off-key. It was obvious he was no longer sober.

Teresa gritted her teeth. No love lost there. "And of course, everyone goes to La Boca. It's a tourist trap, but a colorful one. Promise me tomorrow you'll make the time."

"La Boca is overpriced, and you have to watch your pockets," Carlos said. "Go to El Ateneo Grand Bookstore. It used to be a movie theater. Tim, you will fall in love."

"Tomorrow is a busy day," Silva said.

"Monday is busier." Carlos cut him off. "So much to see. But first we should have some wine, some food, and some entertainment."

Hollis sat beside Finn at one of the tables and touched his thigh under the table. "Okay?" she whispered.

"So far. He's a very entertaining man."

"That makes me nervous."

"Me too."

A trio of musicians set up in the corner—a woman playing cello and two men, one with an acoustic guitar, the other with an accordion. The music started slow and sad but grew faster and more insistent as the piece went on. Carlos stood at the bar watching them intently, his head moving to the music. Teresa sat on a barstool near him, obviously bored, or at least doing a good imitation of the arm candy turned resentful spouse. Silva sat alone at a table watching Carlos. The gunmen had their backs to the musicians and their eyes on everyone in the room.

It was an odd party.

Twenty-Nine

After the first song ended, a woman in a sparkling floor-length gold dress entered the floor. The lights dimmed, and the music started up again. As she moved, it was clear the dress was slit nearly to her hip. She was wearing shoes similar to the ones Hollis had been given—tango shoes. The woman glided across the floor for several minutes, moving her hips and her dress in a way that clearly delighted Carlos. He applauded several times.

Then a man in a pinstripe suit entered the room from the kitchen and walked to the woman. The man and woman circled each other, moving closer until the man grabbed the woman, holding her tightly. At first, he caressed her hair and she moved her lips close to his, then he dipped her and she rolled almost out of his arms. It was planned, clearly, as he caught her at the last minute and drew her back to him. But something had changed in their dance. It was now a passionate, almost angry, tango. The music changed again, and the dance changed with it, becoming sad, as though the couple were saying goodbye.

Carlos had been watching the couple intently, but as the dance ended he slipped over to Hollis and Finn.

"Do you tango?" he asked.

Finn laughed. "I read."

Carlos looked at Hollis. "I'm afraid not," Hollis said. "It's lovely, though. Like the story of a relationship."

"Exactly. It is a story. A story of love and anger, betrayal and desire." He held out his hand to Hollis. "I will teach you."

She took his hand. It didn't seem likely she had a choice. Carlos faced her, holding her right hand in his. She put her left hand on his shoulder, he put his right hand on her back. It all seemed easy enough, Hollis thought. And then he pulled her close with such ferocity, she nearly gasped.

"I don't know the steps," she told him.

"In Argentina, we like to improvise."

"That's interesting. You seem like a man who prefers to have a plan."

Carlos smiled. "Perhaps. But when you tango, you think of nothing but tango."

The music started again, slow but intimate. Carlos moved his foot forward, and out of instinct Hollis moved hers back.

"You are a natural," he said. Then he spun her and she almost lost her balance. "The tango comes from the streets, from the working class. It is the music of pride and desire, of people who are hungry for more. I can see in the way you move your body that you understand this, Señora. You know what it is to want excitement, pleasure ..."

"I have everything I want."

"No one has everything they want."

The music quickened. He dipped her until her hair swept the floor, then spun her. They moved across the restaurant, dancing near the professional couple, then away from them. She began to lose track of where they were, or what was happening. She knew it was important to take the driver's advice and mirror her partner, so she focused on Carlos. It made them move as one.

She held on, realizing she was thinking only of tango. It was as if she'd been swept away somewhere and all she could think of was the music, and the terrifying strength of the man who had her in his arms. When the music stopped, Hollis finally caught her breath. But before she could pull away, the guitar player began a new tune.

"Maybe that's enough for now," she said.

"No." His voice was firm. "You must dance the tanda with the same partner."

"The *tanda?*"

"This..." He nodded toward the musicians. "We dance until they stop, Señora McCabe. If you agree to tango with someone, you must never break the dance. It is the greatest of insults." He tightened his grip on her waist. "You don't wish to insult me, do you?"

Hollis did her best to smile. "Never, Señor Gardel."

The second piece was faster, and Hollis found herself holding Carlos tight just to keep up. By the third song, she was able to glance to her left. Finn and Teresa were dancing a less-intense tango, more swaying and flirting, than the show of power that was her dance with Carlos. Another day she might have been a little jealous watching them, but now all she hoped was that he was getting more information from Teresa than she was getting from Carlos.

"You and your husband have been together many years," he said. "And yet you still have a burning passion for each other."

"Do we?"

"I did not realize though that you were Dutch. Your American accent is perfection."

Hollis was blank for a moment, then remembered the honeymooning couple from Amsterdam. She bit her lip to stop herself from laughing. Finn's instincts had been right about the room being bugged, but at least the couple occupying it was safe.

When finally the *tanda* ended and the musicians switched to something quiet, they went back to the table. It gave Hollis a moment to catch her breath. The tango was more work than it appeared, and it required a trust that had surprised her. It was a perfect dance for a man looking to test her loyalty. She only hoped she'd passed.

Silva sat at one end of the table, an empty chair between him and Teresa, with Finn to her left and Carlos and Hollis sitting across from them. As if on cue, the food arrived. There were large steaks, roasted potatoes, and a strong red wine.

"The best of Mendoza ..." Carlos said, as he poured each glass almost to the top.

The waiter put out bread and chimichurri sauce, both for dipping and for spreading over the beef and potatoes. Hollis put a little on her plate, but after one taste of the fresh blend of parsley, garlic, olive oil, and vinegar, she went back for more.

"Do you know where chimichurri gets its name?" Carlos asked, but without waiting for an answer he continued. "It is from British soldiers who had tasted it asking *gimme curry, gimme curry*." He laughed.

"That's just a story," Teresa said. "No one knows how it got its name."

"But we know it is from Argentina."

"And Uruguay," she added.

Carlos laughed. "My wife—my late wife—she would never think to disagree with me in public. Never in private, either. But I marry this one and she delights in it. So much passion."

Teresa took his hand across the table. She smiled, and it was, to Hollis's eyes, quite a charming smile. The kind that might convince a man she cared for him. She wondered if Carlos believed it.

As they ate, the music played softly and the professional dancers continued to dance. But no one at the table paid much attention. All eyes were on Carlos. He told stories of Argentina's history, of his travels around the world, of a grandchild that lived in America, who he rarely saw but deeply loved. The rest of the table listened. By the time dessert arrived, a chocolate cake with salted caramel decorations, Hollis felt she knew everything about the man. But when she stopped to think of what he said, it was almost nothing at all. His world was funny stories that likely hid dark truths.

Silva said almost nothing but kept drinking glass after glass until Hollis was surprised he could still sit upright. Teresa interrupted to correct Carlos more than once. He seemed to enjoy the banter between them, at least in public.

When Teresa got up to use the ladies' room, Hollis was tempted to follow but Teresa walked too quickly to catch up. She dropped her purse and Eduardo jumped up to get it for her. She smiled at him, perhaps the first genuine smile of the night, and left the room. Carlos told the story of another heist in which he was almost caught. He was enjoying himself, while Hollis could see Silva doing all in his power to hold his tongue.

"You know of course the Borges saying about the Malvinas ... the Falklands War," Carlos said.

Finn nodded. "A fight between two bald men over a comb."

"This is the secret to my life. I sell combs. I don't take sides, so no matter who wins the war, I make money." He laughed.

Teresa returned, sighing. "There's more to life than money."

"If there is, I will still win." Carlos laughed even harder, but this time it seemed the joke was a private one.

The waiter brought more wine and coffee. Hollis knew better than to check the time, but she assumed as she sipped the last of her coffee that the evening would be soon over. She hoped so, anyway. She realized halfway through dinner that she and Finn had been in Argentina less than twenty-four hours. So much had happened that she needed a break from all of it to catch up. And to sleep. She desperately needed more sleep than the two catnaps they'd taken so far. Looking over at Finn struggle to keep his eyes open, she knew the moment they could get away, they would fall into bed. Discussions of what had happened tonight, what he had possibly learned from Teresa, would have to wait until breakfast.

"I'm so grateful you both agreed to be my guests tonight," Carlos said. "You have been so different than I expected ..."

"As have you," Finn said.

Carlos seemed pleased. "Our evening draws to a close, I think," he said. "My new friends"—he smiled toward Finn and Hollis—"my old friend"—he looked toward Silva, who had been silent most of the evening—"my wife"—he nodded at Teresa. "I have enjoyed all of tonight but one thing. I've been saddened to realize that not all is what it seems. I needed tonight to be sure, but now I am sure. I have been lied to."

No one moved, no facial expressions changed. Carlos's voice maintained its lightness. But everything in the room was different. Hollis could see the waiter take a few steps back. Eduardo and Bryan were behind her. She had no idea what they were doing. The dancers were standing still. Hollis could hear the musicians, though. They still played, but it was as if they lost the beat.

Finn locked his eyes on Hollis. He was calm, so she was calm. The door seemed miles away, and they would never be able to make a run for it. Not with guns at their backs. They could talk their way out of it, maybe. That depended on what he knew. Finn smiled a half smile. *It will be okay*, he was telling her. She smiled back.

Thirty

"I'm an old man now," Carlos said. "I have as my pleasures good friends, the woman I love, an occasional call from my children and grandchildren when they want money." He laughed. "I live for these things. They are all that matter to me. That and tango." He smiled at Hollis.

"I know I'm at the end of my career," he continued. "It's been a good one for me, I think. But there have been losses. And there have been betrayals. Some lies are not to be forgiven. And some can be remedied. I hope soon to know the difference."

"What's this about?" Teresa said. Her tone was bored, but her eyes were wide, her body tense.

"We are all as one?" Carlos asked.

"Of course," Silva said. "Like in the old days."

Carlos looked to Teresa. "Yes," she said. "As one."

He only smiled at Finn, then patted Hollis's shoulder. "Let's have more wine," Carlos said, as if nothing had happened. "And fresh glasses."

The waiter moved quickly. He took the used glasses off the table and brought news ones. He opened two new bottles of wine and poured each person a half glass.

"That's not enough," Carlos said. He grabbed a bottle and filled each glass to full. "Let's make a toast." He lifted his glass. "To trust."

"Trust," Silva said. "*Salud.*"

Finn and Hollis lifted their glasses, waiting to see what the others would do. Carlos drank. Then Silva. Then Teresa. Hollis put the wine to her lips. It tasted fine. She drank a little, as little as she could. Finn did the same.

"And to the future," Carlos said.

They each drank again. Hollis felt lightheaded. She knew he was going to do something. She waited for Eduardo and Bryan to make their moves. But there was nothing.

"And to you," Finn said to Carlos, standing up and raising his glass. "For an evening we will remember with great fondness."

They all drank again.

"But now we must go," Finn said. "You brought us here for work, and it's getting quite late."

"Of course." Carlos turned and signaled the gunmen. "Get the car for the McCabes," he said.

Hollis looked around. All the tension from the room was gone. Carlos was a man who liked to talk, she learned that quickly enough. Maybe he gave speeches like that all the time. Teresa stood up and shook Finn's hand. Silva finished his wine. When he stood up, he swayed a little.

"Lovely to see you both again," he said. Then he coughed a little. "*Perdóname,*" he said.

He coughed again, reaching for a napkin to cover his mouth. Hollis could see there were droplets of blood on the napkin. He looked up at Carlos, surprised. A third cough, heavier than before, brought more blood.

"*Lo siento,*" Silva said. Then he dropped to the floor.

Hollis reached out to help, but one glance at Finn and she stopped. It wouldn't have mattered anyway. Silva's eyes were open, there was blood and foam around his mouth. He twitched a little, then went quiet. Hollis moved toward Finn. She wanted to scream, or run, or something. But she knew she had to stay quiet. Killers, she reminded herself, don't collapse at the sight of a murder.

Carlos stepped over the body of his old friend. "He had told me that you were pretenders. It was the reason he gave for the very inappropriate way you were brought to this country. I have known Silva my whole life, so I did not know what to think." He glanced back at the dead man on the floor with no emotion in his face then turned back to Hollis and Finn. "I had to see for myself. To judge for myself. And it's true that you were not what I expected."

"But as I got to know you both, I understood that it's exactly because you were not what I expected that I could see you were the real thing," he continued. "You are very smart, very charming, but you are also cautious. You are calm, but there is passion in you. These are the qualities for people in our business. Silva was all emotion and excitement." Carlos laughed. "He told me you were college professors."

"Why would he say that?" Finn asked.

"He has been jealous of me for many years. He believed I betrayed him once, and it cost him time in prison. I think he sought to betray me now when I am in the midst of a delicate negotiation. Perhaps he thought by kidnapping you, he would anger you enough to keep you from doing your job. Or perhaps he did not trust himself to keep his mouth shut around you. He has not been sober for many years." He sighed.

He signaled to the waiter, who brought him his wineglass. He finished it in one gulp, then snapped his fingers. The musicians got louder, the dancers started dancing. The waiter unfolded a tablecloth and draped it over Silva's body.

It was as if it was the most ordinary thing in the world.

"It has been a most wonderful evening for me," Carlos said. "I hope the same for you both."

Finn stood silent.

"Lovely," Hollis said. "You are a wonderful dancer."

He blushed. "A perfect tango depends on two people in sync. I have felt that with you tonight."

"And I with you."

He smiled. "You have chosen to dance with me, and you will stay until the music ends."

"Of course."

He kissed her cheek. *"Gracias."* He reached his hand out to Finn, who seemed to snap out of his trance. He took Carlos's hand.

"Thank you," Finn said. "I'd been saying I wanted a good steak in Argentina and I think you fed me the best one possible."

"I am sorry to add one more job to your work here, but I hope you will find the compensation I sent to your account more than enough."

"Of course."

"You have your instructions, I hope, Señor and Señora McCabe."

"We're ready."

"By Monday this sad business will be behind us. Thank you for returning to me what is mine."

Hollis didn't want to, but she found herself looking one more time at Silva's body, lying at Carlos's feet. His arms and feet sticking out from underneath the tablecloth.

"We're happy to help," she said.

"I have found the right people," he said. "I think you also are in the business of selling combs."

Thirty-One

The driver was waiting for them with the door open. Bryan and Eduardo had walked them out, but neither Finn nor Hollis acknowledged that. They just climbed into the back seat and waited for the car door to close.

"That was horrible," Hollis said as softly as possible. Perhaps the driver was helping them before, but after tonight his loyalty could switch again. She looked back at the café as the car drove around the corner. She wanted to believe they were safe for the moment, but who knew? "He killed his friend in front of us."

"I think that was the point, doing it in front of us. He wanted to show us that he has faith in us," Finn said. "Or what happens when he loses faith."

"I wonder if he knows about Teresa helping Declan?"

"I got the feeling she's doing more than helping Declan," Finn said. "From the way she spoke about him, she's helped herself to the man. The whole time we were dancing she asked me questions about him. I finally told her he was a bit of a ladies' man, so she might be better off keeping her distance."

"Good advice I don't think she'll follow."

"Not good advice." Declan popped up in the front passenger seat.

Hollis, half startled, half angry, flung her purse at him and the corner of it caught his nose.

"You really are the right person for the job, Hollis. You've got a violent streak in you."

"What are you doing here?" Finn said.

"Checking up on you."

"Shouldn't you be checking up on Teresa?"

Declan turned toward the driver. "I'm not involved with Teresa. Just helping her."

"Like you were helping Silva? Do you know that Carlos poisoned him?"

"How?"

"The wine."

"Did you all drink the wine?" Declan asked.

It took a moment, but Hollis got it. "Carlos poisoned the glass. He asked for fresh glasses." She turned to Finn. "Did you know that? I thought it was awfully brave of you to do that toast."

"I wanted to do what our driver told us, to follow his lead," Finn said.

"It was impressive."

Finn leaned in and kissed her. "I watched you two dance the tango. *That* was impressive."

"This is adorable," Declan interrupted. "And I'm always a big fan of seeing the two of you in love, but can we get back to Silva's death? Are you sure he's dead?"

"Very sure. But you don't care about Silva," Hollis said. "Just like you didn't care about us in that crypt."

Declan shook his head. "For what it's worth, I did send someone to get you out, but you'd managed on your own by then. And as far as Silva, I barely knew him. I came down here because he was trying to pull a job and needed help. I needed the money..."

"How could you possibly need the money?" Hollis asked. "Didn't you make millions from that deal in Ireland?"

"I lost it."

"How could you lose it?" Hollis asked.

Finn wasn't interested. "You said you came down here to help Silva."

"Yeah. It was my understanding that he wanted to move some art. But Silva's always been a bit in over his head, so I should have known better. The paintings were rubbish, not even a complete poser would be fooled. You can't go cheap on the forgers, especially if they're copying A-list painters. But Silva wanted to prove he was better than Carlos. Envy clouds the judgment."

"If you couldn't sell the paintings," Finn said, "why are you still here?"

"I told Silva about the address book. We took an idea to Carlos. He's got connections higher up the TCT food chain. The plan was that the three of us would split the money and the credit."

"But you don't have the book."

"That's a minor hitch. You can't let details stop you from grand plans."

"So while you were trying to execute this grand plan, Carlos double-crossed you?" Finn guessed.

Declan nodded. "Silva and me both, it seems. It was a simple enough idea. I'd get the book, we'd sell the book. But it was going to take time. Carlos was impatient. He wanted someone to track the book, so I told him about Tim and Janet McCabe."

"You gave him the names of hitmen to track us down?" Finn asked.

"The deal was they wouldn't kill anyone. And if it helps, they aren't usually very good at their jobs, but they must have improved some skills. They traced the book to where it was last seen."

"Dublin."

"Yeah. They found out an American woman had taken it. And from there, they found you. Only Carlos changed the deal. He said to kill the woman who took the address book, so there would be no loose ends. When they showed up, I knew it was time to get you out of there."

"They didn't show up."

"They did, Hollis," Declan said. "You met them the day before yesterday."

Hollis was about to argue with him when it hit her. The helicopter parents asking if her husband was a professor. "Arthur and Anne," she said. "They were checking out their targets. Did you kill them?" .

Declan sighed. "I can't get out of this damned country at the moment. I can't even show my face in public, not without one of Carlos's spies finding me. I paid someone else to do it. Not to kill them, just to detain them for as long as was needed. You're welcome, by the way. I saved your lives."

"You turned us into hitmen," Finn pointed out.

"Carlos was expecting to meet the McCabes. It was either let them kill you and fly down here themselves or send you down in their place. I thought you would both be happy with the choice I made. All you have to do to pay me back is get me the address book."

"Why did you put a dead man in our house?" Finn asked.

"I didn't put anyone in your house."

The car turned a corner a little fast and all four of them tilted to the right. "Sorry," the driver said. "I thought we were being followed."

Declan ducked down slightly. "By Carlos's men?"

"I don't know," the driver said. "I hope not. I have tickets to the opera for Friday and I would prefer to be alive to see it. Maybe I can try to lose them?"

"No," Hollis said, more forcefully than she intended. "We go to the hotel. If they're Carlos's men, they'll be suspicious if we do anything else."

"Never argue with Hollis," Declan said to the driver.

"I'm glad you see it that way," Hollis told him. "I want my gun back."

Declan smiled. He reached into his pocket and pulled out the gun he'd taken from her. "Don't take it out again unless you intend to use it."

Hollis realized the handbag she had wasn't big enough for a gun, so she put it in the pocket of Finn's jacket. It hung out slightly. "I'm not going to be able to hide it," Finn said.

"I'll stand close to you when we get out of the car," she told him.

"You can tuck it in your pants," Declan suggested. "Just check the safety first. Do you know how?"

"Of course I know how," Finn insisted, then handed the gun to Hollis, who made sure the safety was on. When she handed it back, Finn kept it across his lap, his hand on the grip.

"Still behind us," the driver said.

Finn put his arm around Hollis. Declan ducked lower in the seat. They all sat silently for a moment, as if noise would put them in more danger. Hollis tried to keep her breathing steady. Finn looked a little pale, but he shook it off. The driver pulled up at the hotel entrance and the car that had been behind them slowed but kept driving. Hollis could see Bryan behind the wheel and Eduardo next to him. She was glad her instincts had been to pretend that everything was normal, but the fact that the gunmen had followed them made something very clear: for all his pleasantness, Carlos didn't trust them.

"We don't have the address book," Finn told Declan. "I wasn't lying when I told you we handed it over to Blue."

Declan nodded. "I know that now. But, here's the thing. You can get it. Go ask your friend Peter for it. And I will do him a favor in return."

"What favor?" Finn was losing his patience. The driver got out and opened the door to the backseat. Thankfully Declan couldn't risk following them inside with Eduardo and Bryan driving around.

"I'll tell him what it means," Declan said. "And once he knows that, he'll know how to put an end to TCT once and for all."

Thirty-Two

The dress and the tux were draped across the chair about five minutes after they arrived back in the room. Finn checked the door locks several times, then put a chair under the handle. He went to the suitcase and took out the guns Carlos had given them, putting them on the nightstand, moving them in different directions until he was satisfied. The gun they'd gotten back from Declan was placed on Hollis's nightstand.

"You just need to reach out your hand and grab the handle part."

"The grip," she corrected him.

"Whatever. In case someone breaks in."

"Do you think someone will break in?" She waved her hand to dismiss the question. It was part of the new normal, she had to accept that. Someone could break into their room to kidnap them, kill them, or just annoy them, as Declan seemed to favor. "If they get in, I'll grab my gun."

"You're going to have to teach me how to use one," Finn said. "I read about it in the books on weapons, but I think this is one of those things you have to learn by doing."

It was a major concession for Finn to believe there was anything that had to be learned by doing. "It's easier than it seems. When we get home, we can take lessons."

"I'll need to know before that. Remember, we're supposed to kill Declan."

"And get the address book. And there's the other job. The one Carlos paid us extra to do."

"Which is what?"

"Silva was probably supposed to tell us and didn't," she said.

"It's too late to ask now."

The image of Silva's body on the floor appeared in Hollis's mind, and it took all of her effort to focus on something else. She knew that what had happened to Silva was a long time in the making. Carlos had killed him that way for effect and it had worked. There was no way of walking away from a partnership with Carlos and living to tell about it. Message received.

"I was thinking that Silva must have wanted us chloroformed so that we wouldn't talk on the way down here. He knew who we were from Declan, but he didn't want us talking about the note he sent us. Remember how he asked where it was?"

Finn listened intently. "Eduardo and Bryan followed Silva's orders because he outranked them, but they were obviously uncomfortable with it. They tell Carlos what happened, and Silva decides to sell us out to save himself. So the party tonight was the test. Us or him."

"I don't want anyone to die, but if it had to be someone ..."

"But why not just kill him later when they were alone? Was that just a show for us," Finn wanted to know, "or was someone else in the room meant to see that?"

"Maybe his gunmen, so they'd know his loyalty is to himself."

"I guess. But whatever the extra murder is, it's somehow giving him back something."

Hollis went through the clothes until she found pairs of pajamas for each of them. Hers were a soft pink, striped satin that reminded her of something that Katherine Hepburn would have worn in the 1940s. Finn's were gray cotton. He put them on the chair and slipped under the covers in his underwear.

"Bed please." He held out his arm, ready to hold her.

"Best offer I've had all night." She climbed in beside him and cuddled up close.

"Did Carlos say anything to you that I should know about?"

"He told me that if you agree to tango with someone you have to stay for the whole dance, otherwise it's incredibly rude."

"Fair enough."

"The problem is, it feels like we're dancing with Peter, with Declan, and with Carlos. Eventually we're going to have to break away from at least two of them."

Finn sighed. "That's a pretty easy call. We stick with Peter. All three of them can kill us, but he's the only one who can also put us in jail."

"We haven't done anything illegal," she said. "Not really."

"Does that matter?"

"For all Peter's bluster, I think we can trust him not to frame us for a crime."

"You trusted Declan and he locked us in a crypt. And I don't believe for a second that he substituted us for the McCabes to save our lives. I bet he recommended the McCabes because they were a couple

181

about our age. He was planning all along to get rid of them and put us in their place."

"That's pretty smart," Hollis said.

"Thank you."

"Not you—okay yeah, you too, for figuring it out. But I meant Declan. Not only does he keep himself from being killed, he puts us in the line of fire so we're more likely to help him get the book back."

"A criminal genius but a lousy ..."

Hollis waited for him to finish his sentence. Nothing. She raised her head and looked at his closed eyes, listened to his steady breathing. A moment later there was a couple of small snores until he settled again.

"He sent someone to get us out," she protested. If Finn were awake, he'd accuse her of having to get in the last word, but he wasn't awake, and it felt good to say it. She did trust Peter, mostly, and she also trusted Declan, to a point. The only one who really scared her was Carlos. And she worried that Peter and Declan couldn't, or wouldn't, step in when Carlos turned his wrath on Finn and her.

Hollis lay her head back on his chest, but sleep didn't come as quickly for her. She was tired, achingly tired. She couldn't remember the last time she'd had an untroubled sleep. It felt like years.

In her head, the soft music of tango was playing. A guitar, an accordion. The music was sad but beautiful. Behind her closed eyes Silva's body lay on the ground, and a young man's body was propped in her favorite chair. If Declan was telling the truth, he had come down to Argentina to sell some forged paintings then decided to trade up to selling an address book he knew he didn't have. He must have figured he could steal it from them. That would have been his first plan. The break-in that Finn had talked about when the menus were in the wrong order ... he wasn't paranoid. She'd have to apologize for that.

But they didn't have the book, so breaking into their house wouldn't have worked. Plan B was to bring them to Argentina? Then who was the dead guy in their house? Why did his ID say Silva?

And where the hell had all of Declan's money gone? He had more than a hundred million dollars after their encounter in Ireland. No one spends that kind of money in a few months. Could anyone spend that kind of money in a lifetime? On what? She tried to think it all through, but she was getting tired. Her head was woozy from wine and fear. As she let her mind drift, she realized something. It was so clear and so obvious. She thought about waking Finn up with a poke, but that would be cruel. She'd tell him in the morning. And then she fell asleep.

Thirty-Three

"Try to remember it," Finn said over breakfast. The hotel offered a buffet of American and European favorites in the restaurant, but also the same ham and cheese sandwiches that they'd gotten at the coffee shop. Hollis thought it was an odd breakfast choice, but Finn pointed out that it was pretty similar to the breakfast sandwiches they bought at home, minus the egg.

"You don't think the egg is essential?"

"Clearly it's not." He took two. "You experience the culture through the food."

"When did you turn into Anthony Bourdain?" She settled on black coffee and a croissant and focused on the moments before she drifted off to sleep. "It was right there. I knew it." She struggled to remember the thing that had seemed so obvious the night before. "It was brilliant too. Whatever it was."

"Maybe you're trying too hard. It'll come back to you."

She hoped that was true. "We're supposed to go to La Boca today," she said. "Teresa was pretty insistent. And that bookstore."

"Bookstore first. I get the feeling we'll be followed, so we'll need to lose them before we go to La Boca. Whatever she wants us to do, we should probably not bring Bryan and Eduardo."

"What does she want us to do? Did Teresa give any hint last night while she was feeling you up on the dance floor?"

"She was sweet. I assumed she was a gold digger, and I guess she is, but there's something kind of innocent about her."

"Then she married the wrong man," Hollis said. She had a certain sympathy for anyone married to a killer, but they couldn't help everyone. "Did she say anything?"

"Mostly she talked about Declan. Or asked about him, really. She must think we're better acquainted than we are because she assumed I knew how devastated he was by the deaths of some close family in Ireland. She said it made him turn away from God, which she thought was the worst thing that could happen. He did lose his uncle, but it's hard to image Declan being devastated about anything. As far as I can tell, he's got the emotional depth of a 1960s romantic comedy."

"Maybe that's just for show."

"Maybe. Teresa did say something about how Declan had women everywhere. When she saw us at the museum, she thought maybe you and he were involved on the side, but she realized that couldn't be true once she started dancing with me." He smiled widely. "Because, obviously ..."

Hollis took his hand. "Obviously."

"And Carlos? Did he say anything while he had you in his death grip? Anything except for the tango metaphor?"

She shook her head. "Not really. Silva said something weird, though. Something about how a sacrifice stays hidden only so long but once it's on display, the world can judge its worth."

"What does that mean?"

"Maybe he was the sacrifice, and he knew that Carlos had figured it out, so now we can decide if what he did was worth it," she guessed.

"It wasn't."

Finn got up from the table and went for another sandwich and some fruit. He glanced back at Hollis. She pointed to her cup.

She had a momentary rush of the panic that comes from having no idea what you're doing. She should have been used to it. Every day since the first time she agreed to help Interpol she'd had at least a few minutes of feeling in over her head. At least she felt rested, was halfway to being fully caffeinated, and had eaten some "calories don't count because I'm not home" baked goods. Self-care for spies.

"Good morning!" A blond woman in her twenties stopped at the table. Behind her was a man about the same age, his arm around her. "You are the McCabes?"

Hollis tensed, but relaxed just as quickly. The arm around the woman, her hand on his, the giggling, over-the-top happiness of the pair practically announced who they were—honeymooners.

"Yes. You're the people we gave our room to."

"It's the most ..." She looked at her husband. "We've never had so much luxury before. We are so happy."

"Hopefully the start of a lifetime of happiness." She wondered how they'd feel if she knew a killer had bugged the room.

"Thank you for your kindness," she said. "What a lovely gift." The couple left the restaurant, still wrapped in each other's arms.

A gift. Hollis remembered what she'd figured out the night before.

Finn put a fresh cup of coffee in front of her and dug in to his sandwich.

"Last night, I was thinking about how Declan lost all the money he got just a few months ago," she whispered. "And a few months ago, the university got a huge anonymous donation to the Art Department, the English Department, and the International Studies Department. All the things we care about."

Finn dropped his food. "Crap. You're saying he donated all of his stolen art money to our school, to our departments."

"I think so."

"Just when you want to hate the guy ..."

"He felt guilty because people died getting that money. People he cared about."

"But why us? Aren't there orphans somewhere he can help?"

"He likes us."

Finn laughed. "Yes, so much that he is using us to get the address book back from Blue. Peter's never going to go for that. If he really liked us, he wouldn't have put us in the middle of it."

"He got rid of the real Tim and Janet. And they were going to kill us."

"Until Declan killed them."

"Or, like he said, they're just out of the way. Whatever that means," Hollis said. "Though Declan did send someone to break into our house and search for the address book."

"Thank you," Finn said a little too loudly. The other diners looked their way, so Finn leaned closer to Hollis. "I told you the house was broken into. You know how particular I am about the recycling. I wouldn't have had the papers out of order."

"It's one of your sexiest qualities."

"I'm just pointing out I was right."

"And I'm pointing out that I think he's trying to protect us, in his own peculiar way."

"So the guy Declan sent to break into the house somehow ended up dead because Carlos killed him?"

Probably. Though it didn't explain why Carlos had killed the man or placed him in their house. "Now all we have to do is find a way to keep Carlos from killing us once he realizes we don't have the book, didn't kill Declan, and have no idea what the third job is."

"How?"

It was a good question. "Carlos said it. We stay loyal to each other as long as we're dancing, so I guess we have to find a way to keep the music playing."

Thirty-Four

The El Ateneo Grand Splendid Bookstore lived up to its name. It had been a theater, built in 1919, and still looked like one, though where there had once been rows of seats, there were now rows of books. The walls were cream, with elaborate gold accents decorating the surfaces. The stage was still intact, but the red velvet curtains, hung on each side, now partially hid a cafeteria. A small sign said that Carlos Gardel was among the performers that had once graced the stage. Like Eva Perón, he was everywhere in the city.

Hollis and Finn walked around the main floor before climbing the stairs to the first balcony, then the second and third. On each floor, people were curled up in the areas that had been box seats but were now nooks for reading and quiet discussion. It was a lovely, respectful use of a beautiful theater and Hollis found herself standing at the railing of the third floor, looking down, mesmerized by the view.

"Buenos Aires has some amazing buildings," Finn said, his voice filled with the wonder of a kid in his first toy shop. "You have the phone, right? Take pictures."

"Who's the tourist now?" She took out the phone and snapped a dozen pictures, but it was impossible to capture the place. She zoomed in on a few of the decorations. "What are we supposed to be doing here?"

"Who cares? Let's see if they have a section on Argentinian history." Finn wandered off. When Carlos suggested the store, it was unlikely he realized he was focusing on Finn's biggest weak spot. So why did he want them there, she wondered.

She took a few more photos, looking down from the balcony to the floor below. As she zoomed the camera she noticed the head of a bald black man. She didn't look for Finn. She went straight to the staircase and down to the floor where Peter was browsing the travel section.

———

Once she got there she wasn't sure what to do. Peter was paging through a guidebook, as any tourist might. He didn't look up as she approached or seem to be aware that she passed him. She moved to another aisle and watched, trying not to look like she was watching.

He put the book back and took another guidebook, paging through that one. Then he picked up another one. Behind him an employee stocked a shelf with guides to Patagonia.

"*Perdon, Señor,*" Hollis said. "Do you sell address books?"

The man smiled. "*Sí, Señora.* Second floor."

"*Gracias.* My friend lost his address book and he really wants one. His birthday is tomorrow, so I have to get it now."

The man nodded in that polite way people do when they don't care.

Peter put one of the books on the shelf behind him, at a slight angle so it stood out from the rest, and kept walking. Hollis waited a moment for the employee to leave the aisle, then she picked up the book. *Essential Argentina.* Now all she had to do was find Finn.

That wasn't easy. There were multiple floors, and on each floor there were places where he could be sitting. She tried the main floor, then went up one, walked in almost a complete circle, then up another staircase. He didn't have a phone anymore so there was no point in texting him. Not that it would matter. He wouldn't look at it anyway if he'd found a book that he liked.

Or if someone with a gun found him.

She walked up another staircase.

English language books. If he were safe, he'd be here. She wandered the rows, trying not to get her attention pulled by the alluring covers and the promises of new authors and new books. It was a drug she and Finn shared. But he wasn't in the section. She circled the floor just in case, finally finding a pair of long legs sticking out from a small corner nook.

She sat next to him. "What are you reading?"

"I have no idea." He showed her the book, a novel in Spanish. "I'm hiding, actually. I saw Eduardo." He looked at the guide book to Argentina in her hands. "What about you?"

"Peter was looking at this, then he put it down pretty much in front of me. I figure it has a clue in it."

"We need to get out of here."

"But before we go, we need to figure out why Carlos sent us here. What did he want us to find?"

"They have an excellent map section."

"Do we need a map?"

"No, but I did want to check it out. It's on the ground floor."

"Let's focus. We can order a map online."

"Says the woman with the suede coat and the guidebook to Argentina. Where's my souvenir?"

"Fine. Map. But also, Carlos. He wasn't just suggesting tourist attractions."

They made their way down the stairs toward the front door. Hollis saw Eduardo wandering the aisles on the second floor. They could try to avoid him, as was Finn's plan, or they could just acknowledge that he was there.

"Let's just leave without him noticing. We have to go to La Boca," Finn reminded her.

"First we have to figure out why we're here." She handed him the guidebook, took a deep breath, and walked over to Eduardo.

"*Hola,*" she said. Eduardo nearly jumped.

"Señora McCabe. You have found me."

"I found you? Weren't you following us?"

"No. This is my day off. I am ..." He searched for a word. "Browsing. I do this every Sunday."

"Carlos sent us here."

Eduardo's face fell. "Yes, okay. I will not make a fuss. I will go with you where you want."

As tempted as she was to ask what he was talking about, she just said, "Good," and looked for Finn. He wasn't where she'd left him, so she walked down the aisle to where she knew he would be. Eduardo followed, head down.

Finn was, as expected, searching through the maps.

"Seriously?" Hollis swatted his shoulder. "I go over to Eduardo and you don't at least stay close enough to make sure I'm okay?"

"Why would I hurt you?" Eduardo asked.

"It's a bookstore full of people," Finn protested. "And anyway, I walked five feet. I could still see you."

"He could have put a gun to my back and forced me out of the store. Your priorities are just insane."

"I told you not to go over to him," Finn said. "You insisted. How are my priorities insane?" He looked over at Eduardo, then back at Hollis. "Don't you have your gun?"

Hollis patted her purse. "Of course, but you should have been watching."

"You brought him to me. You can't feel that afraid of him. What's the plan now, anyway?"

"He's the job Carlos mentioned last night. We're supposed to kill him," Hollis said.

Finn looked over at Eduardo, who just looked sad. "What did he do?"

"He's involved with Teresa. I should have figured it out sooner. The way she smiled at him last night. The thing Declan said about wanting to help someone in love. And what Eduardo said yesterday. The comment about wanting to be us. He didn't mean he wanted to be a hitman, he meant he wanted to be part of an old married couple."

"You and Teresa?" Finn put his hand on Eduardo's shoulder, which made the guy flinch a little. "That's great. You guys would make a nice couple. And don't take us seriously," he said, gesturing toward Hollis. "We argue, but marriage is the best thing that's ever happened to me."

Hollis smiled. "Back at ya. But we still have to do something with him."

"I'm in love with her," Eduardo said. "She should not be with that old man. She should be somewhere safe, with a man who can give her a life and grow old with her. Declan said he would send help. But instead…" He was on the verge of tears.

"Is this an international crime ring or a dating service for killers?" Finn asked.

Hollis stared at him.

Finn rolled his eyes. "Okay. The three of us leave together. We'll take him to La Boca with us."

"Is Bryan here?" Hollis asked Eduardo.

"No. He knows nothing about Teresa and me."

Finn grabbed a poster-sized rolled map, clutched the travel guide to his chest, and headed toward the counter.

"What is he doing?" Eduardo asked.

"Buying a map."

"Why?"

"He likes maps."

Eduardo nodded as if he understood. She wanted to comfort him, to let him know that everything would be okay, or at least she hoped it would. But there was no way of knowing if anyone was watching, so it was better to keep being Tim and Janet McCabe until they could get him away from the store and tell him he was safe.

The only problem with that was if they didn't kill Eduardo, then Carlos would kill them. And as Carlos had proved last night, he wouldn't think twice about it.

Thirty-Five

Outside the bookstore Finn tried to hail a cab.

"Don't you have a car?" Eduardo asked. "We could take my car if you tell me where we are going."

"You're really taking this well," Hollis told him. "Shouldn't you be trying to kill us, or at least making a run for it?"

"If Carlos wants me dead and I get away, he will kill Teresa."

Hollis caught Finn's eye. "It's going to work out," Finn said to Eduardo. "Where's your car?"

Eduardo pointed toward a black BMW and the three got in. Eduardo sat in the driver's seat, Finn next to him, and Hollis in the back.

"Hold the map." Finn passed the package with the map and guidebook to her.

"Hold the gun," she told him, handing over the weapon they'd gotten from Peter.

"La Boca," Finn told Eduardo, who swallowed hard and moved the car into the street.

"We're not killers," Finn told him. "We're college professors."

"Yes, I know the story you told Silva."

"It's not a story. We're going to La Boca because Teresa told us last night that we had to visit the neighborhood. We think it was some kind of clue."

"You're friends of Declan?" His voice lifted slightly, with cautious hope.

"*Friends* is an exaggeration."

From the backseat, Hollis scolded, "Finn. We're friendly," she told Eduardo. "We're helping him, and now we'll help you. You're not going to die today."

Eduardo glanced in the rearview mirror. "Carlos is not a man to be crossed. You must have a plan and a lot of people backing you up."

"You would think," Finn said. "We have each other, a spy named Peter, and ... what else do we have, Hollis?"

She shrugged. "Not a lot." But maybe there was something in the guidebook. Peter had left it for her to find, so Hollis paged through looking for a note, but there wasn't one. However, a small corner of one page was turned down. "This is an entry about San Telmo Market."

"An antiques market," Eduardo said. "Very popular. Teresa's father, he goes there to find spoons. He loves spoons." He laughed. "He's a very nice man, though, as you know. He's very happy for Teresa to be away from Carlos."

"As we know?" Finn sounded confused. "Oh, the driver." He looked back to Hollis. "Did you realize that?"

She shook her head. "But it makes sense why Declan made such a point of telling him last night that he and Teresa weren't involved.

And why the driver is helping us. Because we're supposed to help Teresa."

"Would have been nice if Declan just told us all of this instead of locking us in a crypt."

"He did that to keep you safe from Bryan," Eduardo said. "Bryan is the one who sent you the death threat at your hotel. He wishes to be a hitman and he is unhappy having you come in to do this job to kill Declan that he could do himself. He's going to be very mad when he finds out you were the ones to kill me and not him."

Eduardo pulled onto a small street and parked. "This is the start of the neighborhood. It was originally just shipyard workers who lived here. They built houses from corrugated sheet metal and painted it with the leftovers from the ships. That's why it's so colorful."

"It certainly is." Even from the window of the car, Hollis could see bright blue, green, orange, yellow, and red. And that was just one house. The streets were filled with people and what looked like tables of souvenirs for sale. Many of the houses filled their balconies with giant papier mache people. On one there was Eva Perón and, once again, Carlos Gardel.

"Where would Teresa want us to meet her?"

Eduardo shook his head. "This is not a place we come."

"Maybe that's the point," Finn said. "Maybe she wanted to meet us somewhere that was completely out of character for her. Someplace Carlos wouldn't think to look."

"A *milonga*," Eduardo said. "She hates the tango. She would never go to one and there is a famous one on the next street."

"I thought she met Carlos at one."

"She has known him her whole life, but he doesn't like to admit he married a woman he knew as a baby, so this is the story he tells people. Teresa's favorite place is not a *milonga*."

"So where ..." Finn asked.

Eduardo started to answer, then he thought better of it, jumped out of the car before either Finn or Hollis could react, and disappeared into a sea of tourists.

"What now?" Finn said.

"We run after him."

"Why? We're not going to kill him and it's not our job to keep him safe."

"But if he shows up somewhere, Carlos is going to know we didn't kill him. And it's our job to keep *us* safe."

"I have a better idea." He handed the gun back to Hollis, who put it in her purse. "Let's go."

"Beautiful souvenirs, miss," a man called to Hollis as she bumped and struggled to get through the crowd.

"We can dance?" A street performer put a fedora on Hollis's head. She turned to face him. "Do you tango?" he asked.

"She does not." Finn took the fedora from Hollis and placed it, rather forcefully on the dancer's head.

"If you are hungry, we have menus in English," a woman told them as they walked passed.

"We're never going to find him," Hollis said. "I think her La Boca story was to send us on a wild goose chase."

"Not Teresa. She wanted us to come to this neighborhood. She was sending us..." Finn looked around the square until he saw what he wanted. "There."

It was a small white building, the least colorful of any she had seen so far. "A church?"

"She said that Declan had turned away from God, she found that very sad. It's just a guess but..."

"It's a good guess."

They took two steps inside before they knew it was a great guess. Teresa and Eduardo were sitting in a pew, holding hands. Teresa was crying slightly. When she saw them walk in, she looked relieved.

"You're both safe," Hollis said. "We've got a friend we can call to get you out of the country."

Instead of making her happy, Teresa cried harder. "I'm so sorry," she said. "I had no idea Bryan would..."

"Would what?" Hollis asked.

Eduardo blushed. "I was going to run away once I realized where Teresa was suggesting. She always finds the church in a new neighborhood. Most Argentinians aren't as religious as they once were but Teresa..."

"What did Bryan do?" Finn asked.

"He doesn't yet know that Carlos wants me dead," Eduardo said, "so he just called to tell me that he is going to kill you to prove himself. He is going to your hotel."

"But we're here, so it's fine."

"You said that the room you brought us to was just one of your rooms," he said. "You told me that you had given the other away. I don't know..."

"The honeymooners," Hollis practically shouted. Her words echoed around the small church.

Finn grabbed Eduardo and pulled him up from the pew. "Eduardo, you have to drive us to the hotel, now."

"The plan is to kill Bryan?" Eduardo asked. "It may be the only way."

Finn looked at Hollis and she knew what the exasperated, confused expression on his face meant. Bryan might be the one person they would actually need to kill.

Thirty-Six

"We can't use our phone," Hollis said as Eduardo drove too fast and too recklessly to be legal. "Carlos might be able to trace it."

"He will," Eduardo told her. "Same with mine and Teresa's. I had a burner, but I could not find it this morning. Carlos must have taken it."

"I can't believe I'm saying this, but you may have to kill Bryan," Finn told Eduardo. "If we run out of options..."

"I've never killed anyone! Carlos knew my uncle, and he gave me a job. I am supposed to run errands and stand behind him when he talks to people. Carlos said that his reputation was so bad that no one in Argentina would dare try to kill him. He was training me to be a criminal, but the more I saw, the less I wanted this life."

"A car full of hitmen who wouldn't hurt a fly," Hollis said. "What now?"

"We need Peter," Finn said. "If we actually have to kill Bryan, at least he can do it."

"Is San Telmo far from here?"

"It's on the way to your hotel. But do we have time to wander the stalls if your friends are in danger?"

"Will Bryan kill them once he sees they're not us?" Finn asked.

"I don't know. He can be very ruthless. He thinks it's impressive. Last night Carlos was saying how understated you both were. Ordinary. The kind of people no one would suspect. I think it annoyed Bryan. The last thing he wants to do is fit in." He turned a corner sharply.

Finn tilted toward him in the front seat, and in the back Hollis and Teresa held on to each other.

"Finn and I will run through the market," Hollis said. "We'll spot Peter and bring him to your car. Just keep it running."

Eduardo stopped suddenly, and they all fell forward. "It's there," he said. "Be quick. Even with no traffic we are still twenty minutes from your hotel."

Finn and Hollis jumped out. "You go left," Finn said. "I'll go right."

Hollis wanted to run but it wasn't possible with so many people milling about, looking at the tables of antiques and art. Another day, she thought, and she'd be in heaven. But instead of browsing the booths, she looked for Peter's tall, dark frame, his bald head, and his general no-nonsense attitude. He would stick out in this crowd, if for no other reason than Peter would never relax enough to enjoy a Sunday afternoon in the park.

Luckily it wasn't a large fair, and by the third row she spotted him. She also spotted Finn. Together they flanked Peter.

"Come with us now," Finn said.

"You need to be a bit more subtle," Peter mumbled as he pretended to be interested in a glass seltzer jar, one of dozens at the booth.

"Spy school later. Come with us now."

Peter looked at Hollis. "Bad?"

"Deadly."

He gestured for them to go first and he followed to Eduardo's car. He took the front seat and Finn crowded into the back with Hollis and Teresa. Eduardo drove away without anyone bothering to make introductions.

"You realize that if someone was watching, you just blew my cover. And yours," Peter chastised them. "Somebody better be dying."

"I am dying," Eduardo said, a bit cheerfully. "But Señor and Señora McCabe are saving my life and helping me and Teresa get away from Carlos."

"How romantic. You could have called me."

"We smashed the phones you gave us," Finn said.

"And I suppose you lost the gun. Or someone took it from you."

"Of course not. We're not complete idiots." She glanced at Finn.

"That's something at least," Peter said.

Eduardo abandoned his car in a no-parking zone outside the hotel. Everyone jumped out. Finn grabbed his map and the guidebook. Hollis could have asked why those items would save an innocent couple from an ambitious thug, but she didn't. She felt proud of her restraint.

The five of them rushed into the hotel and ran toward the elevators. Peter barked, "Everyone stands behind me." Only Teresa obeyed.

Matias looked up from the reception desk and smiled, then frowned as he saw everyone. "Everything okay?"

"Yes, perfect," Finn said. "Just some friends stopping by."

"*Bien.*" He did not seem convinced.

The elevator ride seemed to take forever, and when the doors finally opened it was Finn leading the way toward the honeymoon suite. Hollis took out her gun. They looked at Eduardo. He shook his head. "I don't bring my gun on my day off," he whispered.

"We go on three," Peter said.

"We could just knock," Finn suggested. "He might not have gotten here yet."

"We'll do this my way," Peter said. He put up one finger, then two, and just as he was about to put up three, Finn knocked. Peter curled his fingers into a fist but said nothing.

"*Un momento, por favor,*" a woman's voice from inside.

The door opened and the pretty blond from the restaurant smiled, then looked confused. "Is something wrong?"

Peter pushed passed her into the room. Eduardo and Teresa followed so Hollis and Finn did too. Inside the suite, which was far more luxurious than Hollis had imagined, the woman's husband was sitting on a chair in his bathrobe.

Peter walked up to the man and put him in a head lock, his hand over the man's mouth. Eduardo did the same for the woman.

"You need to get dressed," Peter whispered. "Now."

The two frightened people just nodded. The husband moved to the wife and started to speak. Finn shook his head and put a finger to his mouth.

The man whispered something in Dutch to his wife but otherwise they remained quiet, dressing quickly.

They were ready to go in less than two minutes. Peter moved to the door.

There was a knock. Followed quickly by another, louder knock. Peter waved for everyone to move back, and this time everyone listened. He swung the door opened, grabbed Bryan by the neck. Bryan elbowed Peter and got a few steps away from him before Finn rushed forward, punching the left side of his face, then following it with a punch to his chin. The boxing teacher was right, Hollis saw, Finn really did have an amazing cross-uppercut combo.

Bryan fell to the floor, his gun tumbling out of his hand. Hollis picked that up and took the knife from a holster around his ankle. Peter and Finn grabbed one arm each and dragged him from the room. Hollis gestured for the others to follow. The woman started to cry.

As soon as they were all in the hallway with the door closed behind them, Hollis put her arm around the woman.

"We didn't do anything wrong," she said. "You gave us the room."

"Of course you didn't," Hollis said. "It's just that he's trying to kill us, and we knew that he would come to this room looking for us. He was probably going to kill you out of spite. He's like that apparently. I wish I could sugarcoat it, but there isn't time."

"Where to now?" Teresa asked.

"We can't go far," Finn said. "Let's get everyone to our room. Then we'll figure it out from there."

Eight people crammed into the elevator. Peter kept Bryan's neck locked in the crook of his arm, the honeymoon couple clung to each other, Eduardo and Teresa kissed, Finn held onto his map and the guidebook, and Hollis, against all common sense, worried that the room would be a mess. She hated having people over when things were disorganized.

Thirty-Seven

Peter used plastic cuffs to tie Bryan to the bed frame. He grabbed a sock from Finn's suitcase, wet it in the bathroom sink, then stuffed it into Bryan's mouth. He took the belt from the hotel bathrobe and tied it tightly around his mouth, finally tying the ends to the bed frame. When Bryan kept struggling, Peter took his belt off and wrapped it around Bryan's ankles, then around the bed frame, essentially hog-tying him to the bed.

The rest of the group stood watching in varying degrees of terror.

"Why did you wet the sock?" Hollis asked.

"It'll weigh down the sock, make it hard for him to move it. And it also keeps his mouth from drying out," Peter said. "We may need him to talk later."

The Dutch woman started to hyperventilate.

"I'm Hollis." She put out her hand to the woman.

"Elsa Van Dijk. This is my husband, Levi."

"Hallo," Levi said, reaching out his hand.

When all else fails, be polite. It was something her mother used to say when Hollis and her brother would argue. She never really understood it until now. The social niceties had a calming effect on an otherwise insane situation.

"You're safe," Finn said. "Nothing bad is going to happen to you."

"If you have the man who wanted to kill you, why did we need to leave our room?" Levi asked.

"It's bugged."

"Oh."

The couple sat on the bed as far from Bryan as they could get.

Hollis turned to Teresa. "It's not going to be long before Carlos wonders where you are and checks to see if we've killed Eduardo. We have to figure a way out of this. We need to get in touch with Declan."

Peter looked up, stunned. "You don't have a way to call Declan?"

"He just sort of shows up," Finn said.

"That's crazy," Peter said.

"You do the same thing."

Peter said nothing, just frowned.

"I have a number," Teresa said. She took a piece of hotel stationery and wrote it out, handing it over to Finn.

"I'll go downstairs and borrow a phone," Finn said. "Eduardo, you go upstairs and pack up the Van Dijks' belongings."

"We have two more nights here before we go to Patagonia," Elsa said.

Peter grabbed his phone and texted. "My guy will get you a suite at the Alvear Palace Hotel. It's one of the top hotels in the city." He smiled a little, trying to sound comforting. It didn't suit him. "We'll send some champagne to your room. You'll probably need a drink."

Elsa and Levi seemed skeptical. "I can pack up our things," Levi said.

"I can help too," Elsa said.

"No," Finn said. "Not both. Elsa and Eduardo, you go. Levi and Teresa will be here waiting. That way you'll be sure to come back."

Peter smiled. He was obviously impressed with Finn's take-charge attitude. "Do we have any other weapons?"

"Two Walther PPKs," Hollis said. "They're in a suitcase in the closet. I'll get them."

"Good. Well then, you all do what you need to do, and the rest of us will babysit our guest." Peter patted Bryan's head. Bryan did his best to move, but Peter's knots were holding. If eyes could kill, though, the entire room would have been dead.

———

It took ten minutes before Elsa and Eduardo returned, but whatever he had said she was noticeably more relaxed.

"We should go to Amsterdam on our honeymoon," Eduardo told Teresa.

"I have to get a divorce for us to get married."

Peter shook his head. "I don't think you'll need a divorce."

He didn't say why, but it was clear that only Elsa and Levi didn't understand what he meant.

Teresa went pale. Eduardo put his arm around her. "He was my father's employer. He was always nice to me, very charming. And he could give me a good life," she said. "I thought it was better than love." She looked at Eduardo. "I was stupid to think that."

"Might be a good idea to relocate," Peter said. "Spain is one of my favorite countries. The food, the people, the scenery. You really can't go wrong."

"You'll help us?" Eduardo asked.

"You help me, I'll help you. Ask Hollis, um, Janet here."

"He's very helpful," Hollis said, trying to find the right balance between sarcasm and optimism. Eduardo and Teresa did not need to know how much trouble he could be.

Finn opened the door and slid into the room—with Declan following quickly. "He's been tracking us," Finn said in explanation.

"Teresa," Declan said, "your dad is picking up some passports I had made for you. You can be on a plane tonight."

"Peter suggested Spain."

Declan looked at Peter. "The man himself." He reached out his hand.

"Declan Murphy? That's funny. Hollis and Finn gave me a very vivid description of a Declan Murphy in his fifties, blond hair, green eyes."

The brown-haired, blue-eyed, twenty-something Declan smiled. "I understand you've been wanting to meet me."

"I've been wanting to arrest you."

"This isn't a good time. I need the address book."

"I'm not giving it to you."

"Then we're all going to die."

Elsa gasped. Hollis jumped up. "He doesn't mean it. Declan is a big talker."

"Are you all spies or something?" she asked.

Hollis pointed around the room. "Peter's a spy. Bryan's a hitman. Eduardo is a bodyguard, but he's fallen in love with his boss's wife, Teresa. My husband and I are college professors ..."

"And agents for an international organization dedicated to taking down a major criminal group," Peter added.

That made Hollis smile. They weren't actually agents, not on the payroll, but it sounded cool.

"And I'm a forger, art thief, and general mischief maker," Declan said. He shook Elsa's and Levi's hands. "Lovely to meet you."

"Okay, now that introductions are over," Finn said. "What do we do?"

Peter took a deep breath. "It's pretty obvious. We torture that guy," he said pointing to Bryan. "We get the four lovebirds out of harm's way. We figure out a way to kill Carlos, and we throw the Irishman in a deep, dark prison."

"Those are all grand ideas," Declan said. "But if I can, I'd suggest that you get me the address book, which I can copy, with some small but important changes. Then Hollis and Finn get the book to Carlos, making clear they've killed me and Eduardo. We trace who Carlos passes the book to, you take down TCT and become a hero to all your law-enforcement pals."

"And what happens to you?" Peter asked.

"I'll be dead." Declan smiled. "So, I suppose I'll spend eternity on some small island somewhere, far away from any trouble at all."

Peter stared at him for a long time. Declan stared back. The rest of the room watched to see who would blink. Based on what she knew about both men, they could have watched all night.

But there was a knock on the door.

Thirty-Eight

A second knock. Hollis grabbed the gun Peter had given them. Finn took one of the Walthers from the case, Eduardo took the other. Peter took out his Sig Sauer and added a silencer. Declan rolled his eyes at that move, but he took out a gun of his own.

Teresa took off one of her stilettos.

"Could that hurt someone?" Finn whispered.

"They kill my feet whenever I wear shoes like this," Hollis said, pointing to the spiked heel. "They can probably do some damage to a head."

A third knock.

Finn walked to the door. "Who is it?"

Through the door a friendly voice said, "Matias, Señor McCabe. I have a package for Señora."

Finn looked at Hollis. She nodded. Everyone tucked their guns behind their backs. Peter stood in front of Bryan. Finn opened the door halfway, and true to his word Matias was standing in the hall with a garment bag.

"The room is working out?" he asked.

"We're very happy," Finn said.

"I'm so glad. This arrived for you. A leather jacket, I think." He peeked into the room and saw some of the other faces. "Is everything good? Do you need something? A drink, perhaps."

"I could use a cup of tea," Declan said.

Peter's turn to roll his eyes. "I could use a whiskey."

Declan laughed. "You're very competitive."

"Tea would be good for me," Hollis said, looking around. "And some coffee, I guess. A bottle of whiskey. And those little chocolate cookies with the dulce de leche ..."

"*Alfajors*," Matias said. "I'll have room service bring it to you." He looked passed Finn's shoulder to where Peter was standing. Eduardo moved closer. "Okay. If that's everything?"

"Yes, everything," Finn moved one step at a time until the door was closed. One eyebrow raised, he handed the jacket to Hollis. "Your souvenir."

"I'll put it next to your map."

He smiled. "Yeah, all right. Now that we're done with shopping and drink orders, we need to keep at least seven of us alive."

"You've a cruel streak in you, Finn," Declan said. "Unless, aside from Bryan, you meant Peter as the other one we could do without."

"I didn't."

"Look, I understand I've gotten you in some trouble, but in fairness to me, I'm not the bad guy here. You remember the Argentine economic crisis from 2002?"

"Yeah, the peso was devalued so much that the country went into a recession for years. They had overborrowed ..." Hollis said.

Declan shook his head. "Carlos, with the help of some other members of TCT. They've made a lot of money destabilizing Argentina on and off for twenty years, and it's just the beginning. But in order to move forward, they need to protect the information in that book."

"What's in the book?" Peter asked. "It's all in code, and our guys can't figure it out."

"Just being honest here, neither can I," Declan said. "Not entirely. But I know enough to create a near copy. Just enough right to be convincing, just enough wrong to keep it from doing any real damage."

"You came here to sell that address book," Peter said, "and now you want me to hand it over to you? No."

"That was plan B. I thought I was down here to sell some art work, a newly discovered Van Gogh. Some paintings that were lost after World War II made their way to Argentina. Would have been an easy thing to convince a buyer who had more money than sense."

"Fake paintings," Peter said.

Declan shrugged. "Real ones are out of my league."

"Whatever the reason you came here," Finn said, "if Peter can get the book down here, what stops you from selling it yourself?"

"If you haven't noticed, Argentina is going through another round of instability, which, for what it's worth, is not okay with me. People get hurt, real people trying to feed their kids."

"As opposed to the people who buy fake Van Goghs?" Finn pointed out.

"Those are just posers with too much money. They don't pay taxes, they don't help feed the poor," Declan said. "If my cheating them helps redistribute the wealth ..."

Finn put up his hand. "We know the speech, Robin Hood."

"It's not a speech. TCT was supposed to be an organization that helped move money from the exploiters to the exploited by forgeries, internet hacking, an occasional monetary manipulation. All for good."

"With lots of profit for you on the side," Finn pointed out.

"He did give our school most of the money he'd gotten in Ireland…" Hollis reminded him.

"Money he stole," Finn reminded her.

"But still. He gave it away," she said. "He's trying to help Teresa and Eduardo. What could be in that for him? He's betraying Carlos, 'the man who doesn't exist.'"

"Carlos isn't the man who doesn't exist," Declan said. "He's more of a middle man. A dangerous middle man, to be sure. He brokers items, he arranges for people to disappear…"

"He's Jorge Videla?" Hollis asked.

Declan nodded. "It's a name he's used before, and it fits him. I wanted you to know who you were dealing with. He's frightening, but he's looking to make money, that's all. The man who doesn't exist, on the other hand, is after power. A man can be satisfied with a certain amount of money, but those who are hungry for power will always want more. And this man would kill half the world to make just a few people richer."

"And who is he?" Peter asked.

"I'm sorry I have no name for him. No one does, that I've been able to find. All I know is he's been operating for about fifteen years, getting higher and higher until he's essentially the head of TCT. He directs a lot of operations. He calls for a recession somewhere, and trust me, there's a recession exactly where he wanted it. His name is in that book—coded, but it's in there. That's how valuable the book is. If we create a fake copy that's good enough to fool Carlos, and it makes it high enough up the ranks, we might be able to find him."

"We've photocopied the book," Peter said. "I can have an encrypted email…"

"Has to be the real thing, mate. I need to know the paper, the cover, the ink … I don't know who has seen it, what they'll be expecting."

"It's worth a shot," Eduardo said. "To stop mass murder."

All eyes went to Peter. "I don't trust the guy." He nodded toward Declan. "He's a conman. Even if he's telling the truth, whatever value that book has, if I hand it over and he takes it …"

"I won't," Declan said.

"If he takes it," Peter continued, "that's my job, maybe my life. And who knows who else will be in danger. I say we arrest Carlos tomorrow. There are guys in Blue that specialize in extracting information. We'll get the name of his contact."

"And by the time you do, his contact will be long gone," Declan said. "And there goes your chance to finish off a criminal organization."

"I know it's an unpopular opinion," Hollis said, "but I trust him. He's saved my life, he's saved Teresa's, Eduardo's. Call it a feeling, but I think Declan is the one person who can keep us all alive and maybe bring down TCT."

Peter clenched his jaw. "How about you, Finn? You buying this?"

Hollis looked over at Finn. His eye twitched. "I don't want to, but Hollis is right. And I trust her feelings any day of the week. I think we go with this."

"I do too," Levi said. They all looked over at him.

Peter laughed. "I guess I'm outvoted. But if this turns out badly, just remember it wasn't my idea."

"The good news on that," Declan said, "is that if it ends badly, none of us will be alive to remember who had the idea in the first place."

Thirty-Nine

"The room is packed," Hollis told the room service waiter as she pulled the table from his grasp. "We'll sort it out ourselves."

Like Matias, the waiter kept trying to look into the room, but all there was to see was a crowd of people standing in front of the bed. Elsa had thrown a blanket over Bryan, and Levi had joined Peter and Eduardo in standing in front of him. Perhaps she and Finn were a corrupting influence because the honeymooners now seemed to be enjoying the odd turn in their vacation.

"Our agents will make sure that all the lovebirds are safe," Peter said once the door was safely closed and locked. "And the four of us will continue the mission." He poured himself a cup of tea. Declan held out a hand for the teapot, but Peter made a point of putting it down as far from Declan as possible. Declan then stretched himself in front of Peter's tea to retrieve the pot. They were like a couple of kids, unwilling to share their toys. If this was how the four of them were going to work together, they were doomed to fail.

"What happens to Bryan?" Hollis didn't want to know but, she had to. He was a person, someone loved him.

"We'll debrief him. If he's smart, he'll cooperate and we'll be able to relocate him somewhere he'll be able to live out the rest of his life. In freedom, if he plays his cards right," Peter said.

It sounded like a solid plan, one Hollis wanted to believe. But she figured it wasn't true.

"Why don't we ask now if there's anything he knows that can help us?" She sat on the floor next to Bryan. "When my husband screws up," she told him, "he gets very stubborn about apologizing. And it just makes me angrier, because then I'm not just upset about whatever he did wrong, I'm also upset that he won't admit it. He thinks he's avoiding a fight by not admitting anything. But instead of an ordinary fight, it turns into a blowout. We nearly got divorced a few years ago because he refused to admit he hadn't read a paper I'd published on global interdependence in an internet-based economy."

"In my defense," Finn jumped in, "it was baseball season."

Hollis looked at Bryan. "See what I mean? My point is that you can make this worse for yourself, or you can just cut your losses."

Bryan grunted something at her. He was trying to be defiant, but in his eyes, she could see the fear.

"Give up," Peter said. "He won't respond to logic. That's not how killers operate."

"I get it," she tried again, focusing herself on Bryan and ignoring the rest of the room. "I had a plan for my life. I was going to be a spy. I trained for it and everything. I was pretty good, top of my class in some things. But then I made a different choice. I had a quieter life.

216

And then, well, things changed again, and I made a choice to go along with that change. So I understand what it is to have a life planned out for yourself, and then to realize that it's not going to be exactly what you envisioned. I'm not a self-help type person, but there's a certain sense in being open to new possibilities. I think that's what Peter is offering you."

He grunted again, but there was less anger in it. Then he tried to say something.

"Can we take the sock out of his mouth?" Hollis asked.

"He'll scream," Peter said.

She looked into Bryan's eyes. "Please don't scream."

"Señora," Eduardo said. "He wants to kill you."

Hollis untied the sash around his mouth. "Unless he's going to bite me to death, he's not going to succeed."

Bryan opened his mouth and she pulled out the sock. He spit a few times, said what was likely a lot of swear words in Spanish, then looked over at Eduardo.

"*Che*, this is worth it to you, dying for a woman?"

"Yes," Eduardo said.

"Stupid. I told Boss to watch the way you looked at his wife. I told him you would betray him."

Eduardo stood up. "You wanted me dead? It's worth it to you, to impress Carlos?"

Bryan shook his head. "It's not Carlos I'm trying to impress. I need to go to the meeting he has. I need to show the next level what I can do." He looked over at Declan. "I can help you. I know that Carlos has seen the book. Not what was inside, but he has seen it before. He's expecting the McCabes tomorrow at the café. He told me to tell them to bring the book with them."

"What time?" Finn asked.

Bryan bit his lip. "What do I get for telling you?"

"Anything on this table," Peter gestured toward the room service table, with half-finished pots of coffee and tea, and an unopened bottle of whiskey.

"How about you let me walk out of here?"

Finn and Hollis looked over to Peter. He didn't have to say anything. The answer was in his clenched jaw.

"What time?" Peter asked.

"If I don't show up tonight, Carlos will know something has happened to me. They won't be safe, the McCabes, even if I tell you the time. He'll know they've done something."

Finn shook his head. He closed his eyes and sighed. "We killed Eduardo as instructed, but then we realized that Carlos had been wrong. Eduardo wasn't having an affair with Teresa. You lied to get him out of the way, to feed your own ambitions, and then you killed Teresa. So, out of respect for Carlos, we killed you."

Hollis could see that the last thing Finn wanted to do was concoct a story that would give Peter an excuse to remove Bryan as a problem. But he was leaving them no choice. Bryan looked from face to face. He looked about to say something but instead he just mumbled to himself.

"He'll want proof," Eduardo said. "Three bodies is a lot to take your word for."

"Carlos trusts my father," Teresa said. "If he backs you up, he'll believe. But then you have to get my father away from here. He must be safe."

Peter nodded. "You two go tonight. He goes tomorrow. We'll make sure of it."

Bryan laughed a little. "You still don't know when you are to meet Carlos, and he's not a man to be kept waiting."

It was his only card. To convince him to cooperate, they had to take it away from him. Hollis turned to Eduardo. "What's Carlos's number?"

He handed her his cell phone. She typed the number into the burner phone Eduardo had given her. Then she took a picture of Bryan. "I can text him this. I'll tell him you killed Teresa, and we've got you tied up. I'll ask him if he wants us to bring you tomorrow with the address book or kill you now and save ourselves the hassle of keeping you alive all night."

"Go ahead. I'll tell him everything," Bryan said.

"He chose us over Silva, his friend of many decades. Do you think he'll choose you now? Do you think you mean that much to him?" Hollis kept her voice calm, even light, the way she'd speak to a distracted student, explaining the importance of keeping up with the class. But inside her heart was beating fast. This wasn't just a moment of no return for Bryan, but for her and Finn as well. They were committing to a mission no matter who got hurt. They were weighing lives saved against lives lost. This was what real spies did. They looked into the eyes of desperate men and made bargains that would probably not be kept.

She wanted to make clear to Bryan that they couldn't send him back to Carlos without knowing he would help them, and they couldn't leave him with Peter without Bryan's proving his value. There was no win for him anymore, there was only a chance to contain the losses.

"Do what Señora says," Eduardo pleaded. "Just admit you are wrong."

They all waited. It took several minutes but finally Bryan nodded. "If you give me some coffee, I will help you."

Forty

"If you tell Carlos you killed me without consulting him, it will go badly for you," Bryan said. "Eduardo will agree with this."

Eduardo said nothing, but saying nothing felt a lot like agreement.

"You can send a message to Carlos that I am with you, helping you get rid of the traitor Eduardo. This way I get credit for the hit that should have been mine in the first place. Teresa will go back tonight. And I will go tomorrow with the McCabes at one o'clock to have coffee with Carlos at Tortoni's."

"She's not going back to him," Eduardo said.

Teresa's eyes filled with tears. Hollis wondered if Bryan had made the suggestion, one he had to know they'd ignore, for the pleasure of seeing the fear in Eduardo and Teresa.

"Tell him you're staying with your father," Declan suggested to Teresa. "Text him now and say your father is ill. Carlos respects your father. He'll leave you alone and it will buy us some time."

"But if my father talks to Carlos ..." she started, between tears.

"Once he has the passports, the plan is for him to wait at a bar for me to text that you're leaving Buenos Aires," Declan said. "I can tell him any plan we come up with and he'll go along. He just wants you out of harm's way."

"And I want that for him," she said.

"We'll get your father out," Peter suggested. "But Declan's right. If your father backs us up, it gives us time to get you out of here without anyone raising alarm bells."

"And tomorrow, we just let Bryan go back and tell Carlos the truth?" Hollis asked.

"What truth can he tell?" Peter asked. "He sat in a hotel room eating cookies and drinking tea with a couple of Dutch honeymooners, an Irish art thief, a South African spy, and two American college professors. All of whom were using the resources of an international spy ring to help a young couple in love? You think Carlos will believe that? I'm here and I don't believe it."

"Just a small point," Declan interrupted. "Not really an art thief. I make and sell forgeries. I leave the real things where they are."

"Van Goghs," Hollis said.

"Not just Van Goghs."

"You know what's interesting," she said, "my teaching assistant had Van Goghs in her apartment the other day. Pretty paintings but obvious fakes."

Declan smiled.

It was a hunch, but his smile had confirmed it for her. "It bothered me when you said you'd paid someone to get the real Tim and Janet out of the way," Hollis continued. "If you gave all your money away, what did you pay with? And just now it hit me, you paid with the fake Van Goghs."

"*Angela* is a criminal?" Finn said. "Timid grad student, doesn't say a dozen words without apologizing Angela? She's a criminal?"

"No," Declan said, "but her dad is. She just watched over you and reported back. And, okay, she did a quick look around for the address book."

"She was the person who broke into our house?"

"A quick look. She didn't take a thing."

"It makes sense. She gave me the envelope from 'her friend Tommy.' There is no Tommy Silva. She made that up because you asked her to use that name. She knew we'd find the passports and the note you wrote pretending it came from Silva," Hollis said. "Silva, the real Silva, wanted to see the note when he came to our house, but Peter had taken it. I'll bet he didn't know what it said, and he was worried."

"She didn't kill the guy that was put in our living room, though," Finn said. "She couldn't have. I don't see her having the strength to move the body."

"She didn't kill anyone," Declan told him. "I promise you, whoever was left in your house had nothing to do with me. I don't know who he was or who put him there."

"Silva must have put him there," Hollis said. He was the only person left who could have, since neither Declan nor Peter would have reason to. Why, she didn't know. And there was something else she couldn't figure out. "So, Angela watched us, broke into our house, and delivered your message, and you paid her with two obviously fake Van Goghs? That's getting away pretty cheap for all she did."

"Actually, I paid her with a bit of the money Carlos paid Tim and Janet to kill me." He smiled at his cleverness. "The paintings were just my way of saying thank you. Can't sell them, so I've decided to give

222

them to people who help me out. And in case you're wondering, you both are worthy of a field of sunflowers for saving my life."

Hollis, against her better judgement, smiled. "Stop being charming," she scolded him. "We haven't saved you yet."

Bryan finished the coffee that Hollis had held to his lips. He seemed to relax. To Hollis, it seemed he was thinking it all through, and she hoped, realizing his life depended on getting in Peter's good graces.

"Carlos has a meeting tomorrow to hand over the address book," Bryan said. "He needs the plane to get to it. I know this meeting is late in the afternoon. Dusk. He didn't like the time, he said he prefers complete darkness, but he did not have the influence to change it. He told me to have the plane ready at three p.m."

"Where's the meeting?" Finn asked.

"I don't know."

Finn looked at Eduardo, who shook his head. "He said nothing to me."

"He told Silva," Bryan said. "But of course that's no use to us now."

Peter began pacing. "Okay. So I get the book down here. Declan copies it. We put a tracker in it, follow Carlos to his meeting, see who the contact is, and track that person to your nonexistent guy."

"You can't put a tracker in it." Declan poured himself a second cup of tea. The rest of the room waited for him to explain, but instead he grabbed a cookie and sat in the desk chair, enjoying it.

"That's non-negotiable," Peter said. "Once the professors hand over the address book, it'll transmit even from the air."

"Carlos will find it," Declan said. "He's paranoid. And as it turns out, rightly so. People keep betraying him."

"I've been doing this for more than twenty years—" Peter started.

"And Carlos has been a criminal longer than you've been alive."

Peter stopped pacing. "Then he takes the book and gets on a plane and we never see it again. Is that a better idea?"

"Or we find out where the meeting is," Finn suggested. "If he told Silva, maybe he'll tell us."

"You know I admire your can-do spirit," Peter said to Finn, "but there's no way Carlos tells you where that plane is headed."

"I'll bet you a million dollars they get the information," Declan said.

"Blue isn't in the gambling business."

"That's good because I don't happen to have a million to spare," Declan said. "So how about you put me in prison if I'm wrong and let me go if I'm right."

Peter spun around and faced Declan. "You know what, Murphy, I'll take that bet."

Forty-One

Peter's guy from Blue, the one who had followed them on their first day, arrived with two others. They took Elsa's and Levi's suitcases. Elsa hugged Teresa and they promised to keep in touch. How that would happen with Eduardo and Teresa on the run, Hollis didn't ask. Maybe they would find a way.

"Promise me you will email, even just once," Elsa told Hollis, "so I know the story ends well."

"I'll use a different name," she said, "and I'll probably tell you I'm a teacher in Michigan."

Elsa smiled. "But I'll know you are Mr. and Mrs. James Bond."

It was almost seven when Finn and Hollis left the room. The plan was for Declan and Peter to stay, babysitting Bryan. Peter's man was coming back for Eduardo and Teresa. Teresa's father had picked up the false passports they needed, and Peter had arranged for the address book to arrive by morning. Hollis and Finn agreed to spend the night in the suite now that the honeymooners were safe in another hotel. Hollis spent twenty minutes explaining to a maid why she needed fresh sheets and towels when they'd already been changed that morning. Finn said it didn't matter, but it did.

"Dinner?" Finn had asked moments after they got in the elevator. She wasn't hungry, but she was anxious to talk through everything and obviously that wasn't possible if someone was listening. They'd saved lives, captured a killer and put together a plan to fake the address book, but something felt off, and she needed Finn's assurance that everything was going the way it should.

Unfortunately, she didn't get it. Instead, they sat on barstools at a pizza place near the hotel, watching a drizzle turn into a steady rain, laughing and worrying about what might happen with Declan and Peter left together in the room.

"They'll either come out as an unbeatable team of super spies, or one of them won't come out at all," Hollis said.

"I'd put money on Peter to kill Declan."

"I don't know. Declan's got pretty solid survival skills."

"I'm not in love with the crush you have on that guy," Finn said.

Hollis laughed. "Come on, Declan is everything you would want an art thief—"

"Art forger."

"Whatever," she said. "He's charming, good-looking, has an Irish accent. And he has that whole social justice thing."

"Which I admit is probably not a put-on. Crazy that he gave millions of dollars to the university."

"It's a pretty flattering gesture of friendship."

"Or some angle he's playing."

"Probably. He did manipulate Carlos into using the McCabes so he could get us in their place. And he wanted us so we would help him get the address book. But maybe he wants the address book because he really does want to save the world from some terrible guy hell-bent on causing some economic tsunami," Hollis said.

"Or maybe he's going to steal it and sell it to replace the money he gave the school."

"Then why give the money away in the first place?"

"Maybe it's not about the money for him, it's about the game," Finn said. "If he does steal that address book, Peter will kill him. Actually kill him."

"Or he'll just put him in prison." The idea made Hollis a little sad. She was fond of Declan, that much was obvious. He was like a younger brother. A really troublesome, completely unpredictable, but somehow still loveable younger brother. When he wasn't locking them in crypts or getting them misidentified as killers, he was quite sweet.

"Either way, what happens to Bryan?" Finn asked. "I don't buy what Peter said."

"Neither do I. Maybe we can talk him into putting Bryan in witness protection."

"Can Blue do that?"

She shrugged. Bryan wasn't a good man, but as much could be said of Peter and Declan—each were killers, each had secrets. She didn't want to see either of them die for their past deeds, and she certainly didn't want to have helped capture Bryan only to let him be murdered. "Bryan's made clear that he's looking out for himself. That's a survival instinct Peter will understand and work with. Criminals can reform, right?"

"Apparently they can get graduate degrees at small but prestigious Midwestern colleges."

Hollis's eyes widened. "That's crazy. I spent so much time worrying about how Angela was going to handle lecturing a room full of students. I didn't think she had the courage." She let out a dry laugh. "I guess it's good that Declan had Angela there, she was protecting us in a way."

"I don't know how protective she was. Someone managed to put a dead guy in our house while we were upstairs in bed."

It seemed like a million years earlier that they'd come downstairs and found Peter and the young man in the chair. But it had been two and a half days.

"Who is that dead guy?" she wondered aloud. "And what does he have to do with any of this? If we're right that Silva put him there, why did he do it?"

"It had to have been part of the larger scheme."

"How? If it was revenge against Carlos, why not stick the kid in his living room instead of ours?"

"Maybe we need to know who he was, to know why he was there."

Sensible but there wasn't much hope of finding out, Hollis realized, so they might never know who had ended up on their chair, and why Silva—if it was Silva—had done it.

The rain showed no signs of letting up, so it was either get wet or wait for who-knows-how-long until it stopped. They decided to get wet.

"We've lived through worse," Finn said. He grabbed Hollis's hand and they ran, barely missing puddles but getting soaked anyway.

When they ducked under an awning to avoid an especially heavy downpour, Hollis looked at the streets lit only with streetlamps and the moon. A group of teenagers passed them, ignoring the rain. Across the street an old man huddled in a doorway with a small dog in his arms. But otherwise the streets were quiet. She realized it was the first time since they'd arrived they hadn't been hungry or scared or chased by killers.

She had a chance to just be in the moment in this amazing place. The buildings were still beautiful even in the weather, the shops were stocked, the smell of food wafting out of the restaurants was still heavenly. But without the noise of people, she saw something she hadn't before. There was a melancholy about Argentina. It was as if they understood the hardness of life in a way that most Americans did not. But along with the sadness, a passion and joy. It was a complete contradiction, sort of like the dance she had seen at the café, a mix of hope and resignation.

Once you know the tango, you know everything there is to know about Argentina. Silva had said that.

As if on cue, she heard the sounds of tango coming from a nearby bar. She curled into Finn's arms.

"Dance with me," she said.

He wrapped himself around her and slowly moved his feet. She moved with him, more swaying than dancing. But it was their version of a tango.

She caught the eye of the man across the street, and he and his dog began swaying to the music as well. That was the other thing about Argentina. It was romantic.

By the time they got to the hotel their clothes were clinging to them and they were laughing and hugging and trying to catch their breath.

"I'm getting old." Finn coughed as he tried to catch his breath. "It's depressing."

"I'm older," Hollis pointed out.

"Two months. And you look younger." He grabbed her the way Carlos had, but instead of dancing, he kissed her. "I'm proud of the way you handled Bryan."

"I hope he's telling the truth."

"He is. I've been listening to student's lies for years. I have an ear for it. You do too. It felt like the truth to me."

He was right. She'd have known if Bryan was lying about the meeting and the plane, just like she knew when a student's "my grandmother died" line was real and when it was just an excuse. Well, usually knew. The real Tim and Janet had fooled her. And that gave her pause. Maybe, even without their experience, Bryan was as good as they were.

"Do you realize we'll be done with all of this in the morning and we can go home?" she said. "That's good, right?"

"It's good," Finn agreed. "We've done our bit. More than our bit."

It was just hitting her that they would be on a plane in maybe fifteen hours, and in class the next day. When someone asked how her long weekend was, she'd have to say she spent it on the couch reading. Even if she told the truth, no one would believe her.

"I'm sorry I didn't read your paper on global whatever in an internet economy," Finn said.

"It was really boring."

"In that case, I'm glad I didn't read it."

"I'll write something even more dull, and now you'll have to read it. The Cubs are out of the playoffs."

"Ah, but it's basketball season. I have a lot of hope for the Bulls this year." He kissed her a second time.

There was a woman behind the desk. Hollis felt a little disappointed. She'd gotten so used to finding Matias there, it almost seemed as if he never went home. But it was also a relief. One more bit of odd behavior from them, and he'd probably call the police.

Forty-Two

"We need to use a computer," Hollis told the woman at reception.

"Our business center is open," she pointed toward a glass door. "You need to be guests of the hotel."

"We're in the penthouse suite."

The woman nodded, smiling. "Of course, the honeymoon couple. It's obvious."

Finn laughed and kissed Hollis's cheek.

———

In the business center, Hollis opened her emails. If they were going to answer Finn's question about who the dead body was, leading them to the why it was put in their living room, they needed the DNA. She was planning to send Elaine Richardson a reminder that those results would be very helpful to have, but she didn't have to. Elaine had emailed her that morning with a short message. *Call me.*

They went back to the receptionist and used the hotel phone to call Elaine. There was no thought of using the burner phone and they decided that going back to Peter would only open a can of worms. They wanted the answers first, then they would tell him what they had learned.

"Sorry," Hollis said once Elaine answered, "I know it's after nine your time ... I mean, it's after nine and this is your personal time, but I just got your email and it sounded urgent." Finn leaned in close and Hollis tried to position the phone she he could hear, but it made it almost impossible for either of them to get every word.

"I don't know if it is urgent," Elaine said. "But the body of a young man turned up in the alley behind O'Brien's Pub a couple of days ago."

"Okay. What does that have to do with the swabs I gave you?" What she wanted to ask was how Elaine had connected the body back to them so quickly.

"The police came to see me a few hours ago. The DNA from the swabs you gave me, I'd put them in the databases this morning. I expected it would take a week or so to get any results. But it matched the body. The police wanted to know why I had been typing his DNA."

"What did you say?"

Finn pushed in close, to hear what Elaine was saying. Between the height difference, and the odd looks from the receptionist, it made an awkward call even worse.

"The truth," Elaine said. "That you had an attempted break-in a few days ago and the burglar or whoever had left some blood near a window. You and Finn had an argument about whether it was an animal or a person, so you asked me to settle the debate."

Hollis exhaled. It sounded reasonable. Some kid tried to break in and then later got into deadly trouble. Nothing to do with them, not really.

"Okay, we'll talk to the police," Hollis said, "and explain."

"There's more, Hollis. The police said the DNA was a partial match to a man named Vincente Martinez. Do you know who that is?"

"No." Hollis looked at Finn. He shook his head. "Should I know who that is?"

"I hope not," Elaine laughed. "I didn't, either. He's some kind of master criminal from Argentina, seems to sell to all sides. He was arrested several times. Once in the US, once in Chile, and a third time, in 1990, in Argentina with a man named Tomas Silva. But while Silva went to prison, Martinez disappeared."

"So the person who ..." She hesitated, trying to figure it out. "You're saying the DNA belonged to Vincente Martinez?"

"Not him, but related to him. Not close enough to be a son or brother, but maybe a cousin ..."

The dead kid couldn't have been alive in 1990. "A grandson?"

"Yeah, that would fit."

Carlos had a grandchild in the States that he loved dearly, he'd said at dinner. Somehow that grandchild had ended up dead on their chair.

In the elevator on the way to their room, they debated whether to tell Carlos. "The police will contact Argentina's consulate in Chicago," Finn said. "They'll find his parents. His parents will tell Carlos."

"That his grandson happened to be found dead in the same small university town where Silva, Eduardo, and Bryan found us? You don't think that makes us look suspicious?"

"What I think is Silva killed him for revenge," Finn said. "He would have done anything to hurt Carlos."

"If it was Silva, why would he put his own name in the kid's wallet?"

"Why not? He wanted credit for the crime. He knew that Carlos had betrayed him, not just once but over and over, so why not get one last lick in? He had to figure Carlos was going to kill him for one reason or another."

"Silva told the truth about us," Hollis reminded him. "That's why he was killed."

They walked down the hall toward their room.

"Or," Finn suggested, "Silva told the truth about us because he knew he was going to die."

Hollis stopped. "*A sacrifice stays hidden only so long. Once it is on display, the world can judge its worth.* Silva said that to me the night he died. He told me to remember it. Maybe he told me the truth too because he knew it was his last chance to get back at Carlos by ruining his final deal."

"That makes sense. Silva knew who we were. He knew we were helping Declan, that we worked with Blue." Finn was excited. "So he knew we'd use what he said to you … except, what does it mean? A sacrifice stays hidden?"

"It has to be a riddle to the meeting tomorrow. Silva was the only other one who knew where it was. Wherever Carlos is going, it's got something to do with a once-hidden sacrifice."

At least most of the group was safe. Eduardo and Teresa were in hiding with her father. Levi and Elsa were hopefully enjoying a new hotel suite. Bryan was under the very watchful eyes of Peter and Declan, assuming the last two hadn't killed each other. And she and Finn were together. How long they would all be safe once whatever sacrifice Silva meant became public was another question entirely.

They were at the door of the room. Hollis was bursting to continue talking about this, but that couldn't happen in the room, which was likely still bugged. Neither could they stay downstairs in soaking wet clothes. They decided to go inside and do their best to communicate. Peter's men had placed their luggage just inside the door, and on the desk was Finn's package with the map and the guidebook. At least they could get out of their clothes and into bed.

After she changed, Hollis sat on the bed and paged through the book. Finn was right, Silva had said those words as a clue, so he'd meant them to be solved. Whatever he was pointing to had to be an identifiable place. At least she hoped so. While she looked through the book, Finn spread out his map on the bed, studying it from north to south.

She had no idea how big a country Argentina was. It was about a quarter the size of the US, which meant it was about the land mass of the States from the East Coast to the Mississippi River. After Brazil, it was the largest country in South America and it seemed all its size was in its length. It went from Bolivia to the edge of Antarctica, with the Andes mountains, Pampas grasslands, and glacial lakes all within its borders. Even assuming the meeting was in Argentina, it was a tremendous amount of ground to cover.

Finn kept shaking his head. He was getting nowhere. "We should go to bed soon. It was a hard day."

"A little longer."

He nuzzled his face next to her ear. "Could be fun to have an audience," he whispered.

She shook her head.

He kissed her neck.

She shook her head and pointed to her book.

"Why don't you lie down," she suggested.

He grabbed her thigh. She laughed but shook her head again. She didn't even like the idea that Carlos, or Jorge, or Vincente, or whoever he was, might be listening in while she brushed her teeth. Anything else was out of the question.

Finn went back to his map, and Hollis kept paging through the book. Bryan had said the meeting was late afternoon, dusk. That would make it about six. The days in Argentina were getting longer but it was still early spring. Bryan had also said Carlos wanted the plane ready no later than three. So the flight was less than three hours. Based on Finn's map, that left out the bottom part of Patagonia.

She grabbed the hotel's pad of paper and pen and wrote down, *Start with cities?*

Finn searched the map, pointing out cities. His finger landed on Mendoza. Hollis went through the guidebook. A beautiful area known for wines, but nothing that made sense with what Silva had said. Finn pointed to Cordoba. She looked it up, nothing. San Miguel, Mercedes, Santa Rosa, Catamarca … nothing. Salta. A city in the north. Without much hope, she paged through the guidebook. The first page of the Salta entry showed a leathered figure that looked like a sleeping child. The Museum of High Altitude had an exhibit of sacrificed children. She silently cheered. Finn grabbed the book. He nodded.

This was it. The children of Llullaillaco. Discovered in a cave in 1999 at the summit of Mount Llullaillaco in Northern Argentina, the children were part of a religious sacrifice from about five hundred years before they were found. This had to be what he meant. *A sacrifice can stay hidden for only so long. Once on display, the world can judge its worth.* The children were on display. The meeting would have to be at that museum, in front of the exhibit.

They'd figured it out. Silva had gotten in one last betrayal, taking up Declan's habit of leaving them puzzles to solve in order to get the clue.

She assumed he meant it as a clue. But as she crawled into bed beside Finn, she wondered if he actually meant it as a warning.

Forty-Three

"Here's the thing," Peter said.

That was not a good start. No one ever said, *"Here's the thing. You've won the lottery."* *Here's the thing* was always the beginning of something you didn't want to hear. Then, just to drive the point home, Peter hesitated the way people do before they deliver bad news. Hollis took Finn's arm and waited.

"Declan's book looks amazing. The agency sent down leather address books that were a near match..."

"A near match?" Finn asked.

"The real book is a dark brown," Declan held up an address book. "And the fake is just a wee bit lighter." He held up a second book.

From a distance they looked the same. So Hollis got closer. The fake was a chestnut brown, the real one more of a dark chocolate. A subtle difference, admittedly. But having had her hair dyed the wrong shade a few times, she knew even a subtle difference mattered.

"It's not like they'll be side by side," Finn reminded everyone. "And Carlos saw the book, we know that, but he hardly memorized it."

They all looked toward Bryan for confirmation. At some point he'd been unshackled, allowed to shower, and was now eating a roll with his coffee. "He won't notice," he said. "Carlos is easily fooled."

His transformation from loyal employee to government snitch was complete, and it had only taken twelve hours.

"The inside work is amazing," Peter said.

Declan, still sitting at the desk where he had been working since dawn, blushed. "It was a rushed job, but I think it was some of my best work."

"I'll feel bad putting you in prison," Peter said.

Hollis laughed. "You can't. We know where the meeting is going to be. At least we think we do."

Peter's eyes darted toward Bryan, then back to her and Finn. "Good," he said, before she could say another word. "In case the tracker doesn't work…"

Hollis could see Declan roll his eyes. A battle he'd obviously lost.

There was evidence of a couple of false starts in the litter of fake address books. One looked complete, but apparently Declan had made a mistake and started again. When Finn said it was good, Declan took it and threw it in the trash.

"Had to be better than good. It has to fool Carlos and whoever the contact is. Otherwise it's useless to us."

Peter put the real one in his pocket, then wrapped the near-perfect fake in paper, put it in an envelope and handed it to Hollis.

"It should be safe in your purse," he said.

"Almost everyone who has wanted to kill us is either dead or in this room," Finn said. "We'll be fine."

"My guy will tail you but not too close. Just in case," he said. "And Bryan will enter just after you do. I don't want him alone with Carlos until after you've safely left the café."

"Are you sure we can trust him?" Hollis asked.

"He can help us identify the man at the meeting this afternoon. He has been persuaded to help us. And in return, we've agreed to help him. Informants are the lifeblood of the spy business."

Hollis took a piece of the hotel stationary and wrote down *Museum of High Altitude in Salta. The children who were sacrificed.* She folded the paper in three and handed it to Peter. "Just in case."

Peter put the paper in his pocket. "Guns?"

Finn lifted his jacket to show a gun tucked into the waist of his jeans. Hollis opened her purse.

"Hold on to them," Declan said.

Finn clenched his jaw. "We'll do fine."

Declan stood up and shook Finn's hand. "Ah, you will do. You two continually amaze me. If I don't have a chance again, thank you."

"Why won't you have another chance?" Hollis asked.

He didn't say.

All that was left to do was go to Café Tortoni, hand over the package, and hope for the best.

———

This time the café was packed. A combination of tourists and locals at every table and every seat at the bar. Carlos was at a table in a back corner, sitting alone and looking unhappy. He signaled to a waiter when they arrived.

"Hot chocolate and churros, it's a must," he said.

"You okay?" Finn asked. "We did what you wanted. I thought you would be happy."

"Teresa spent the night with her father. She said he was ill."

"You don't believe that?" Hollis tried to keep her voice even.

"She is in mourning for Eduardo. I know that's what it is. You must go with me to see her. You need to tell her that he died a coward. That he didn't love her."

If Peter's men had kept to the plan, she and Eduardo were likely in Spain or wherever they'd decided to go with their fake passports and their new lives.

"I don't think that will make things better for you," Hollis said. "Give her time to grieve and she'll come home to you."

Carlos considered it. "No. We will finish our business here, and then we will go see her."

"We have a meeting first," Finn said. "We can meet you this afternoon."

"What meeting can you have? You came here to do work for me."

"And we've done it. All that you've asked," Finn said. He was calm, slightly annoyed. It was impressive. "Now we are moving on to other clients. We can meet you this afternoon to explain to Teresa whatever you want. But as my wife has said, I don't think it will help you. Give her time."

Again, Carlos considered it. The hot chocolate and churros arrived. The chocolate was more dipping sauce than drink, but it was good. Very good. And a nice complement to the crispy and chewy churros.

Hollis took the address book, still in the envelope, and slid it across the table to Carlos. He ignored it and focused on his churros. For a moment, she thought he wouldn't even look, he was so distraught over Teresa.

But he wiped his fingers on a napkin and opened the envelope. Underneath the table, Hollis put her hand on Finn's thigh. She could feel his leg tense up, ready to run if need be. She got ready too.

"The Irishman is dead?" Carlos asked.

"Yes," Finn said.

Carlos glanced toward Hollis. "You had a fondness for him. I think he has that effect on a lot of people. Silva found him funny. I thought he was full of it, all that talk of helping the people. What people did he ever help?"

"Some in our business need to justify their actions," Finn said.

"If you want to be greedy, you should be greedy. No point in feeling guilty about it."

He opened the envelope and unwrapped the book. He held his breath. They held their breaths too.

"I only saw this once," he said. "I didn't understand what was in it, and I don't now. But it was heartbreaking to me later when I realized it had great worth and I had let it slip from my fingers. Another man knew, another Irishman. He took it, talked of destroying it. But thankfully he died before that could happen."

One of the people Declan lost, Hollis knew, but she didn't acknowledge it. "We're finished here?" she said instead.

"You think I should let Teresa come home when she's ready?"

"I do. Women can't be rushed."

He seemed to accept that. "She's with her father. He called me last night. She won't get into much trouble as long as she's with him."

Carlos looked past them as if he recognized someone and was slightly annoyed by it. Hollis turned around and saw Bryan walk in the café. He came straight for their table, smiling. He pulled up a chair and sat between Finn and Carlos. Hollis knew he'd agreed to cooperate. But as soon as Bryan arrived, a chill went through her.

"You had a good night?" Carlos asked.

241

"Didn't they tell you?

"I prefer not to know the details, you know that."

Bryan reached his hand out to take the address book, but Carlos batted his hand away.

Finn took one last bite of the churros, then put his napkin on the plate. "We have a meeting, then a plane to catch."

"Boss has a meeting this afternoon as well," Bryan said.

Carlos slammed his cup onto the table. "Enough. We will conclude our business with the McCabes and then you will do as I tell you."

Bryan looked at Hollis. He was making a decision, she could see it. And it was obvious by his smirk that he was making a bad decision. He'd told her he would, and she hadn't listened. He'd said he wasn't interested in Carlos, but in using Carlos to get to the next step on the ladder. He would use them too, if it helped further his ambition. The only thing they had going for them was the crowd enjoying their coffee and snacks, the waiters moving through the tables carrying trays almost too heavy to lift, the folks at the bar enjoying an early afternoon drink. Too many people for Bryan to kill them there. Peter probably had someone watching them, someone who looked like a tourist. Maybe. Could they take that chance?

Forty-Four

"I would take a long hard look at that address book," Bryan said. "You want to be sure. The McCabes"—he said the name with sarcasm—"have a way of taking a perfect plan and turning it inside out."

"I don't know what you're talking about." Carlos was getting annoyed.

"The book has a tr—"

Finn gasped. "It was you."

"It was me, what?" Bryan seemed amused and completely untroubled.

Finn, on the other hand, was suddenly and uncharacteristically angry. He leaned forward and grabbed Bryan's shirt. "You put that dead kid in our house. You kidnapped him, tied him up, shot him, then placed him on our chair where you thought Silva and Eduardo would find him. Eduardo would report back that Silva's name was in his wallet. It was a way of pointing the finger when the truth would come out. When Carlos would learn who he was."

"What are you talking about?" Carlos growled. "What kid was shot?" He turned to Bryan. "Do you know what he's saying?"

Bryan opened his mouth, but Hollis spoke first. "We use a house sometimes as part of our cover identity. It's where Silva, Bryan, and Eduardo came the night they spirited us to Argentina. Earlier that night we'd been awoken by some noise and came downstairs. There was a young man, long brown hair, probably twenty years old, in our living room. He'd been shot somewhere else and brought there. Naturally we moved the body."

"Your home in the States?" Carlos said. "And the boy, describe him exactly."

"The local police did a DNA test on him. He was a partial match to a man named Vincente Martinez. A grandson perhaps."

Carlos went pale. "They're sure?" he asked quietly.

Hollis nodded.

"Silva killed him." Bryan was glaring at Finn, but it was clear he was still looking for a way to spin it. "He hated you, boss. He wanted revenge for the time he spent in prison, the money you stole from him."

Carlos sat, unmoving. "Silva hated me," he agreed. "But he loved my grandson like his own." He turned toward Bryan. "You whispered in my ear about Teresa and Eduardo, about Silva's disloyalty, and now you try to get me to turn on my new American friends. You killed my Nicolas for what? To become my right-hand man?"

"You're just a stop on the way," Finn said.

Carlos was shaking. He pointed a finger at Bryan. "You are a dead man."

Bryan got up, leaned over to Carlos, "No, old man. You are the dead one." He said something in Spanish, but Hollis only picked up one word—*patetico*, pathetic. He pushed Finn and moved through the restaurant, nearly knocking over a waiter. He was out the door before any of them could react. Peter's men were supposed to be outside. Bryan knew that too. Hollis was sure he could evade them.

What now? They couldn't just leave a grieving man to finish his hot chocolate. They couldn't stay and risk Bryan returning. Hollis looked to Finn. He didn't seem to have an answer, either.

"What can we do for you, Señor?" she asked.

Carlos reached out and grabbed her hand so tightly she thought he would break it. "I think the music is ended. I think it is time to be done with my business." With his free hand he brushed aside the book.

"You're not going to the meeting?" Finn asked.

Carlos shook his head.

Finn glanced toward Hollis. He had to go to the meeting, or else the book would not get passed to the next man or, hopefully, to the head of TCT itself.

And what if Bryan had been lying about not knowing the location? He would get there and tell the contact what they'd all been up to. Bryan knew where they lived. Hollis and Finn would never have a moment's rest if all of TCT were looking for them, if Bryan were free to show up anytime.

Peter and Declan would have lost an important chance. And the others—would Bryan go looking for Elsa and Levi? For Teresa and Eduardo? He might want to eliminate anyone who had seen him offer to cooperate with Blue. Or he might kill them all just because he could.

Carlos had to go through with the meeting and that book would have to go up the chain of command, just as they'd planned.

"Bryan will poison TCT against you," Hollis said.

Carlos shrugged. "My grandson was not in my business. He was studying in Nebraska. He said it was all cornfields, but he loved it. He wanted to be an architect. He was a good boy. Why would Bryan do this to him?"

"Bryan killed your grandson because you had hired us to do the hit he felt was his opportunity," Hollis said. "He wanted your permission to kill us, and Silva along with us. Silva's name in your grandson's pocket. I think he believed that Eduardo would see it as Silva's revenge, and report to you what had happened. But we moved the body before they came to our home. Bryan couldn't admit it was supposed to be there. That's why he kept searching the house." She realized she was speaking more to Finn than to Carlos, but what came out of her mouth next was for both of them. "If he would do that to an innocent young man, what's next?"

"What happens to Teresa?" Finn suggested. "Can anyone you love ever be safe?"

That woke Carlos up. "I must see Teresa. I'll go to her father's house and insist she comes home. She loved Nicolas. She'll want to know what's happened."

Hollis felt herself starting to panic.

Finn signaled for the waiter. "A glass ... *Un vaso* ... um ... *de agua, por favor.*" He was buying them time.

The waiter nodded and soon returned with three glasses of water. Finn sipped his, and Hollis realized how dry her mouth was. She drank half the glass in one gulp.

"Let me call Teresa," Hollis said. "If she's angry at you, let me talk to her first, smooth things over."

"She will be angry at you as well. You took Eduardo from her."

"She doesn't know it was us. That's not how we work."

Carlos looked relieved. "Maybe do not tell her yet about my grandson. She's already grieving, and I need time to think about how to tell my daughter, if she doesn't yet know. Just tell my wife that I am sorry and I want to see that she's okay."

Hollis got up from the table. She pulled the phone Eduardo had given her from her purse and walked toward the exit of the restaurant. She couldn't use the phone to call Peter. Eduardo had said it was bugged. She had absolutely no idea what plan Peter would come up with to get them back on track. But she kept walking toward the door as if she did, knowing each step got her farther from Finn, who was doing his best to comfort a killer.

As she almost reached the door, she saw a cell phone on a table. The man was reading the paper. She got her hand ready. She could just take it. She could feel herself tense, her face get warm. Someone could see her and then it would all be over. Police would be called. Or she could just take it, and no one would notice. Maybe Declan could teach them how to pick pockets. He'd no doubt protest he'd never done such a thing, but he knew how. She knew he did.

She moved close to the table, her purse on the arm closest to the man. She casually moved her arm down her purse, brushed the table. Her fingers found the phone and she picked it up, dropped it into her purse, and kept walking.

Nothing. No one said a word.

Outside, she dialed Peter's number and filled him in as quickly as she could.

"We put Teresa and Eduardo on a plane hours ago," he said. "Maybe we can get someone to play Teresa."

"I think he knows what his wife looks like. How do we get away with that?"

"From a distance. She won't talk to him, but he can see her. But from yards away. Maybe the window at her father's house?"

"No." But Hollis suddenly had an idea. "A church. She's in mourning for her dead lover, angry at her husband. Probably full of guilt. Teresa would go to church. Is her father still in Buenos Aires?"

"Yes, he leaves in an hour," Peter said.

"Don't let him. If he's with Teresa, it will sell it."

"I can try and get an agent to play her. It will take a couple of hours."

"We don't have time. It's nearly two and Carlos has to be on that plane at three."

"Maybe you say that Teresa won't see him. Only the father will talk to him."

She didn't think it would be enough. But it might have to be. Teresa, a dark-haired beauty, was long gone and there was no one else. "Wait," she said, as she remembered another brunette she'd met in Argentina. "It's a long shot. I mean a very, very long shot."

"Are you going to suggest putting Declan in a wig, because I don't think even Carlos's old eyes will be deceived."

She could hear Declan laugh in the background. It was a little disconcerting to think of their budding friendship, created over too much caffeine and a rushed forgery.

"Actually no, but that would be fun," she said. "I was thinking of a waitress named Gabriella who was very kind to us. She works at that restaurant in Palermo where you met with us in the kitchen. She's got dark hair like Teresa. She's shorter, but if she's sitting in a pew, her back to Carlos, with Teresa's father by her side … maybe."

"Gabriella. Yes. She could work. Hold on …"

She could hear Peter and Declan talking quickly. A plan was being put in place.

"Declan is on the phone to Teresa's father. He said to go to the Nuestra Señora de los Santos Church. Our Lady of the Saints. He said there is a mass for the dead being said there at two fifteen. It's by your hotel, he said. If you go at two thirty, mass will be underway. Keep Carlos at the back of the church. We'll put Gabriella and Teresa's father in the middle. Close enough to see but not too well."

"I think we can do that. Carlos doesn't strike me as a religious man, but I doubt even he would interrupt a church service."

"One problem. I don't think Gabriella will say yes to me. When she saw me in the kitchen, I had my gun out. She looked terrified. And as charming as Declan can be, she's never met him, so I doubt she'll follow him, either."

"I'll go to the restaurant. I'll talk her into it," Hollis said. "And I'll have Finn bring Carlos. Two thirty at the church."

It was 1:38. There wasn't even an hour. It was impossible.

Forty-Five

Hollis walked back into the restaurant, palming the phone in her right hand. She bumped against the table where the man continued to read his paper. She bent down as if she were picking something up from the floor.

"Sorry," she said and put the phone back on the table.

The man nodded but then went back to reading.

Finn and Carlos were still sitting together. Carlos was leaning forward in his chair, his elbows on the table, his eyes closed. Finn was sitting close, talking to him. As she got closer she heard Finn say, "'I always imagined paradise would be a kind of library.'"

Carlos smiled a little. "Borges had a saying for everything." He sighed. "I hope that he's right. Nicolas would be happy in a library."

Hollis looked at Finn, tilted her head. Finn glanced toward Carlos. They had to talk, away from him, but that was impossible. They couldn't leave him and risk his calling Teresa or cancelling the meet.

"I'll go to our meeting alone," Hollis said to Finn. "And I'll meet you at the hotel. Perhaps you can stay with Carlos a little longer."

"That is very kind of you," Carlos said to Finn, who hadn't answered yet.

"And Teresa?" Finn asked.

"She won't talk to me over the phone, so I'm going to her father's house. She said I must go now because she intends to go to mass at Our Lady of Saints Church at two thirty."

"I know that church," Carlos said. "It's where we were married."

Hollis looked at Finn. "Perhaps you and Carlos can meet us there, and they can have a moment together before the mass."

Finn looked startled. "Are you sure?"

"Yes. Two thirty at the church."

Carlos nodded. "Of course she would want to go to mass. Teresa hasn't yet given up on God. I should have thought of that."

Finn took Hollis's hand. "It's a plan," he said, more question than statement.

"It's a plan."

Carlos began to cry and Finn put a comforting arm around the man's shoulder. Hollis did her best to seem calm. She walked slowly toward the exit, but as soon as she was through the door, she dashed onto the street and hailed a taxi. She fidgeted the entire time to the restaurant. If Gabriella said no, if she wasn't working, if she thought the whole idea was insane ...

Of course she'd think the whole idea was insane.

―――

"So I need you to go to the church and sit in a pew for just a few minutes, that's all."

Gabriella had been at work and was delighted to see Hollis and know that she was enjoying Argentina. That is, until Hollis launched into the story about how they needed her to pretend to be this old man's long-dead wife sitting at mass. He had dementia and was convinced she was alive and young and at mass. The only way to calm him was to give him what he wanted, and Gabriella looked enough like her, at least from the back, to pass for his wife, for a few minutes from a distance.

Gabriella stood listening to the whole story. "I knew you were in trouble," she said. "I knew when you came in before. You both looked so frightened. And now your husband is missing." She gasped. "Does someone have your husband? Has he been kidnapped?"

That was a better story. Hollis wished she'd thought of it.

It was 1:52.

"Okay, I'm going to tell you the truth and you won't believe me, but I don't have time to keep lying. I work for an international spy ring. So does my husband. The man who came to the restaurant, he does too. We're trying to get a very bad man who is sometimes called Jorge Videla."

Her eyes widened. "Do you know who he was?"

"Yes. And this man we're trying to get, he did not kill as many people or ruin as many lives, but like Videla, he is a bad man. Videla died in prison and maybe this man will too. But first we need to fool him into thinking that his wife is at mass with her father. It will only take a few seconds, and you will not be in any danger but I need you to say yes now because ..."

Gabriella looked at Hollis. "This should not sound true, but it does."

"Will you help? I'll get you money to pay ..."

"I don't need to be paid to put a bad man in prison." She called out to Saul, the restaurant owner and spoke to him in Spanish. He grunted but nodded. "Okay," she said. "I need to be back at three. Is what I'm wearing okay?"

Hollis looked at the tie-dyed t-shirt Gabriella had on. Teresa would never wear it. There was one more stop to make.

———

At 2:11, Gabriella sat in the middle pew of the church, wearing the rose cashmere and silk sweater that Teresa had bought for Janet Mc-Cabe. Teresa's father sat next to her. Hollis sat with them. She told her that Teresa was grieving for her lost love, a man who had been killed.

"But he's not dead?" Gabriella asked.

"No. We sent them away together to start a new life."

"You must feel very good about your work, helping people that way."

"I guess I do. When I'm not feeling terrified."

Gabriella shook her head. "You are a strong woman. I can see that. I'm proud to help you if it helps others be safe."

Hollis needed that, a reminder that the world is mostly good people wanting good for others. It was easy to forget when surrounded by killers.

———

Mass started exactly at 2:15. Gabriella, from the back and several yards away, did look like Teresa. She played the part too. She sat close to Teresa's father and even seemed to be crying.

Hollis walked outside the church and waited. It was an unusually warm day and she could feel a trickle of sweat run down her back.

253

She could see Peter and Declan in a car, though Declan ducked down when Carlos arrived in a black sedan. He and Finn walked up the church steps.

"Mass already started," Hollis told Carlos.

"Then I will wait."

"You can't," Finn reminded him. "The meeting."

Carlos looked annoyed and upset. And, worse, as if he were about to burst into the church.

"Why don't you peek in from the back and see her?" Hollis suggested. "You'll know she's okay. And then you can talk to her when you get back tonight."

Carlos walked up the final step and pushed open the door of the church. Hollis and Finn followed. He stood at the back, his eyes searching for her. Hollis could see Gabriella kneeling at the pew, her head bowed, her hands folded in prayer. Teresa's father put a comforting hand on her shoulder. At the altar the priest was standing, looking out at the congregation, while a choir sang in Spanish. A few tourists stood in the back, but otherwise the pews were filled with mostly older woman, praying.

Hollis pointed. "She's there."

Carlos squinted. They waited. For a moment it looked like he might walk up the aisle to sit with her, but he stayed put. "Yeah okay. I'll leave her to God. But tell her I must talk to her tonight. She cannot avoid me forever."

They walked back outside into the sunlight.

Carlos shook Finn's hand and then Hollis's. "I have made many wrong choices in my life. I have trusted the wrong people. I'm grateful at least today I did not go wrong."

"I'm sorry about your grandson, Carlos," Finn said. "I really am."

"*Gracias,* my friend. You've finished the dance, staying through many changes in music. I won't forget this."

He waved goodbye and walked down the steps. When he got to the bottom he hesitated. He looked back at the church and for a moment Hollis worried he'd changed his mind about waiting to speak to Teresa.

"I have one more thing to ask of you. Come with me to this meeting. My colleague will be expecting me to come with, what you would call, muscle. And it seems I am fresh out of bodyguards. But this is just one reason. The truth is I do not trust myself today. I need the support of friends."

Going with Carlos meant more delay, more danger, but it also meant a chance to get a description of the man he was supposed to meet. Hollis was ready to say yes. She looked to Finn for his answer.

"I know I shouldn't," Finn whispered to Hollis, "but I feel guilty."

Hollis did too. "There's confession after mass."

"Except we won't be here. We'll be on our way to Salta."

Forty-Six

The plane ride was quiet. Carlos looked at photos of his grandson on his phone. Hollis looked out the window. Finn napped for a bit. Aside from the fact that they were on a private jet with a dangerous criminal on their way to meet another dangerous criminal, it would have felt like any commuter flight they'd ever been on. Except instead of peanuts, there was a fruit and cheese plate, expensive wines, and several options for dessert.

Carlos took the address book out of the envelope and put it back again. He smiled to himself as if he knew a joke no one else did. Finn looked over at Hollis. She shrugged. If he knew the book was a fake, it seemed self-destructive to go to the meeting. Hollis and Finn could always say they had no idea. They'd never claimed to know what the book looked like.

They'd been tasked with finding it, or rather the McCabes had. They would have no responsibility for it afterward. If it came to that, she hoped Carlos would agree.

"It has a bug in it," Carlos said.

"A bug?" Finn swiveled his chair to face Carlos. "An insect?"

"No, no. A device, about the size of a thumb nail, stuck between the endpaper and the cover of the book. I ran my hand over every page, just to be sure. You can't be too cautious. It is very small, but I discovered it."

Carlos held up the book. It didn't appear there was damage to it.

"What did you do with the bug?"

"Nothing yet." He took a small metal file from his pocket and ran the lengthwise edge of it from the bottom of the endpaper to the top, moving slowly, carefully. It seemed to Hollis that he wasn't doing anything that would matter, but as his metal file got to the top, she could see a small, paper thin plastic disc moving out from between the endpaper and the cover. Carlos took it in his fingers.

"I've been a criminal a very long time. I've seen many advances in technology that have made things easier for us, and harder. But I have rarely been fooled by the tricks of other criminals."

"You think Declan put that in there?"

Carlos nodded. "He thought he could find me and outsmart me. I didn't order his death, but I can see now why it was a necessary part of this transaction. He was too smart for his own good. The Irishman was going to get in his way."

"His?" Hollis asked. Though she knew the "his" was the man who didn't exist. She hoped Carlos would supply a name, but he didn't. He just looked at the tracker.

"Amazing what they can do now," he said. Then he bent it with his fingers until it snapped in two.

When they landed, a limousine was waiting. Carlos directed the driver to play some music, a guitar instrumental, then he sat in the back, leaned his head against the seat, and closed his eyes. Hollis and Finn sat in the seat in front of him. They held hands but didn't speak. Instead Hollis looked out the window at what seemed to be a pretty rural, almost desert landscape. She hadn't worried much that Carlos found the tracker. Peter would know where they were headed based on her note. But in the car, as they drove through an area so different from Buenos Aires, it occurred to her that she wasn't absolutely sure they had gone to Salta. It was just a guess. A good guess, but what if there was another museum, a different sacrifice?

Within twenty minutes they came into a town. There was a large square with a pretty park, and long, Spanish-looking buildings around it. One street seemed to lead to a pedestrian shopping area. There was a church painted a dark terra cotta. Hollis looked for anything that might tell them where they were but couldn't see anything.

The car came to a stop in front of a peach-colored building with ivory decorations that gave it a Moorish feel. Finn pointed toward a word on a sign, *Museo*. They were at a museum. That was a good start.

They got out of the car and walked toward the building with Carlos in the lead. It wasn't just any museum, it was the right one. The Museum of High Altitude. They were actually going to do this. She saw Finn smile when he realized they were in the right place.

But as they got to the door, Carlos took a left, passing the museum and heading toward a small side street. They followed.

"Where's the meeting?" Finn said. "It'll be easier for us to help you if we know what's going to happen."

"It's just an exchange, nothing to it." Carlos pointed to a stall with *empanadas* painted on the side. He spoke to the man in Spanish and bought a bag full. "My favorite empanadas are from the north. They're smaller than the ones you get in Buenos Aires but so flavorful." He reached into the bag and handed each of them one. "You must try it."

So they did. And he was right. Hollis had eaten a lot of empanadas over the years, a spicy hand-held meat pie, but this was particularly good. They stood in the street, enjoying two each, and watched people as they walked by.

"They're more the indigenous peoples of Argentina here than in Buenos Aires," Carlos told them. "In the city we have many European imports. My grandfather was from Italy. On my mother's side, her family was from Wales. But here, the Europeans didn't settle. So these are true Argentinians. It's a beautiful area. There are mountains all around us. If you don't have to hurry back, you should travel a bit. Argentina has everything. Each province its own beauty. Here in Salta it's the mountains."

"And the empanadas," Finn added.

Carlos laughed. He did not seem in a hurry to move. Hollis looked around. No one seemed to be watching, no one was coming toward them. It didn't seem likely that the meeting would be in a busy street, but maybe that was the perfect spot. She had a lot to learn about being a criminal.

After Carlos finished his last bite, he crumpled up the bag and tossed it in the trash. "We'll go inside now. It's almost time."

He immediately started walking back toward the entrance to the museum. Finn and Hollis followed. He wasn't a man used to explaining himself, obviously, especially to the people he hired to protect him. At least that's what Hollis assumed they were there to do. Which hopefully they wouldn't have to.

The Museum of High Altitude, which Hollis immediately decided was the best name for a museum she'd ever heard, was a three-story building with exhibits mainly in the archeology of the Andes, largely focused on Incan history. Carlos moved quickly so Hollis and Finn rushed to keep up, but even at a glance, Hollis could see a remarkable display of textiles, pottery, and religious objects.

They made it up to the third floor, passing visitors until they got to a room that held the exhibit they had come to see.

Through the doors were the 500-year-old frozen bodies of three Incan children killed in a ritual sacrifice. They were found in 1999 by a team of archeologists, surrounded by a treasury of objects made of gold and other materials. A sign on the wall near the exhibit explained that it was believed they were drugged and allowed to freeze to death at the top of the 22,000-foot Mount Llullaillaco. In the cold and dry air, the bodies were naturally mummified.

There were two girls, one about fifteen, the other about six years old, and a boy of about seven. But for preservation purposes, a sign stated, only one was on display at a time. When Hollis, Finn, and Carlos walked into the darkened, heavily air-conditioned room, La Doncella, the oldest girl, was the one in a glass case. She had long black hair, her chin tucked onto her chest, her legs crossed. She looked as if she were sleeping.

Carlos was nervous. While Finn and Hollis were mesmerized by the mummy of the young girl, Carlos began to fidget. He reached into his jacket pocket, patted what was there—the address book, Hollis assumed, then crossed his arms. A minute later he repeated the gesture. He reminded Hollis of someone who had just given up smoking and had no idea what to do with his hands.

"I'm done after this," he said. "I will retire to my ranch, and Teresa and I will spend whatever time I have left together."

Finn nodded toward Hollis. She turned and saw an Asian man, about forty, dressed in jeans and a gray t-shirt, flanked by two other men dressed nearly the same, except both were wearing jackets. Better to hide guns. To anyone else they would have looked like tourists, but their expressions were too serious, their strides too purposeful. They walked toward the exhibit, the first man moving close to Carlos. Finn and Hollis stood behind along with the other muscle. Hollis had never felt more ridiculous.

"Mr. Sato," Carlos said.

"You have it?"

Carlos reached into his pocket and pulled out the envelope. He handed it over. Sato took the book from the envelope. He looked at it, he frowned. He turned to the other men and said something. Hollis assumed it was Japanese. Sato, she knew, was a popular Japanese surname. One of the men took out his cellphone and pressed the flashlight app, shining it on the book.

A guard rushed over, "No light. Outside."

"Let's finish in another room," Sato said.

"No," Carlos said. "I've given you what you asked for. We cannot draw this out."

Sato ignored him. He walked out of the exhibit room without waiting for an answer. His men walked after him and Carlos followed. The pecking order was clear. Carlos was the king of criminals in Argentina, but whoever these men were, they were not impressed.

Finn and Hollis followed, but as they entered a well-lit room of Incan textiles, Hollis saw Peter focused on one of the exhibits. Beside him was a woman, standing close enough to give the appearance of being a couple. Coming out of the mummies room behind them,

Hollis recognized the man from Blue who had come for the honeymoon couple. Across from him, standing near the entrance to the next room was a tall woman reading a brochure, but her eyes were darting toward Carlos.

For a moment Hollis felt home free. Whatever was going to happen in this room, they were surrounded by heavily armed, well-trained spies. She and Finn could just hang back and make their escape when necessary.

But just beyond the woman reading the brochure, in a corner of the next room, Hollis saw a familiar head of brown hair. Declan had shown up. The man they were supposed to have killed had decided to crash the party.

Forty-Seven

Sato kept walking until he was directly under a light. His men followed, then Carlos, then Finn and Hollis. Sato held the book up, examining it in the strongest light in the room. He stared at the front, flipped it to the back and stared again. The color, the slight difference in the brown leather from the real to the fake. He was looking for a reason to declare the book a fake, and a shade or two was going to give it to him.

She tried to be optimistic, but she saw Finn go pale. *Declan*, he mouthed. She nodded. His eye twitched. They each took a deep breath. They'd have to hope that whatever he was doing there, he was smart enough to stay out of the way.

"We need to conclude our business," Carlos said. "I must return to Buenos Aires as soon as possible. I have personal business ..."

"I don't care about your personal business. There is something about this book."

"It was gotten from the source."

Sato glanced at him. "The Irishman? He's dead?"

Carlos nodded toward Hollis and Finn, and for the first time Sato looked at them. "They took care of him personally, so there would be no doubt."

Sato looked them both up and down. Hollis was sure he would realize they weren't capable of murdering Declan, or anyone.

"You look like American tourists," he said. Then he paused. "Good cover." He went back to looking at the book. "You got it directly from Declan?"

"No," Hollis said. "An American woman had taken it from Ireland." It felt odd to talk about herself in the third person but that was the story that Carlos knew, so that was what she had to stick to.

"But Declan was the one who had it previously?"

"He had access to it," she said, honestly.

"I didn't know the man personally. But I know he was a forger, and a good one I hear. I think he forged this."

"That's ridiculous," Carlos said. "I had an arrangement. I take care of the Irishman for your boss, bring you the book, and you pay what I am owed."

"Only if what I have is authentic."

Sato looked around the exhibition room. An elderly woman with a teenage granddaughter wandered into the hall and began studying one of the displays. Peter chatted with the woman agent, who wandered out of the room, leaving him alone. Then a man Hollis hadn't seen before walked in. She sensed that the agents were getting nervous. With civilians looking at exhibits and Sato taking too long with the book, the odds of something going wrong were growing.

And there was Declan. Wherever he was.

"This is enough," Carlos said. "I've given you what you asked for."

Sato flipped through the pages, but it was clear by the casualness with which he did it, that he wasn't looking for a particular entry. Hollis assumed he was just making sure there was writing in it.

"I saw the book two years ago," Sato said. "There's something about this ..." He turned to Hollis and Finn. "How do you know this is the real thing?"

"Because Declan didn't want us to have it," Finn said. "If you had met the guy, you would know he could convince you of nearly anything. So you had to watch what he didn't say."

Carlos nodded. Out of the corner of her eye, she could see Peter quietly nod too.

"If this book were a fake," Finn continued, "he'd have led us right to the American woman who had it, he would have made us believe it was the real thing."

"As it was, he tried to protect her from being killed," Hollis said.

"Did you kill her?"

"That was the order from Carlos."

"You don't seem like someone who could ever hurt anyone," Sato said to her. He looked over at Finn. "How did you kill the Irishman?"

"I didn't," he said.

"You said he was dead."

"She killed him." He nodded toward Hollis. "She shot him in the neck, from behind, while he was chatting with me. That's the thing about my wife. Some men are dumb enough to forget just how capable she is of anything she wants to do."

Hollis bit the side of her lip, so she wouldn't begin to cry. After a while couples stop complimenting each other, especially in front of others. Even if he was telling Sato she could kill a man in cold blood if she chose to, she wanted to kiss Finn for saying it.

"Did he bargain for his life?" Sato asked. "My boss will want to know."

"I don't think it occurred to him that we would ever harm him," Hollis answered. "He believed we were friends."

There was truth in what she said, and it seemed to satisfy both Sato and Carlos. Sato put the book back into the envelope. "I understand it's a new account."

He took out a cellphone, handed it to Carlos, who punched in a long series of numbers, pressed "send," and handed the phone back to Sato.

"It will take fifteen minutes to get confirmation that the transfer has taken place," Sato said. "We can wait together over coffee."

"I will have to trust you," Carlos said. "I don't have time to wait." He shook Sato's hand and turned to walk out of the room. They were almost out of danger.

But blocking his exit was Bryan.

"*Hola*, boss."

He pushed Carlos aside and moved toward Sato and his men.

Sato had turned his back on Carlos and appeared to be interested in a colorful blanket behind a glass case, likely made hundreds of years earlier. Sato pointed to it and said to one of his men, "My grandmother would have appreciated this workmanship ..." before slipping into Japanese.

"You and I have something important to discuss, but it should not be here," Bryan said.

Sato turned and looked at him, with a slight smile. "You're the underling," he said. "The muscle I met before with the other one, the tall one. I was wondering why Carlos had brought new people with him today, but I can see now why he would. Insubordination."

"You need to talk to me."

Sato smiled. "I need my gin and tonics to have ice in them, my friend. I need my wife to remind me where I've put my car keys. I have just begun to need reading glasses. But I do not need anything from you."

Smooth.

Carlos moved closer to Sato and Bryan. "My apologies."

"This is not the place," Sato said. "We're attracting attention now because of this man."

Sato walked out of the main exhibit area, took a left, and pointed toward a men's room. His men went inside first, came out, nodded an all-clear, then went back in. Sato, Bryan, and Carlos joined them. Carlos turned toward Hollis and Finn.

"Both," he said.

So they both walked in. As the door closed behind them she saw Peter walk into the hall. He looked at her, pointed his finger to the floor. He'd be there, he was telling her. Close, but if there was trouble, not close enough.

Forty-Eight

The room was empty except for their group, but it was still uncomfortable for Hollis to be standing in the men's room. She positioned herself as far from the urinals as possible, but then she had another problem. All the men were taller than her. Standing where she was, all she saw were the backs of men's heads. She nudged Finn to move over. He put his hand on her back and guided her toward the center. That also seemed like a mistake. Away from the public, everyone was showing their guns except for Hollis and Finn. She briefly considered getting it from her purse, but she was worried that there'd be another incident like happened with Declan. Better to look like she wasn't concerned than look like an amateur.

Sato noticed that Hollis and Finn hadn't gone for their weapons. "You're interesting bodyguards."

"We're not bodyguards," Finn said. "We take care of problems, and it doesn't look like this is our problem."

Once again Hollis wanted to kiss him. He was amazing under pressure. She wondered if his throat was dry, like hers, and his heart was pounding.

"They're working with Blue," Bryan said. "They're helping Declan and the South African agent to bring down TCT."

Now all eyes were on them. And all the guns.

"What gave you that idea?" Sato said.

"Last night, I was in their hotel room. They took me, tied me up."

"You're here now. They had you and they let you go?"

Bryan hesitated. Bless Peter, he wasn't joking when he said it would be an absurd story to tell.

"They are setting me up to be the fall guy."

"They're doing an excellent job."

"He killed my grandson," Carlos said. "Please give me the pleasure of killing him."

Sato looked at Carlos. "If this is true, why is the man still alive?"

"He isn't," Carlos said. "He just doesn't know it yet." He stared at the young man. "You came to me hungry and poor, and I gave you a purpose. I gave you clothes, a place to live. I taught you about wine and food. I took you with me around the world. And you betrayed me for a promotion?" His eyes filled with tears.

"I'm switching partners," Bryan said.

"But the music is still playing." Carlos's voice was soft.

"Not for Silva," Bryan said. "Not for Eduardo. When would it have been my turn to die?"

An interesting choice. He was letting Eduardo remain dead. Or, he was pointing out, dead or not, Carlos had ordered the hit. Either way Hollis was grateful, for the moment anyway, that the real fate of Teresa and Eduardo was staying under wraps.

Sato was impatient with the drama that had nothing to do with him. "This is what you had to tell me?"

Bryan turned to him. "No. I came to save you money. Maybe your life. I saw Declan make the book that Carlos gave you. It's a fake."

Hollis felt herself go numb. Sato already had doubts.

"He put a small plastic tracker in it between the end page and the front cover. He and the South African argued about it, but the spy won," Bryan continued.

Hollis glanced over at Carlos. She saw the color drain from his face. He knew. And he was stuck. To say that he found the tracker would be to admit that the book was a fake, and that he'd been fooled. He'd be a dead man. So he said nothing. It would keep Hollis and Finn alive. For now.

Peter was just outside the door, she told herself. Hopefully it was close enough.

Sato took the book out and opened it. He removed a small file from his pocket, and just like Carlos had done, he ran it carefully up from the bottom of the page to the top. They all watched in silence. He reached the top.

"There's no tracker."

Bryan started breathing heavily through his nose. "Then these guys removed it."

Sato sighed. "These two Americans are working with Declan and a South African spy. They kidnapped you and held you last night, then let you go this morning so you would be free to come here and ruin their mission. They put a tracker in the book so as to follow its where-abouts, then took it out before it was delivered," he said. "This is your story?"

Bryan shook his head. He looked once more at Carlos, then pushed Hollis back, and ran for the door. One of Sato's men aimed his gun, but Sato stopped him. "Too much attention for something that isn't our problem."

"And these two?" the man asked, pointing his gun at Hollis and Finn.

Before the door to the men's room could fully close from Bryan's exit, it swung open again. Declan walked in. The men quickly put their guns away.

"Seriously?" Finn mumbled.

Declan looked at all of them with the innocent face of a stranger looking to relieve himself. He rested his eyes on Hollis.

"This is the men's room?" He said with a flawless American accent.

"I'm sorry," she said. "We're done in here."

Sato turned to Carlos. "Your operation is sloppy, old man. You should think of retiring."

Carlos stared at Declan. Hollis could see that it took every bit of effort not to say his name, not to admit that Bryan had been right. Instead Carlos left the room. Finn was a few steps behind. Hollis lingered. She felt as though something was about to happen, though she wasn't sure what. Then she realized Declan was walking toward Sato. He stood inches from him, his hand moved up as if he were reaching for his own pocket, then swiftly down again. In one more step, he walked into one of the stalls and closed the door.

She wanted to play the moment in slow motion to make sure she'd witnessed Declan taking Sato's cellphone, but before she could process the information, Sato and his men walked past her and into the hall.

"Are you coming?" Finn whispered.

She nodded. It was time to go home.

Forty-Nine

Sato kept walking. His men followed. Carlos walked too, but slowly and with his head down. Peter was standing at the entrance to the museum, reading a brochure.

Carlos walked to the front door. His eyes blinked as they reacted to sunlight, and then he stepped through the exit onto the street.

"Do we follow him?" Finn asked.

Peter came up behind them. "No. He has nowhere left to go." Then he moved toward Carlos.

Hollis took Finn's hand and they walked outside the museum. The sun was beginning to get low and streak in purples and pinks across the sky. They stood on the sidewalk outside. There were tables for nearby restaurants, but they were empty in the quiet space between lunch and dinner. There was a family across the street and some people Hollis could see at the end of the block but otherwise it felt as if they were alone.

Carlos was standing under a restaurant's canopy, looking quite alone and unsure of what to do. Around him, there were several agents making it clear he was no longer a free man.

"He brought this on himself," Finn said.

"I wasn't feeling sorry for him."

"Yes, you were. That's a man who made so many bad decisions in his life, betrayed so many people that he deserves whatever comes next."

"You're right."

"I'm always right."

She smiled and leaned into his shoulder. Maybe he wasn't always right, but he was right often enough. "It's over," she said.

"Yes, it is."

A black SUV pulled up and parked just down the block from where they were. A second SUV followed. "It's time to go," Peter said to Carlos.

"You're mistaking me for someone else," Carlos told him.

"Then you can tell me again when we get where we're going."

Carlos turned to Hollis. "I thought at least you understood the rules of the dance."

"I do," she said. "It's just not the same dance."

Carlos put his hands in the air to show that he held only a cell phone. "I need to make one call. In America the suspect always gets one call."

"We're not in America."

"Please. My grandson died. I thought I could tell my daughter in person, but she should hear it from me."

"Your grandson?" Peter asked.

"The kid in our house," Hollis said.

273

Carlos didn't wait for an answer. He pressed a button and let the phone ring. For a moment he spoke in Spanish. Hollis understood one word. *Muerto.* Dead. He finished the call, handed the phone to Peter, and said, "I don't think I will need this again."

Peter pointed him toward a car. Carlos took several steps away from the canopy onto the street. Just inches from the car, his head jerked to the side, he stopped walking, looked up, and fell to the ground.

Peter waved Finn and Hollis against the wall. They ducked into a small doorway, but the shop was closed. Peter took out his gun and pointed it up, as if someone was on a rooftop. Hollis hadn't heard anything, not even a ping, certainly not a gunshot. But Carlos was on the ground, and there was a small but steady stream of blood coming from the side of his head.

A half-dozen men and women moved toward one building just next to the museum. They waited. A few minutes passed and Peter got an all-clear. Whoever was on the building was gone.

"Where was Declan?" Finn whispered to her.

"It wasn't him."

"He's a sharp shooter. He could have made that shot."

"He was pickpocketing Sato's cell phone in the bathroom. When would he have had time to get to the roof?"

"He was what? Why would he do that?"

Hollis shrugged. She didn't know. She didn't care. But then she realized. "Carlos put the numbers of some bank account into Sato's phone. It's where the money for the address book was going to be transferred."

Finn let out a dry laugh. "It's strange, but I'm relieved if all he's doing is stealing millions of dollars."

"He's growing on you."

"I wouldn't say that."

Peter pointed them toward the second SUV. Agents returned from the roof and huddled around Carlos. As Finn and Hollis got in the car, an ambulance pulled up.

A couple came out of the museum. Peter said, *"Ataque al corazón."* The woman blessed herself and they walked in the other direction.

Peter leaned into the car where Hollis and Finn were waiting. "It's all clear. No one on the roof. But Carlos is dead. The man he met with…"

"Carlos called him Mr. Sato," Hollis said.

"Well Mr. Sato's men aren't taking any chances. They probably got their money back too."

"Declan has it by now," Finn said. "Hollis saw him do it."

Peter smiled. "I guess he earned it. When he rushed passed me into the men's room I thought he was going to blow the whole thing."

"He may have saved us," Hollis said. "When he walked in, all the guns went back in their holsters. But the tracker is off the book. Carlos found it and removed it before we ever got to the meeting."

"At least we know who was picking up the book. It's a start." He tapped the door of the car and nodded to the driver. "I'll see you at the hotel tonight."

The car drove off just as the ambulance was putting Carlos's body in the back. The latest version of Jorge Videla was dead, but instead of being a terrifying killer he'd turned out to be a sad old grifter who had played one too many cons.

Fifty

There was a private plane waiting for them. They sat together on the couch and let a movie play on the TV, *Barefoot in the Park* with Spanish subtitles. Hollis silently wondered how she was going to feel going back to commercial flights after the luxury of private jets, but Finn wasn't cheered by the offer of food and wine.

"We helped Teresa and Eduardo," he said, after nearly an hour of silence. "We did some good."

"We also found out another member of TCT, someone closer to the man who doesn't exist."

"And we paid Declan back for saving your life. So we're even now."

"And life can go back to normal."

Finn shook his head. "What's normal anymore?"

"Me nagging you about the garbage. You not listening when I nag you about the garbage."

He stretched his body across the couch, laying his head on her lap. She stroked his hair with one hand and rested the other across his arm. He reached up and took that hand. His breathing steadied, and hers did too. Just being together, sitting close, lowered her blood pressure and made her feel like whatever craziness there was in the world, she was safe as long as Finn was with her. She'd picked the right dance partner.

———

Back at the hotel, they went to the suite. No one was listening anymore and their clothes were there, so it seemed the sensible choice. They ordered room service and lay on the bed watching television. There was no word from Peter on when they should be able to go home, but the flight was twelve hours, and if they flew commercial it was extremely unlikely they'd get a direct flight anywhere near close to home.

"I don't think we'll get back in time for class tomorrow," she said.

"I can get my teaching assistant to sub for me, and if Angela is still around maybe she can teach for you."

"That seems unlikely." But worth a shot, she thought. Everything that happened in her life lately seemed unlikely.

"I have a meeting with the head of my department Friday," Finn said. "I meant to tell you but with everything that happened…"

"What's the meeting about?"

"I was going to propose teaching a class about forgeries in the world of art and literature. I'd been researching it…"

"I remember. You said you were going to write a paper."

"I didn't know how you'd feel about me taking on a new class. It's going to be a lot of work."

She laughed. "Not really. You can draw on real-world experience."

"I thought it would be fun. Not so sure I feel that way anymore."

She put her head on his shoulder. "We helped people. Let's focus on that, and not on Silva or Carlos."

"Or Bryan. As long as he's out there somewhere, we're not really done with this."

"Peter must have him in custody. He would have had to walk right past him when he left the men's room. I'm not worried."

But she was worried. Declan got by Peter. What if Bryan had too?

━━━━━━

An hour later, there was a knock on the door. Peter was there. Behind him was a room service waiter with a pot of tea and three cups. "I would have asked for champagne to be brought up, but we're not celebrating."

"Why not?" Finn asked as the waiter left, closing the door behind him.

"When did you last see Declan?"

"In the men's room. What happened to him?"

"Your guess is as good as mine. He went by me. You all came out. We got into position to get Carlos, but I had a man at the door. He waited, went in, no Declan. There's a window in that bathroom but to get to it, he'd have to climb something and there's nothing to climb."

"He obviously found something," Finn pointed out.

"What's the big deal if he got away?" Hollis asked. "He did what he promised. He made a copy of the book. You have the real one back."

278

You have a lead on another thread of TCT. And you pulled down Carlos, their main guy in Argentina. Silva is dead. Eduardo seems like he's going straight, and you have Bryan in custody. After all that were you really going to put Declan in prison?"

"Here's why there's no champagne. Bryan was arrested, but in the commotion of the sniper shooting, he got away. He was cuffed and in the back of a locked SUV. He's more of a Houdini than Declan," Peter said. "And speaking of the Irishman, he didn't give me back the book. Remember that almost perfect forgery he said wasn't good enough?"

"He threw it in the trash," Finn said. "I saw him do it."

"He must have retrieved it. I sent the book back to DC as soon as we were done with it. It's just arrived. It's a fake. Declan has the real thing."

Hollis couldn't help herself, she laughed. Finn laughed with her, and much to her surprise, so did Peter.

"You do realize this is my career," he said, and the laughing came to an end. "And when I get the guy, I'm going to kill him."

"You guys were getting along so well. I'm surprised he would do that to you," Hollis said.

Finn shook his head at her. "Unbelievable. You keep trusting him."

"I thought he was growing on you."

"Yeah, like mold."

Peter got up. "I'll come back in the morning to get you and make sure you get out okay. You did good, both of you. Handled yourselves well. You should know we traced the final call Carlos made. It was to a man named Evans, a Scotsman who does business throughout South America."

"What kind of business?"

"The same business as Janet and Tim. I recorded the call. He told Evans that he was followed to the meeting and the man needs to be dead. I assume he meant Bryan, or maybe Declan. Either way. He didn't mean you two or he would have said *they*."

"That makes me feel better," Hollis said. "Not just that he didn't order a hit on us. But that he knew it was his last chance to reach out to someone, and rather than talk to his daughter like he said, or even try to talk to Teresa, he focused on revenge. Says everything about who he was."

"Where are the real Janet and Tim McCabe?" Finn asked.

Peter smiled. "At the house of your teaching assistant, Angela. Behind one of the doors that looked like a college student's bedroom, she had the two of them locked up. She put a call into the FBI and was gone before they arrived. They've got a dozen different identities, so I'd say they'll be in custody for quite a while."

"Eduardo and Teresa and her father?" Hollis asked.

"They're all safe, far from Argentina. We'll send word to Teresa that she's a widow. I suppose she could come back now if she wants to. It doesn't appear Carlos had many friends. Certainly no one to have an issue with what Teresa or Eduardo do now."

"Bryan might kill them. Or us. He knows where we live."

"We'll get him. And we'll keep you safe. Blue owes you that much," Peter said. "I owe you that much."

She wasn't surprised by what Declan had done, it's what he had said, over and over, was his plan. It's just that she'd stuck up for him. She'd believed him. She knew he was a con man, she just didn't realize he was conning her and Finn.

After Peter left, Hollis packed the clothes Teresa had brought for them. She added her leather jacket, the wallet, and the guidebook, zipped them up and put them by the door. She rested Finn's poster-sized map next to them. He was just going to have to carry it separately, she decided.

She crawled into bed but didn't sleep well. By morning she was just anxious to be in her own bed. And hopeful that when they got there, there would be no angry Argentinian hitman hoping for revenge.

Fifty-One

Matias was at the desk when they checked out. "How was your stay?"

"Complicated," Finn said.

"You were left a note," he said. "For the señora." He handed Hollis a folded paper.

It was a short note. *The world is ending and it's left me with an awful thirst.*

"Did someone deliver this?" she asked.

Matias shook his head. "No. It was a call. A man with an Irish accent."

Another puzzle from Declan, but this was one she had no idea if she wanted to solve. If he had the address book, that was Peter's problem. She was ready to go home. Peter walked in just as she put the note in her pocket.

"Ready?"

"All packed, souvenirs and everything," Finn said.

"Great. But you're not going home. We have to catch a flight to Iguazu Falls. We have a lead on the Irishman."

Before either of them could protest, or talk about getting home for class the next day or even say a word, Peter had their bags in the trunk of a car. They were on a plane, and two hours later landed at a tiny little hook of land in Northern Argentina in a place where Paraguay, Argentina, and Brazil met, and where one of the world's most beautiful waterfalls brought people from all over to see it.

As they drove to the falls, Peter had filled them in on why he was so optimistic. "I knew he'd try something. It's just who he is, so I slipped one of the extra trackers in his wallet while he took a short nap the day before yesterday. I thought it was kind of funny, honestly, since he hated the idea of the thing so much. But I also figured it would come in handy."

"How do you know he didn't just find it and toss it?" Finn asked.

"I wasn't sure, but when he showed up yesterday at the museum, exactly where the tracker said he was, I knew he hadn't found it."

Peter was a little too happy about it, but Hollis decided he had a right to be. Declan knew that Peter's career would be over if the book was gone, and he took it anyway. Maybe it was about the money or about the game, but for someone who risked his life to help two lovers, he seemed pretty cavalier with the ripple effects of his other choices.

Except he was a criminal. Hollis had to remind herself of that.

She showed Peter the note.

"What's it mean?" Peter asked.

"I think it's that he's dropping out of sight," Finn said. "He's supposed to be dead, remember. And the thing about the thirst. That must mean water, so Iguazu Falls makes sense. He must be crossing the border into Brazil from here. He's got to have a fake passport…"

"And he did a perfect American accent yesterday," Hollis agreed. "He could pretend to be a dozen different nationalities."

"I'm sure he could," Peter said. "It's a shame too, because I was beginning to see what you two see him in. He's a good guy. Or he could be if he wasn't…" He didn't finish the sentence. He didn't have to.

Hollis knew that Finn would happily bring up the crypt thing again. And yes, he had locked them in there. But if Eduardo was telling the truth—and why wouldn't he have been?—Declan locked them in there to protect them from Bryan, who had come to the cemetery intent on killing them. Finn could say that Declan had gotten them kidnapped and brought to Argentina as fake hitmen, which he had. But he'd also kept the real hitmen from killing them. And when he said that the McCabes were alive, he was telling the truth. Plus the money he'd given away, and the help he'd been to Teresa and Eduardo.

Had he really done all of that and then stolen the address book?

"He's a criminal," Finn said, as if he were reading her thoughts. "But if it helps, I'm disappointed too."

Iguazu Falls was everything that it purported to be. It wasn't one fall; that surprised her. It was two hundred and seventy-five water falls, with a mist that sprayed a rainbow across the water. They walked the platforms, looking for Declan. Peter handed them a walkie-talkie and told them to give him a shout if there was any sighting.

"I'm in radio contact with a dozen more agents, and we've even brought in the border police to help," he said. He wasn't taking any chances.

"What do we do if we see him?"

"Kill him," Peter said. Then rolled his eyes. "Nothing. Just tell me where he is. Someone will be in the area to pick him up. There's a lot of ground to cover but he's here, and with all the platforms, with fencing on both sides, it's not that easy to get away."

"Unless he wants to jump in the falls," Finn joked.

"The good news for us is that he's neither stupid nor suicidal," Peter said. "We'll get him, and then I'm going to put that guy in an interrogation room and keep him there until the smirk is wiped off his face."

"And then you'll let him go?" Hollis asked.

"No, then I'll put him in prison."

They spread out. Finn and Hollis walked the Argentinian side, while Peter walked the Brazil side. Hollis could see speedboats in the water below, where tourists were enjoying a wet, wild ride under the falls. Above them, more tourists were taking helicopter rides. There were easily a couple of hundred people walking around. The tracker couldn't pinpoint an exact location, but Peter radioed them that Declan was there, somewhere, among all the people.

As they walked she could see the border patrol also walking the crowd. Any man with brown hair was looked at, his picture taken and sent to Peter. They were hardly being subtle.

Hollis looked to her left, Finn to his right. They walked slowly, scanning the crowd. Hollis thought she saw a man reach for a gun. She grabbed Finn's arm. Could it be Bryan? But it was just a tourist taking out a selfie stick from his back pocket.

They were safe, she reminded herself. Or nearly safe. Bryan could be among the faces they scanned, but what were the odds?

"This is pointless," Finn said, stopping as they reached the end of the walkway. "If Declan's here, it's got to be clear by now that someone is looking for him."

"What if he takes a helicopter across the border? Or one of those boats?" Hollis asked. "I don't see how just wandering the crowd will get us anywhere."

"So we give up, right?"

She was about to agree when their radio crackled. *"Found him. We have him."*

Fifty-Two

A tour boat moving back toward the dock noticed something floating in the water and reported it to the park police, who alerted a border agent, who told an agent from Blue. When they'd gone to get a closer look they realized it was the body of a brown-haired male in his twenties. And he was dead.

"Not a drowning," Peter said. "A bullet to the back of his head, execution style."

"Who knew Declan was alive?" Finn asked.

"Carlos. That call he made." Peter shook his head. "Whoever killed him might not have taken the book. It could still be on the body."

They waited for more than an hour as the body was taken from the water and brought to an area where it could be examined. Peter, Finn, and Hollis were driven to the room where he was held and asked to wait.

Hollis opened the note. "'The world is ending and it's left me with an awful thirst,'" she read. "Why would he call the hotel and leave this for us if he were trying to get away with the book? It's a clue."

"It sounds like a suicide note," Finn said.

"But he didn't kill himself, and he didn't know Carlos had ordered a hit. Why did he want us to come here?"

"He wouldn't have had to spend the rest of his life behind bars. If he'd have been useful ..." Peter let the sentence go. "My life is over, though. I can't believe some grifter stole a valuable piece of evidence against TCT right from under my nose and then ended up at the bottom of a waterfall."

"That's not going to be his body," Finn said. "He wants us to believe he's dead, but he's not. Hollis is right, it just doesn't make any sense."

A man in a police uniform came out of the room and signaled to them. "I guess we'll find out now," Peter said.

They walked into a small medical office, set up for tourists who had injured themselves on hikes or in the boats that went under the falls. It was now a make-shift morgue. On a table there was the body of a man, covered in a sheet.

At Peter's signal the sheet was removed from the man's upper body. Hollis recognized it immediately. It was Bryan.

"He was recently arrested," the police officer said. "He has marks on his wrists from plastic handcuffs."

The cuffs that Peter had used to tie Bryan to the bedframe had left red marks on his wrists. Hollis didn't want to smile in front of the cop, so she nodded as solemnly as possible. Finn thanked the man but otherwise played dumb. There might be someone missing Bryan, Hollis realized, who would never know what happened to him. But that was the life of a criminal. And a spy.

"Is this the man named Declan Murphy that you've been looking for?" the officer asked.

"Yes," Finn said, before Peter could speak. "That's Declan Murphy." He nodded toward Peter, who followed them out of the building into the bright sunlight.

"Look, mate, I know you're fond of the guy, but you just lied to law enforcement about the identity of a body to protect a known criminal," Peter said. "And I'm hoping you have a good reason. Because if you don't…" He didn't finish. He just looked beaten. Hollis realized he had nothing to threaten them with—certainly not jail. The whole mission was likely beyond the scope of even an organization like Blue. Two civilians with guns chasing bad guys in South America. It might have been explainable to his superiors if Peter would have gone back with Declan in custody. She felt oddly protective of Peter in that moment, even though she was as in the dark about Finn's declaration as Peter was.

"Of course he had a good reason," Hollis answered for Finn. "It's all going to be okay."

She looked over at Finn for reassurance, but he said nothing. He walked briskly with Peter and Hollis following until they got to the lot where the car was parked. Once there, Finn opened the trunk and took out the map he'd bought.

"You are obsessed with that thing," Hollis told him.

"Good thing I am." He unrolled it, searched it for a moment, then pointed to a spot at the very bottom of Argentina. "Ushuaia."

"What about it?" Peter asked.

"*El fin del mundo*. The end of the world. It's what Ushuaia is called— the city at the end of the world," Finn explained. "Declan said *the world is ending*. I saw this on the map the other night, and forgot about it. But

Declan's note bugged me. When you brought us here, I figured you were right about the *awful thirst* line being the falls. But I think he was telling us where he was going next, the end of the world."

Peter looked at the spot Finn was pointing to. "You think he slipped the tracker into Bryan's pocket in the museum?"

"He's an excellent pick-pocket," Hollis attested.

"There's plenty of water at Ushuaia," Peter said. "The Beagle Channel is right there. Maybe he's planning to meet us there? Maybe he just needed to get somewhere safe?"

"Pretty good idea, this map," Finn said.

Hollis laughed.

Peter laughed. "That stupid Irishman. I could kiss him. I'll call the plane."

Fifty-Three

P eter drove, rushing to the airport even as Hollis reminded him that the plane wasn't going to leave without them.

"No, but Declan might," Peter said. "If there's any chance of getting that book back…"

And he kept saying that for the more than five hours it took for their plane to reach Tierra del Fuego. They landed at the Ushuaia Airport and sped through a rugged, rural area. Peter made hotel reservations as they drove, two suites with access to the spa.

"The spa?" Finn whispered to Hollis. "I thought this was a sleepy town in the middle of nowhere."

But it wasn't. As they reached town, they drove through the main street, passing high-end shops with designer hiking gear.

"Isn't this supposed to be the last stop before you board a ship for Antarctica?" Finn asked.

"I guess people want a last bit of luxury before they do," Hollis said, amazed and slightly bewildered by the isolated mountains and choppy waters as a backdrop for restaurants with white tablecloths and fine Argentinian wines. "Where do we go now that we're here?"

Peter pulled into a parking lot. "We walk until we see a clue of some kind. Unless either of you has a better idea."

Neither of them did. They walked toward the water, wondering if Declan's awful thirst might lead them to something there. The wind went right through Hollis. Finn wrapped his arms around her to keep her warm, but he also kept her steady. It was really stunning, she thought. The town was built on a hill that ended at the water, and nature took it from there. Blues and grays and greens all danced together to make up the water as it played against the shore. Little islands dotted the landscape. Seagulls flew overheard.

"You don't think he came all this way to drown himself here?" Peter asked.

"He must have meant something else."

"*An awful thirst,*" Hollis said. "That doesn't sound like drowning."

"No," Finn agreed. "It sounds like he wanted a drink."

They looked at each other, all of them realizing the clue. "He meant a bar," Peter said.

"There's got to be a hundred of them in this town," Finn pointed out.

"Not for Declan. He'd want a very particular kind of bar."

Hollis walked toward a small red building with a sign that read, Visitor's Center. She talked to a man there, asking one question and getting the answer she hoped for. Smiling she returned to the Peter and Finn.

"Follow me," she said.

They walked a block over, crossed over the main street, and went up the hill. They were halfway up when they saw it. A green building made of dark wood and green corrugated metal. An Irish pub called The Dublin.

Inside, it was as if Saint Patrick's Day were a year-long holiday. Irish flags lined the edges of the bar. Shamrocks and signs for Irish towns hung around the walls, and Guinness was on tap. The tables were crowded with hikers and travelers from all over the world, based on the many languages Hollis was hearing. She looked around for a familiar face, but he wasn't there. Peter walked one side of the small room, with Finn walking the other. They both came back empty-handed.

"He isn't here," Finn said.

"Maybe he's going to come," Hollis told them. "We'll just wait."

Finn clenched his jaw. "How long?"

"As long as it takes," was Peter's answer. "Three." Peter nodded toward the bartender then pointed to the beer.

The bartender pulled three pints.

"A friend of ours may have been here recently," Finn said. "Shaggy-haired Irishman, very charming but you can't trust him."

"What's your name?" the bartender asked.

"Finn and Hollis," Finn said. "And Peter."

The bartender nodded. "Based on your description, you obviously know him well." He reached under the bar. "Declan left this for you." He handed over a large box.

"That's not an address book," Peter grumbled.

"Maybe it will tell us where it is." Hollis was trying to be optimistic. He had brought them all the way here, and it had to be for more than the scenery and a pint. But she worried the book was long gone. He was a criminal, she had to keep reminding herself that. And criminals like Declan would never hand back something that valuable.

She hated to lose faith in the man that had once saved her life, but there it was. He'd left them a consolation prize.

Finn opened the box. Inside was one of the fake Van Goghs, a pretty version of one of his sunflower paintings. Good, but not quite good enough. Even she could see it wasn't the real thing. But it was sweet of him. As Finn said, he was a hard man to hate. She pulled it fully out to have a good look at it.

"I guess this is our field of sunflowers to thank us for helping him," she said. "He kept his promise to give us one."

"How thoughtful." Peter took the box and looked inside. There was nothing else. "Too bad he kept the wrong promise."

She didn't know what to say to Peter. Clearly Finn didn't either. He leaned against the bar and sipped his drink.

Before she put it back in the box, Hollis held the painting up to look at it. It was quite nice and they could use a new picture in the living room. And a new chair. They would definitely be getting a new chair.

"You have a photocopy of the book," Finn said to Peter. "Declan knows that, so maybe he figures you'll still be okay."

"Exactly," Peter said. "He knows that. And he made a fake version. He could have duplicated the book exactly, kept the fake and sent me back with the real one. If all that matters is the information in the book, that's what he would have done. It must be something about the book itself. He knew there was more to it than the words on the page. That's why he took it, and that's why I will never be able to explain how I trusted a forger with a valuable clue to the head of TCT."

"We have the name of Mr. Sato."

"And so far, that's gotten us nowhere. We took photos of the man in the museum yesterday, but our identification software has turned up nothing. If the guy's never been on our radar before, we may never find him."

It was all pretty hopeless. Reminding him again that Carlos and Bryan were dead, and Teresa and Eduardo were safe, was probably not a big enough win to offset the serious loss of that book. Hollis reached for the box and began to put the painting back inside it, but it caught against the cardboard, so she pulled it out again to readjust.

"What's at the back?" Finn asked.

She turned the painting around. An envelope was taped there.

"It can't be," Peter said. "I can't be this lucky."

Peter pulled it off the canvas, ripped open the package.

The address book.

He grabbed his glasses, checked pages. "I made a small imprint with my fingernail on page fourteen, just to be sure which one was real," Peter said. "Declan didn't see me do it. It was right after you two left." He flipped to page fourteen and held it up to the light.

Finn and Hollis waited for more bad news, but Peter laughed.

"The real one. He actually returned the real one." Peter seemed bewildered. "Why would he do that?"

"That's what you wanted him to do," Hollis pointed out.

"But he could have made a fortune with this," Peter said. "In his shoes, I don't know that I would have returned it."

"He's probably made half a dozen copies and is selling the fakes all over the world," Finn said. "Adding it to the money Carlos thought he was paying Tim and Janet, he's doing okay."

Peter nodded. "I don't care as long as I have the original. Besides, if I've learned anything about that guy, he's made up the information in every one of those copies so they're all useless." Peter examined the book again. "I wonder what's in this and why he gave it back."

"Maybe with Carlos's real name and Sato, you can figure that out," Finn said. "It's a place to start anyway."

"Maybe." Peter put the book in his jacket pocket and lifted his beer. "To Declan." He swallowed half his beer, then lifted it again. "And to Tim and Janet McCabe. Another successful mission."

"To our retirement," Finn said.

Finn and Hollis drank to that, but Peter didn't.

Fifty-Four

The next morning, Hollis and Finn boarded a boat to tour the Beagle Channel. It was a small tour boat with only about ten people. They'd had to visit the expensive outdoor shops to buy good boots and warm jackets, something that made Finn remark about how expensive being a spy had turned out to be, but Hollis didn't care.

She also didn't care that they had missed another day of school. The official story was that they'd both come down with the flu. A little suspicious maybe, but that was the third thing she didn't care about. She was just excited by the chance to see a little of the extraordinary beauty of this legendary part of the world.

It was odd, the sheer terror, followed by a moment of bliss, like this one. Pretending to be someone else, then forgetting themselves as they explored another culture and another life. She linked her arm with Finn's. They could have gone their whole lives without knowing each other the way they had these last few months, without ever depending on each other for their survival, or seeing just what the other person could do when the chips were down.

She was glad they were safe and that bad men were dead. But she was just a little bit sad that it was over.

Just as the boat was about to take off another passenger came on board. "All that talk about seeing penguins and seals last night," Peter said, half blushing. "Even with a hangover I knew I had to come."

He took a seat next to Hollis and the three of them watched as the town got smaller and the sea and mountains around them took over the view.

Soon they stopped at a small island, no more than a large rock, where seals were sunning themselves. Everyone, including Peter, took out cameras and phones to snap pictures. It was a situation the seals were well used to; they seemed to pose for the cameras. It must be odd, Hollis thought, to hang around a rock all day and watch a boat full of humans come to take pictures of you. It was finally a life stranger than her own.

"I'm glad you two are done being amateur spies," Peter said as the boat moved toward another rock, this one containing small birds.

"We are too," Finn said. "I mean, it was fun in a way. I had no idea what either of us were capable of until we were required to step up, but..."

"But you're not trained," Peter said.

"Exactly."

"And you're not being paid."

"That's another thing."

"How would you like to be?"

Hollis looked at him. "Are you hiring us to work for Blue?"

"Not full-time. Your cover as professors is brilliant."

"It's not a cover," Finn reminded him. "It's who we are."

"Is it all you want to be though, mate? Because I've seen your skills in the field, and you could be so much more than a guy behind a book. Besides, don't you want to know who Sato is, or where Declan has gotten off to? And the next time someone shows up at your house with a dead body, wouldn't it be better if you actually knew how to use a gun?"

Finn swallowed hard but said nothing. Hollis had imagined she would jump at an offer like that, or run screaming from it. Now she just felt numb.

"Is it what you want, Holly?" Finn asked.

"Sometimes," she admitted.

He smiled. "I think *sometimes* is what Peter's offering."

"What do you want? I think you're awfully good at this, but I don't want to push you into it. And we have to get your heart checked."

"My heart is fine," he said. "And so is yours. You had faith in Declan all along."

"Except he obviously was still playing us. He did steal the book, if only for a day."

"So you want to say no?"

Hollis hesitated. "Either way. As long as we're together, no matter what."

"Better or worse, richer or poorer, in failed assassination plots and despite crazy art forgers..."

Peter shook his head. "I don't think that's how that goes."

"It does for us." Finn leaned in and kissed Hollis.

The boat stopped again at an island where penguins were watching the tourists watch them. Tomorrow would be back to classes and raking leaves and making sure they brought the trash out in time for the garbage men, but today there were penguins in a city at the end of

299

the world and an offer to chase some of the world's worst bad guys around the globe.

A sometime spy, Hollis realized, was the balance they'd been looking for.

Margaret Smith

About the Author

Clare O'Donohue is the author of the Kate Conway Mysteries and the Someday Quilts Mysteries. She was a producer for the HGTV show *Simply Quilts* and has worked on shows for the History Channel, truTV, Food Network, A&E, Discovery, and TLC.

WWW.MIDNIGHTINKBOOKS.COM

From the gritty streets of New York City to sacred tombs in the Middle East, it's always midnight somewhere. Join us online at any hour for fresh new voices in mystery fiction.

At midnightinkbooks.com you'll also find our author blog, new and upcoming books, events, book club questions, excerpts, mystery resources, and more.

MIDNIGHT INK ORDERING INFORMATION

Order Online:
• Visit our website www.midnightinkbooks.com, select your books, and order them on our secure server.

Order by Phone:
• Call toll-free within the U.S. at
  1-888-NITE-INK (1-888-648-3465)
• We accept VISA, MasterCard, American Express, and Discover
• Canadian customers must use credit cards

Order by Mail:
Send the full price of your order (MN residents add 6.875% sales tax) in U.S. funds, plus postage & handling to:

> Midnight Ink
> 2143 Wooddale Drive
> Woodbury, MN 55125-2989

Postage & Handling:
Standard (US). If your order is:
> $30.00 and under, add $6.00
> $30.01 and over, FREE STANDARD SHIPPING

AK, HI, PR: $16.00 for one book plus $2.00 for each additional book.

International Orders: Including Canada
> $16.00 for one book plus $3.00 for each additional book

Orders are processed within 12 business days. Please allow for normal shipping time.
Postage and handling rates subject to change.

31901064820857